THE
HOUSE OF EVIL

THE
HOUSE OF EVIL

WILLIAM LE QUEUX

WILDSIDE PRESS

Originally published in 1927.
Published by Wildside Press.
wildsidepress.com

THE HOUSE OF EVIL

CHAPTER ONE

"HUGH, old man, you're growing as close as an oyster. This is twice this week you have dined out, leaving me solitary, and refused to tell me what you are up to. I wonder what it is you have got up your sleeve?"

Two young men were strolling down the lovely Promenade des Anglais at Nice. The elder, the Honourable Hugh Craig, was twenty-seven; Leonard Lydon, his companion, about six months younger.

They had been fast friends at Harrow, where Craig had risen to be the Head of the School, and afterwards at Balliol, and the friendship had continued after they left Oxford till the present time.

Craig, the youngest son of Viscount Clandon, was a member of an old aristocratic family which, for generations, had been closely connected with the government of the country. Several of the heads of it had sat in the Cabinets of their day and generation; other members had filled high civil and military posts in England and its Dependencies. Hugh himself was in the diplomatic service, and was enjoying a brief holiday with his friend on the lovely Côte d'Azur.

Leonard Lydon was of humbler stock than his aristocratic companion. His father, a wealthy Liverpool merchant, had risen from small beginnings. He had laid the foundations of his fortune very early in his career, so that he was able to give his numerous family the advantage of a liberal education. Each of his five sons was sent to a public school, and subsequently either to Cambridge or Oxford.

The Liverpool merchant had died a couple of years ago, leaving behind him a handsome fortune, half of which was left to his widow for life, the other half divided between the five sons and four daughters.

The two elder sons inherited the business, as well as their share of the private fortune. As there were nine persons to divide the half of the total amount, nobody received a very huge sum, but enough to bring in a comfortable income.

After taking his degree at Oxford, Leonard had become deeply interested in wireless research, and had studied until he became a full-blown radio engineer, a profession which he followed in the Admiralty during the later years of the War. After peace he joined an American Wireless Communication Company which had a branch in England. At the time this story opens, he had been appointed this Company's chief engineer and designer. As he was in receipt of a handsome salary, his financial position was a very comfortable one.

His friend, Hugh Craig, was not so well off as himself. His family, though very ancient, was poor for its position. He was still in the lower grades of the diplomatic service, and his private income was a small one. But the Clandon influence would later on be sure to secure for him a snug post. He was, however, better off than a good many members of impoverished families, as he had been left a moderate legacy of a few thousands by a near relative.

When his friend rallied him upon his secretive mien, Hugh gave one of his disarming and diplomatic smiles.

"I expect you'll learn all about it in good time, my dear fellow. You know I was always rather a reticent sort of chap, fond of making a mystery of small things."

Lydon laughed. "That's one of the truest things you have ever said, Hugh, and nobody who didn't know you thoroughly, like myself, would ever guess it. On the surface, you give the impression of being one of the frankest men living. That appearance of yours will be one of the greatest assets to you in your career. How easily it will enable you to hoodwink people when you want to!"

Hugh Craig smiled in his turn. "From all I can learn this peculiar characteristic has run in the Clandon family for generations. I suppose that is why so many of us have taken so readily to statecraft and diplomacy."

That evening, Leonard Lydon dined by himself at the Hôtel Royal, as he had done a couple of nights ago. During the progress of his solitary meal, he speculated a good deal upon the cause of his friend's absence. Of an ordinary man, the man whose type he had met in scores, he would have said there was undoubtedly a woman at the bottom of it.

But Hugh Craig, good-looking, self-possessed and *débonnaire*, with that smiling, charming manner, was by no means an ordinary man. Even as a boy he had been a complex character, and the transition to manhood had deepened the complexity.

Intimately associated as they had been all these years, Lydon was forced to confess that he knew very little of the inner personality of his friend, the part which he hid so successfully from the world under that smiling, *débonnaire* mask.

Did he care greatly about women? Did he care at all about them? For the life of him, Leonard could not give a definite answer to that question. As was natural on the part of such young men, they had often lightly discussed the other sex together. But out of these conversations nothing of a hidden vein of romance had been revealed by Craig. His comments might have been those of a rather cynical philosopher of twice his age.

Only once had he made any remark bearing directly upon himself, which might be taken to represent his well-considered opinions on the subject, and on this occasion he had spoken with more gravity than was his wont when the conversation touched upon the themes of love and marriage.

"No man who intends to make a career for himself should ever commit the folly of falling in love," he had said. "Because the chances are ten to one that he will fall in love with the wrong person. Marry for sound, sensible reasons perhaps. Even then I think I should postpone the step as long as possible, so far as I am individually concerned."

Lydon, whose temperament was rather of the romantic kind, looked the surprise he felt.

"But surely you will marry some day, Hugh? Not too early perhaps, but when you have got a comfortable post?"

The answer came very deliberately. "It might be an absolute necessity of the position. But putting that on one side, I feel no great yearning for the married state. If I were the eldest son, it would be necessary for me to provide an heir; but the Clandons are so prolific, they are not likely to die out for want of representatives."

On the whole, Lydon would have said, from these and other remarks dropped by the calm, smiling young diplomatist, that Hugh Craig was very little attracted by women, and the last man in the world to be capable of a grand passion.

But he was not at all sure. During the long term of their friendship, Hugh had so often surprised him by sudden revelations of a side of his character totally unsurmised, that he could not reckon upon him with any degree of certainty.

It was just on the cards that he had suddenly met a woman who had the power to stir his languid pulses. And Lydon had always suspected that, deep down under that placid exterior, there was something volcanic slumbering which would one day burst into flame. If Hugh ever did love, it was more than probable he would love with an unreasoning ardour.

If there was a woman, who was she? Where had they met? The two young men had been so much together during their stay at Nice, that opportunity did not seem to have offered itself very abundantly. And one thing was quite certain. If Hugh had a serious love affair, nobody would be told about it till the very last moment. Secretiveness about his personal concerns was the keynote of his character.

Having finished his dinner, Lydon went into the lounge. He had not been there long when the Stormont family came in. It consisted of Howard Stormont, a stout, rubicund, clean-shaven man of about fifty, who bore his years gaily; his niece, Gloria, a pretty, blue-eyed, fair-haired girl with a slender, graceful figure, and his widowed sister, Mrs. Maud Barnard, a woman who dressed in a rather extravagant style.

They had struck up a slight acquaintance with the two young men, chiefly with Lydon, who was a very cosmopolitan fellow. Craig had not taken greatly to the party, being a person of very fastidious taste. When he talked them over with his friend, he admitted that Gloria was a remarkably pretty girl, "would have been quite worth cultivating if she had possessed different relatives." The rubicund Howard Stormont he declared to be an aggressive type of profiteer, and Mrs. Barnard he evidently considered to be an unrefined, over-dressed woman.

Lydon did not take this severe view of the uncle and aunt. Mrs. Barnard was a trifle flamboyant in dress perhaps, but she was also exceedingly amiable and good-natured. Stormont's manners were possibly too hearty for perfect refinement, but he was a genial, cheery fellow, and full of a shrewd wit.

As for Gloria, Leonard though he had never come across a more charming girl. In the few chats they had enjoyed together when Craig happened to be absent, she had told him a good deal about herself. Her parents lived in China, where her father held a high position in one of the European banks. As the climate did not suit her, she had made her home with her uncle, the rubicund Howard Stormont and his widowed sister, at Effington in Surrey.

He also learned that, like many modern young women, she was an athletic girl, passionately fond of all outdoor games and sports. As he was no mean athlete himself, he admired her the more for this fact, which rather surprised him, as her appearance did not suggest any particular robustness, but rather the reverse.

Presently Mr. Stormont went away to write some letters, and soon after Mrs. Barnard followed him. The young people were left alone.

"What has become of your friend, Mr. Craig?" the girl asked him. "This is the second time this week he has left you to dine in solitary state. I feel quite sorry for you."

She had a very sweet, musical voice. In fact Lydon thought everything about her was dainty and refined, far above the average.

The young man smiled. "Yes, Craig has been very mysterious the last few days. He goes off on his own, and he won't tell me a word about it. He parries all hints with his usual diplomatic ability and sang-froid. You can't ruffle him, you know."

"I should say it would be quite impossible," was Miss Stormont's answer. "You are very great friends, are you not? I have often wondered why."

"What is it that causes you to wonder?" asked Leonard.

Miss Stormont blushed a little at being called upon to explain her rather unguarded remark.

"You seem such exact opposites. You are perfectly open, impulsive, not to say impetuous. If asked for your opinion, you blurt it out at once, sometimes without very deep thought, if you will forgive me for saying so, as I have often known you to alter or modify it as you go along. Mr. Craig is so different. Behind that smiling urbanity is an intense reserve, a profound caution. Somehow, if you ask him a straightforward question, his answer is so fenced about with subtleties that you don't feel satisfied."

Lydon laughed heartily. The girl was very frank, even to the point of indiscretion. But she had certainly judged his friend pretty shrewdly. Even those who loved him and admired his very considerable gifts were forced to admit that there was a good deal of the Jesuit about this young descendant of diplomatic ancestors.

They had the longest talk they had ever enjoyed together that evening in the almost empty lounge.

As she prattled gaily along, with that frankness which was natural to her, he learned a good deal about the rubicund Howard Stormont himself. He was engaged in business, a very busy man and possessed of boundless energy. He was not fond of London life, and so far as was compatible with his business interests, played with great gusto the rôle of country gentleman. He had purchased a charming place some five years ago, and was never happier than when strolling around Effington village in his country tweeds, and chatting familiarly with the inhabitants.

This estate had been acquired from an impoverished and hard-living young sprig of the nobility, a grandson of the Earl of Sedgemere, who had originally owned the fine seat known as Effington Hall. Under his short tenure, the revenues which should have gone to the upkeep of the property had been diverted to gambling and riotous living. The once big estate had been disposed of bit by bit.

Stormont, the wealthy man of business, had soon altered this. The mansion and estate had been vastly improved, and pretty Effington village had been renovated out of all recognition. Upon the completion of his purchase, he had given a donation of five hundred pounds towards the restoration of the exquisite thirteenth-century church with its grey square tower, such a well-known landmark in the Surrey landscape. In the "county" he was highly respected for his generosity and magisterial work, for very soon after his purchase of Effington he had been put upon the roll of Justices of the Peace for the county of Surrey.

So, somewhat to his surprise, Lydon learned that this homely, rather commonplace-looking man, whom his friend Craig described as an aggressive profiteer, was a person of importance in business circles, and not altogether undistinguished in the more select sphere of county life.

"I enjoy travelling very much," she told the young man, after she had furnished him with these details of her uncle's biography. "But my happiest time is at Effington with the dear dogs and horses. I know everybody in the place, and the hours seem to go as if they were minutes."

"You seem to me rather a lucky girl," remarked her companion, "and I expect you are spoiled by both uncle and aunt."

Miss Stormont admitted with a pretty smile that he was not very far out in his guess. Howard Stormont was one of the most generous and easy-going men alive, and nobody could be more indulgent towards youth than Mrs. Barnard. She was very young in spirit herself, and preferred the society of her juniors to more staid company. They indulged her in every reasonable wish, and kept open house and practised an almost lavish hospitality.

No wonder, thought Lydon, that the county had taken them to its bosom. And although Craig had conceived a quite pronounced dislike for both the man and his sister, Lydon, less fastidious and critical, thought them very delightful people. Stormont was probably a self-made man, but he detected in neither him nor his sister any offensive signs of the newly-rich. He was not a snob, as affable to a waiter as he would have been to a duke, and never bragged. Mrs. Barnard was perhaps a trifle too flamboyant and juvenile in her attire for a woman of her years, but this, after all, was a very venial weakness.

The tall, elegant girl he considered perfection; he could not see in her anything that he would have wished altered. And so she was the adopted daughter of a wealthy man! It was not much use allowing his feelings to stray in that direction. Howard Stormont would certainly have different views for her future. His friend Craig perhaps, with that fine old family record behind him, might have been considered favourably. But what had he, Leonard Lydon, a man of moderate income and no particular position, to offer such a peerless girl? Better put the idea out of his head with the least possible delay.

Still, it was very delightful sitting there and chatting to her. She talked to him as if she had known him for years, and there was not the faintest symptom of coquetry about her. She seemed a perfectly frank and open girl and quite free from conceit, unconscious that her undeniable personal charms were bound to work havoc on the opposite sex. She was not one of those sophisticated modern maidens who are always out for conquest and admiration.

They sat there for a long time, as neither Howard nor his sister reappeared. Presently Craig returned from his mysterious visit and came into the lounge in search of his friend. It struck Lydon, who could read him more easily than most people, that, in spite of the urbane mask which he so rarely removed, he was preoccupied and gloomy.

Craig was too well-bred a gentleman to be absolutely rude to anybody, much less to an attractive young woman. He addressed a few polite remarks to Miss Stormont, but it was not difficult to see his mind was elsewhere while he was making them. His presence seemed to have a rather chilling influence on both young people. Miss Stormont evidently was affected by it, for, after a very brief interval, she rose and bade them good night, saying that she must go and look after her relatives.

The young men smoked together for about half an hour, and during this time the conversation between them was desultory and fitful. Lydon was more sure than ever that his friend had something on his mind, but in spite of their close intimacy he did not venture to question him. Craig had a chilling manner of repelling confidences which it required a very callous man to put up with. If he did not think fit to unbosom himself, wild horses would not drag anything from him. When he had finished his cigar, he rose and rather abruptly intimated he was going to bed. Lydon stayed a little longer, thinking of Gloria Stormont and her exquisite charm, and then followed his example.

In the morning he came down rather late to breakfast, and was surprised to see the Stormont family in the hall, in the act of departure. The portly man addressed him in his usual breezy and genial manner.

"Glad to have a chance of saying good-bye to you. Amongst my letters this morning, I found one summoning me back to England on urgent business that brooks no delay. Very pleased to have come across you. The world is small, I expect we shall meet again some day. Come along, Maud. Gloria, hurry up."

There were hasty hand-shakes. Gloria smiled very sweetly and flushed just a little as she bade him farewell. Lydon felt his spirits sinking very low at her departure. He went into the dining-room and found Craig half-way through his breakfast. He imparted the news to his friend.

Craig made the very briefest comment. "I suppose you will miss her. You seemed on very good terms when I came upon you last night. Well, my dear chap, perhaps it is better. A very undesirable family, although I admit the girl is vastly different from her uncle and that overdressed aunt."

Leonard did not make any reply to this unkind speech. He knew his friend too well. He was not a man of violent likes or dislikes; but when once he formed an unfavourable opinion of anybody, nothing would ever alter or modify it. Howard Stormont and his widowed sister were anathema to him, and anathema they would remain till the end of the chapter.

They were staying on for the best part of another week, and during that period the young men were together the greater part of the time. But on several occasions Craig absented himself for short intervals, giving no explanation of his movements.

And one day, by the merest chance, Leonard saw him in a side street, engaged in conversation with a shabby, rather furtive-looking foreigner. As they were too occupied to notice him, he soon removed himself from their neighbourhood.

He had come across a few acquaintances at Nice, and Craig a great many. But this shabby furtive-looking foreigner was not the sort of companion suitable for the fastidious young diplomatist. Clearly there was some mystery going on, which his friend was carefully hiding from him. Probably it might be connected with his diplomatic business, but Lydon had an uncanny idea that a woman was at the bottom of it, whatever it was.

Never did he forget that early morning of the day which they had fixed for their departure. In the evening, Craig had gone out to dinner for the third time during their stay. Lydon went to the masked ball at the Casino, and returned early in the morning. He concluded that Craig had come home and gone to bed, knowing that his friend would not leave the Casino till late.

He was about to undress when he was called to the telephone by the police, who gave him alarming news. Would he go at once to the Villa des Cyclamens at Mont Boron, as his friend Mr. Craig was dangerously ill?

He had felt a little nettled the last few days by what he considered Craig's unfriendly reticence; but when he received this message, all his old affection for the staunch comrade of so many years returned in full force. As soon as possible he was at the Villa des Cyclamens of which he now heard for the first time.

CHAPTER TWO

GREAT was his astonishment at finding the pretty villa overlooking the moonlit Mediterranean in possession of the police, amongst whom he observed the shabby furtive-looking man whom he had seen talking to Hugh in the side street of Nice.

The chief official approached him and addressed him in excellent English. "We sent you a rather guarded message, Mr. Lydon, as we felt we could break the news better to you when you came here. A very terrible tragedy has occurred."

Lydon held his breath. He knew now that the mystery about Hugh Craig's frequent disappearance which had so puzzled him was about to be solved by this bland, courteous official.

"A terrible tragedy?" he faltered. "In Heaven's name what has happened?" The man proceeded to explain. "This house is tenanted by a Madame Makris, a widow. Her husband was a Greek merchant, she is an Englishwoman. She lived here with her daughter, Mademoiselle Elise Makris, the only child of the marriage. Mademoiselle and your friend, Mr. Hugh Craig, were very close friends; according to the mother's statement, they were more than friends, very devoted lovers. It seems a few days ago they had a violent quarrel—I am still quoting Madame Makris—the cause of which was not divulged. To-night Mr. Craig dined here, and after dinner he and the young lady went and sat on the veranda, according to their usual custom on the occasions when he visited the house."

Lydon interrupted with a question. "There are only three nights on which he has dined away from the hotel where we were staying together. I suppose he paid several day visits?"

"Madame Makris tells me hardly a day has passed that he did not come here, staying for longer or shorter periods. The young people have known each other for some five years. Well, the mother upon those occasions did not intrude herself very much; she left the lovers alone as much as possible. She followed her usual course this evening, occupying herself in writing letters and attending to her household accounts.

"Suddenly she was startled by the sound of shots proceeding from the veranda where Mr. Craig and her daughter were seated. She rushed hastily from the room in which she was sitting and was horrified at the sight which presented itself. Mademoiselle was bleeding from a wound in the neck. After shooting her, the young man turned the pistol on himself and sent a bullet through his brain. The young woman was still alive, Mr. Craig was dead when she reached him. The second shot had done its work instantaneously.

"Madame Makris at once rang up the police. We came with a doctor and Mademoiselle was taken to the hospital behind the railway station. For the unfortunate young man nothing could be done. After Madame had made her statement to us, we telephoned to you to come up."

Dazed as he was by the tragic occurrence, Lydon could grasp the fact that, although Hugh had never breathed to his friend a word of his secret connection with the denizens of the Villa des Cyclamens, he had been perfectly frank with them as to his relations with Lydon. Otherwise, how did Madame Makris know that they were staying together at the same hotel?

So the volcano which he had always suspected was slumbering under that placid exterior had suddenly burst into flame with these awful consequences to Elise Makris and the man himself.

"Can Madame suggest any explanation of this frenzied act?" was Lydon's next question.

The courteous official shook his head. "Madame says she knows nothing, that the whole thing is inexplicable to her."

"Mademoiselle Makris is in the hospital, you say. Do they give any hope of her recovery? Is the wound a serious one?"

"Very serious, I am told," was the reply. "They can pronounce no definite opinion at the moment. From what I can gather she seems to be hovering between life and death. Perhaps you would like to see the body; we have laid it in one of the bedrooms?"

Leonard went to the chamber, and gazed upon the pallid features of the friend whom he had last seen in full health and strength. As he stood there, looking down on the rigid form, he felt overcome by the memories of their long association. They had been intimate so many years.

A little under the age of fifteen they had foregathered at Harrow, drawn together by that strange attraction which sometimes unites totally opposite temperaments. They had gone up form by form in company. Hugh the mental superior, beating his friend at the last lap of all, and attaining the proud position of Head of the School. In the same year they had been put into the cricket eleven and had done battle against Eton at Lord's. At Balliol, whither they both proceeded, the intimacy grew stronger, and here again history repeated itself. They both represented their University in cricket against Cambridge, as they had represented Harrow.

And now this life, so full of promise and opportunity, had been blotted out by his own rash act. And, even more terrible, Hugh Craig had gone to his last account with the sin of murder, or at least attempted murder, on his soul. What terrible thing was it that had so unhinged his mind?

14

The police had found the pistol clutched firmly in his dead hand. This fearful deed, then, was not due to some sudden temptation of the moment. It must have been premeditated or he would not have taken a loaded weapon with him to this peaceful villa. When Hugh had bade his friend good-bye, he must have had murder, and afterwards self-destruction, in his mind.

When the young man had left the death-chamber, he inquired after Madame Makris, and was informed that she was prostrated with grief, as was quite natural. He exchanged a few words with the furtive-looking man whom he had seen talking to Hugh in the side street a short time ago.

"I saw you together the other day," he said, "but you did not see me, and I hastened as quickly as possible out of sight, as I did not wish to appear to be spying upon my friend. Do you know anything that can throw light upon this?"

The shabby individual lowered his eyes as he answered. "No, monsieur, I am sorry to say, nothing. My acquaintance with Monsieur Craig was very slight."

If the man was not actually lying, it was obvious there was nothing to be got out of him. Lydon impatiently asked him if he was one of the regular police. To this question he replied that he was not, that he followed the profession of private inquiry agent, as it would be called in England. That he was naturally in the course of his business frequently in communication with them, and that having heard of the terrible tragedy at the Villa, he had begged permission to accompany them there.

Later on, Lydon put himself into communication with the dead man's family, and Hugh's elder brother came over to Nice at once to superintend the arrangements. Geoffrey Craig, a rather severe-looking man, who held a minor Governmental post, was as much bewildered by the catastrophe as Lydon himself. He had never heard of the Makris family in connection with his brother.

Hugh Craig was buried in the beautiful English cemetery out beyond the Magnan, what time the girl whom he had tried to kill was lying between life and death in the hospital.

Lydon was obliged to defer his departure for a few days in consequence of these tragic happenings. Before he left he called upon Mrs. Makris, who was now sufficiently recovered to receive him.

She was a stoutly-built, rather over-dressed woman, with a face which still showed traces of good looks. He had been told by the police she was an Englishwoman, and her thoroughly British accent confirmed the fact. But he had a shrewd suspicion that Jewish blood ran in her veins.

While he was waiting in the pretty *salon* of the Villa des Cyclamens for the unhappy mother, he noticed upon a writing table a gorgeous carved sapphire made into a pendant, the stone worn upon the breastplate of the High Priest of the Hebrews as the sign of Issachar. He rather marvelled that such a valuable article was allowed to lie there. In the distraction occasioned by the tragedy, it was of course possible that neither Madame Makris nor any other member of the household had heeded it.

The Jewish-looking woman bore upon her still good-looking face the deep traces of her grief. When Lydon murmured a few words of sympathy, the ready tears fell immediately.

"My darling Elise was all the world to me; we were devoted to each other," she said in a broken voice. "And this state of suspense is awful. Two whole days have passed, and still they are not certain whether she will live or die."

Lydon again expressed his deep sympathy. "I have been very terribly shocked too, although I cannot for a moment pretend to compare my feelings with yours. Hugh Craig and I have been friends from boyhood, and I should have judged him the last man in the world to have given way to such an awful impulse. Have you no inkling of the cause which led to such an unexpected catastrophe?"

Madame Makris shook her head, a head covered with thick dark hair in which there was not a trace of grey, in spite of her years, which might have been anything from forty-five to fifty.

"Not the slightest, Mr. Lydon. There had been some disagreement between them a little time previously, for I discovered my poor girl in tears after he had left. I pressed her to tell me the reason of her agitation, but she parried all my efforts to extract the truth from her. She assured me it was quite a trifling matter, and that she would not have been affected by it, except for the fact that she was in low spirits."

"May I ask, madame, if they had known each other for long?"

"Some few years," was the answer. "There was no regular engagement between them, but it was understood that they would marry as soon as they could. Elise was always rather reticent on the subject, but I gathered that there was some difficulty in the way with regard to Mr. Craig's family. It was a very old and honourable one, and it was expected of him that when he did marry he would choose somebody of his own order. We are, of course, quite middle-class people, and by no means wealthy. My husband was a merchant."

Lydon pointed to the writing-table. "That is rather a valuable thing to leave lying about, if I may say so, madam."

The dark-haired woman looked at it with an air of indifference. "I had forgotten it in the preoccupation of my great trouble. It belongs to Elise. Her uncle, Monsieur Lianas, gave it to her on her twenty-first birthday. She was wearing it when the tragedy occurred. I only brought it back from the hospital this morning, and heedlessly laid it down there. But you are quite right; it is too valuable to be left lying about. I will lock it up directly. Heaven knows if my poor child will ever wear it again," she concluded with a burst of tears.

Leonard went back to England the next day, very sad at heart at the loss of his lifelong friend. He pondered much over the meagre information that Madame Makris had given him. The young people had known each other for some years. There had been no formal engagement between them, but it was an understood thing they were to be married as soon as they were in a position to do so.

And during those years, although they had met so frequently, Craig had never dropped a word about Elise or her mother to his friend. So strange a silence passed beyond the bounds of ordinary reticence. There must be some reason for it, most likely some mystery behind it. He could quite understand that Hugh might find some difficulty in reconciling his family to his marriage with a foreigner of no particular position. But it was strange that a man should be in love and never say anything about it to his closest friend.

As was natural under such painful circumstances, his thoughts of Gloria Stormont had been temporarily pushed into the background; but after a little, when the first violence of the shock had passed away, her charming image again recurred to him.

What a beautiful girl she was, and how delightfully unaffected! Was it likely he would ever come across her again? Her uncle had spoken of it as a probability when he remarked that after all the world was a small place.

And a fortnight later, Howard Stormont's prophecy was fulfilled. Lydon suddenly made up his mind to run down for a week-end to the *Metropole* at Brighton. As he ascended the steps of the well-known hotel about an hour before dinner-time, the first person he encountered in the vestibule was the genial Stormont, looking more prosperous and rubicund than ever.

Nothing could have been more hearty than the greeting Lydon received.

"Well met, my dear fellow, glad to see you. I said it would not be long before we ran across each other again. My sister and Gloria are with me. Are you alone? Good, you must join our table. Well, as soon as you have settled about your room, let us celebrate the occasion with a cocktail. Good old *Metropole*, you can't beat it. I'm not very busy just now, so we're here for a week. My sister is a bit run down, and the sea breezes will set her up."

What a good-hearted fellow he was, Lydon thought. Gloria had said of him he was one of the kindest and most generous of men. Over their cocktails the young man told him of the tragic happenings at the Villa des Cyclamens. But Stormont had read it in the papers. Of course it was impossible that anything could be kept quiet in the case of a man of Hugh Craig's position.

"A very mysterious affair, and I suppose nobody will ever know the rights of it," he remarked when Leonard had communicated all the details he knew, which, as we know, were somewhat meagre. "Well, I cannot say I ever took very kindly to your poor friend, for the reason probably that he took very little pains to conceal his dislike of me. But it is a terrible ending to a promising career. I suppose, in the course of time, he would have ended up as an ambassador. The Clandon family have a knack of falling into soft jobs. Now, you won't see the womenfolk before dinner, as they are in their rooms, and I shan't mention I have met you. When you walk up to our table it will be a pleasant surprise for them. We all took a great fancy to you at Nice."

The young man had no reason to complain of his welcome at the hands of the two ladies when he met them at dinner. Mrs. Barnard told him it was a most agreeable surprise, and although Gloria did not make flattering speeches, she flushed prettily and her eyes looked very bright when she shook hands with him.

They spent a very delightful evening together. Early the next morning Stormont expressed his intention of taking his sister a long motor drive, with a view of getting as much fresh air as possible; they would be back to luncheon.

"You two young people can do what you like with yourselves," he said gaily. Certainly, he was a most complaisant person. Lydon was rather surprised that he should throw them into each other's society like this. Surely he must have ambitious views for his niece's future. And he could not help wondering what it was his friend Hugh had seen in the man which made him dislike him so intensely. Little vulgarisms in speech and manner peeped out now and again, but surely those were not enough to account for such a fierce aversion, more especially as Craig, in spite of his aristocratic lineage, was rather a democratic sort of fellow at heart, and a thorough cosmopolitan.

The two, thus dismissed to their own resources, went on to the West Pier, where they sat for some little time, then they walked up and down the Parade for a couple of hours, till it was time to return to the hotel. During these happy and precious moments Leonard felt that he was making great headway with the charming girl. She talked to him with as much freedom as if they had been friends of old standing. She told him all about her uncle's place, Effington Hall, and of her mode of life there. According to her account, it was a very beautiful place, with lovely gardens, and the rather commonplace-looking Howard Stormont appeared to dwell in great luxury, with a large retinue of servants. As he listened, he wondered if he would ever be asked to join the numerous company which the owner invited there.

Stormont did not seem to mind his enjoying the girl's society on a casual visit to the seaside, but would he draw the line at the familiarity born of a long stay in a country house? Had he been in the uncle's place, he was inclined to think he would.

His visit did not terminate with the week-end. He stayed on another couple of days, being pressed to do so by Stormont himself during this extension of time. The brother and sister left the young couple very much to themselves, and Lydon made splendid running with Gloria. So much so that, before he left, she had promised to run up to town from Effington soon after they returned there, and lunch with him in town.

Lydon had suggested it with rather a shamefaced air. "I don't feel I have the cheek to ask you in front of your uncle and aunt after such a short acquaintance," he explained. "I expect they would think it confounded impertinence on my part."

Gloria had blushed very becomingly when she answered him. "Well, one cannot be quite sure. They are pretty modern, considering all things, but perhaps not quite so modern as you and I. I often run up to shop; it is really no distance from London. I will give you good notice when I am coming, and I can tell them about it later when we have all got to know each other better."

Lydon went back to London very delighted that the girl liked him well enough to take the bold course of meeting him secretly. In due course, when he went in to breakfast in his comfortable chambers at Ryder Street, he found the expected note from Miss Stormont appointing two days later for their luncheon.

There was another letter from the well-known firm of Shelford & Taylor, solicitors in Lincoln's Inn Fields, asking him to give them a call, as they wished to hand him a communication from one of their clients.

He knew these people had attended to the affairs of most of the members of the Clandon family, Hugh included. Greatly wondering, he called on them that morning, and was received by the head of the firm, who handed him a bulky letter.

"This was received from our client, and your friend, the Honourable Hugh Craig, very shortly after the terrible tragedy, with instructions to hand it to you after the lapse of a certain period which has now expired. I am filled with curiosity to know if this letter, dispatched to us on the morning of the day on which this awful thing occurred, throws any light upon the affair."

Leonard read slowly through the long communication, and, laying it down, met the inquiring gaze of the solicitor.

"Yes," he said, in a sad voice. "This reveals the motives which impelled him to attempt the life of Elise Makris, and make an end of his own. I will tell you."

CHAPTER THREE

"First, I will read you the opening sentences of the letter," said Leonard. And this is what he read:

"To you, my very dear friend, whose friendship has been one of the most pleasurable things in my life, to the memories of which I look back with a feeling of great tenderness as I pen these lines, the last I shall ever write upon earth, I reveal the secret of the tragedy which will shortly take place. In Nice the affair will, naturally, be a nine days' wonder. Nice, this fair and lovely city of aristocratic crookdom, where vice and virtue rub shoulders at every hour of the twenty-four, and where the cleverest criminals of the world congregate in the pursuit of their nefarious calling! Nice, where I first met the only woman who ever stirred my pulses, who made me realize the meaning of ardent, overmastering love! When you read these words, perhaps you will smile at the idea of the cautious diplomatist, the rather cynical young man of the world, confessing to being violently in love. But it is the truth. I had passed unscathed up to a few years ago, indifferent to the charms of the many beautiful women I had met in my own country and elsewhere, until I made the acquaintance of Elise Makris. Then suddenly I realized, poor fool as I was, that I had found my ideal. To me she stood for the perfection of womanhood.

"To-night I am going to kill her, because she has betrayed my faith in her, because I have proved she is base and unworthy. And when I have accomplished this justifiable vengeance, there is nothing left for me but to end my own life. By the time you receive this letter the nine days' wonder will have died out, and the memory of Hugh Craig will only linger in the hearts of one or two faithful friends like yourself. The details I am about to relate will not interest the world, but you are at perfect liberty to communicate them to anybody you think it may concern."

"As you are such an old and confidential friend of the Clandon family, Mr. Shelford," said the young man when he had finished reading this preliminary portion of the letter, "I feel quite justified in reading to you what my poor, unfortunate friend has disclosed to me."

From the astounding narrative to which Mr. Shelford listened, he learned the following remarkable facts: Mrs. Makris, the mother of Elise, a very beautiful young woman, had posed, ever since Craig knew her, as the widow of a Greek merchant who had left her comfortably off. Her late husband's fortune was settled upon her for life, she told him, and her daughter would inherit it at her death.

It was on Craig's last visit to Nice, and then only towards the end of it, that his suspicions concerning the truth of her story were aroused. Elise had addressed to him by mistake a letter intended for somebody else, a letter of a most suspicious character, betraying her acquaintance with a very questionable set of people. When he asked her for an explanation, her replies were evasive and unsatisfactory, so much so that he at once came to the conclusion that both the girl and her mother were quite different from what they seemed.

He did not at once break off with her, wishing to test the truth of his suspicions. For this purpose he secured the services of a private inquiry agent, without doubt the shabby furtive-looking man to whom Leonard had seen him talking in that quiet side street.

This man soon discovered the horrible fact that both the woman and her daughter were connected with a well-known gang of international crooks. Elise, with her beauty and charm, was one of their most useful decoys, and under another name had served a term of imprisonment a short time before Craig had made her acquaintance. The woman Makris had never been married, so he alleged; the girl was her illegitimate daughter, the father having been a member of the same gang. To the young man, whose affections she had captured, Elise had represented herself as a model of simplicity and purity. As they did not see each other very frequently, it was the more easy for her to maintain the double rôle of sweetheart to him and the clever decoy of these unscrupulous scoundrels. But for her own carelessness in putting the wrong letter into the envelope directed to him, Craig had made up his mind to marry her privately and tell his family afterwards.

"A most astounding story," was the remark of the shrewd and experienced lawyer when the narrative was finished. "Poor fellow, one cannot but pity him in spite of the fact that he took the law into his own hands. The discovery of her baseness must have overthrown his reason. How deceptive are appearances. One would have judged him the last man in the world to be swayed by violent passions. Clearly the mind must have given way under the shock."

"There are some rather obscure hints that he had been subjected to blackmail, and that through this man he employed, he was able to trace it to her agency. That of course would have a maddening effect upon any man in a similar position."

Mr. Sheldon knitted his brows. "I wish he had been a little more explicit on that point. We do not know whether this girl is alive or dead. When Hugh's brother left Nice, she was hovering between life and death in the hospital to which they had taken her. If she has recovered, I should very much like to find the young woman, although it doesn't appear that it would serve any very useful purpose if I did."

Lydon also expressed his wish that, if she had escaped her lover's vengeance, Elise Makris, the decoy of blackmailers, should be found. Mr. Shelford promised to instruct his agent in Nice to make inquiries at once.

The tragedy had cast a deep shadow over Lydon. Even the prospect of meeting again with Gloria Stormont could not restore him to his old cheerfulness, nor blot out the memory of those sinister happenings at the peaceful-looking Villa des Cyclamens.

Gloria looked very charming and radiant when she arrived at Waterloo Station, where Leonard was awaiting her.

"It was a little indiscreet of us to arrange meeting here," she said with a blush as they shook hands. "Somebody who knew me might have travelled in the same train; that would have been awkward. It was silly of me to overlook that."

"And equally silly on my part," replied the young man. "Well, on a future occasion, we must avoid a similar mistake. Well, now about lunch. I was going to suggest the *Berkeley* or the *Savoy*. But perhaps we had better get off the beaten track?"

Miss Stormont agreed. Several people she knew frequented both these popular places. They finally went to a excellent restaurant in the Strand.

They had a very enjoyable time together. There was not a trace of coquetry about her, but she seemed to envisage the situation with perfect frankness. If Lydon had not been attracted by her, he would not have asked her to lunch. If she had not been equally attracted by him, she would not have accepted his invitation. They might therefore take for granted the fact of their mutual attraction, and not pretend an embarrassment they did not feel.

When they parted, and he pressed for another meeting, she consented quite readily, adding, "I hope, however, we shall not have to keep up this *sub-rosa* business very long. Uncle was speaking last night of you and saying how much he liked you. You can guess how difficult it was to keep myself from blushing. I suggested that as he liked you so much, why did he not ask you to pay a visit? He did not exactly adopt the suggestion at once, but I'm sure the idea is germinating in his mind and will presently blossom forth."

Lydon looked the delight he felt. "So you think I may receive a formal invitation to go down to Effington. That would be very pleasant. In the meantime our engagement for next week holds good."

"Most certainly," was the girl's unaffected answer. He put her in a taxi and directed the driver to take her to Waterloo Station. It was not safe for him to go with her, much as he would have liked to do so. At this hour of the day some of the early birds might be returning home, and at this stage of the proceedings it was not politic for Miss Stormont to be seen by any of her neighbours in the company of a good-looking young man.

The next week when he met her, almost the first words she said were, "Have you heard from Uncle Howard?"

He answered that he had not, and she proceeded to explain: "Well, the idea has blossomed. Two days ago at breakfast, he announced solemnly to auntie and myself that he was going to write to you at the address in Ryder Street you gave him, and ask you down for a week-end. To-day is Wednesday; you ought to have had the letter by now. But perhaps he didn't intend to ask you for this week-end but the next. Uncle is very impetuous in some things but slow-moving in others. And if it is for the following week, naturally he wouldn't be in a hurry."

It was, however, this week-end that the genial Stormont had fixed in his mind. When Lydon went home that night the precious letter was awaiting him, having arrived by a midday post. If Mr. Lydon had no previous engagement, would he spend next Saturday to Monday, or, if possible, Tuesday, at Effington? If so, Stormont would meet him at Waterloo by a certain train and they would go down together.

Of course, he sent an immediate reply. So, at last, he was made free of Effington; he would see his beloved Gloria in her own home, and be able to feast his eyes upon her for several hours. If Howard Stormont was as unconventional as his appearance and manners proclaimed, there would be an end of the *sub-rosa* meetings. In these advanced days, when the chaperone is nearly as extinct as the dodo, he would be able to ask her openly to lunch with him when she came up to London to do her shopping. It was a great step gained.

On the Friday before his visit, he had a summons from Shelford, the solicitor, who had heard from his agent in Nice.

Elise Makris was alive, wonderful to relate. For some days the doctors had entertained little or no hope. Then suddenly the tide had turned, and she had made a remarkable rally. Three days before Shelford's letter of instructions reached Nice, she had been discharged from the hospital, still somewhat weak, but in no danger of a relapse. She had returned to the Villa des Cyclamens, which on the next day was evacuated. Madame Makris had paid up all she owed, and she and her daughter had gone away, nobody knew whither.

The agent had made some inquiries of the police, and had also found out the man employed by Craig in his researches into the past of the girl whom he had so passionately loved and found so unworthy. He gathered that she and her mother were members of a big organization belonging to the exclusive circles of what might be called aristocratic crookdom. Many of the subordinates were known to the guardians of the law under different aliases, Madame Makris, a very old offender, and her daughter being amongst them. But the chiefs of the gang, the daring spirits who engineered the great coups, remained in seclusion, men not only of great ability, but possibly of considerable wealth. They never came out into the open, and nobody could lay hands on them.

So Elise Makris, after that lucky escape from her enraged lover's bullet, had disappeared where, in all human probability, no friend of Hugh would ever be able to find her. She and her mother had no doubt gone to another country, and would conceal their identity under other names. That of Makris had been made too public by recent events.

The only description Lydon had of her was a somewhat indefinite one, taken from the *Phare du Littoral*, the Nice daily newspaper. There were, however, two clues still remaining, if ever he should chance to be thrown into contact with her. She would carry to her grave the mark of her dead lover's bullet; no surgery could obliterate that. And she would wear that remarkable carved sapphire pendant which her mother declared she always carried about with her as a mascot. By those signs he would recognize Elise Makris under whatever alias she chose to masquerade.

"That seems to close the chapter," remarked Mr. Shelford, when he had imparted all that he had learned from his agent. "A terrible blow to the Clandon family. I saw his brother yesterday; he tells me the old people are prostrated with grief. That a man of the promise of Hugh Craig, with a brilliant future stretching in front of him, should have sought to imbrue his hands in the blood of such a shameless creature! It passes comprehension."

On the Saturday morning Lydon met Stormont at Waterloo Station, and they travelled down to Guildford together by an early train. At Guildford they were met by a splendid Rolls-Royce car driven by one of the smartest of chauffeurs. Profiteer or not, as the case might be, Howard Stormont knew how to do things properly.

They went through a few miles of the beautiful Surrey country, till they came to some big open lodge gates. Passing through these, they drove up a broad avenue, shadowed by some splendid trees which would look magnificent later on in their summer raiment, and drew up before the low picturesque house.

The coming of the car had been heard evidently, for the hall door stood wide open to receive the owner and his guest. Behind the decorous form of the stately white-haired butler, Duncan, appeared the gaily-apparelled Mrs. Barnard, and the slim exquisite figure of the smiling Gloria.

Stormont sprang out of the car and grasped Leonard's hand in a hearty grip. "Welcome, my dear boy, to Effington," he said in his loud, ringing voice.

CHAPTER FOUR

THERE was a big dinner party in the evening, somewhat to Leonard's disappointment. He had hoped they would have spent the first night by themselves, so that he would have an opportunity of appropriating more or less the charming Gloria. Instead of this, she would be lost to him amidst a crowd.

Perhaps it was Howard Stormont's way of impressing a new guest. Craig had always said the man was a vulgarian at heart, and that the vulgarity was always peeping through the thin veneer of a lately-acquired refinement. Lydon was far from prepared to go this length, but he did wish his host had avoided so much ostentation the first time he sat at his table.

The house was run on very magnificent lines, and the rather overpowering sense of wealth depressed him a little. In spite of her frank and unaffected manners, it made Gloria seem very far away from him. Even if she reciprocated his feelings, how could he dare to think of taking her from such a splendid home as this to share his own very moderate fortunes?

There were about a dozen people to dinner besides himself and the Stormonts. The white-haired Duncan was assisted by four footmen. The majority of the guests were neighbours, a few obviously with the stamp of the county on them. Two married couples were London friends and had come down to dine and stay the week-end like Lydon himself. The dinner was a very lengthy affair, exquisitely cooked and served with the utmost elegance. The wines and liqueurs were of unexceptionable quality.

Lydon's father, probably a man of greater wealth than Stormont, had lived in much the same profuse style. But Leonard had not seen a great deal of it; he had been away from home so much. His own tastes were very simple, and he had no hankerings after luxury.

To judge by Howard Stormont's beaming countenance, as he sat at his end of the table, with a rather severe-looking "county" lady on his right, he seemed to revel in it. Lydon did not think for a moment that the man had been born to it; from many little signs he could deduce the contrary. But possibly he was one of those ambitious souls to whom magnificent surroundings seem a quite commonplace part of their environment. What to Lydon seemed ostentation only appeared to the other ordinary comfort.

And what about Gloria? Was all this wealth and luxury, these dainty, never-ending dishes, this army of deftly-trained servants an absolute necessity of her well-being, as it seemed to that of her uncle and the richly-dressed Mrs. Barnard, who beamed as benignly on their guests as her portly and rubicund brother?

Well, he did not know enough of her yet to decide. All he did know was that she looked very beautiful in some soft shimmering fabric that displayed to perfection the ivory white of her well-poised neck and rounded arms. Now and then he caught a kindly glance, speaking of more than ordinary acquaintance, from the soft, pretty blue eyes. Now and again he caught her low, sweet laugh at some remark of her neighbour.

Lydon had for his partner one of the county people, a young married woman, Mrs. Lycett, not very remarkable for good looks, but very lively and voluble. He learned afterwards that she was a very important person in her set, by reason of her various accomplishments. She was a keen and prominent golfer, a daring and fearless rider to hounds, an adept at every kind of sport.

As Lydon was no mean sportsman himself, he got on very well with this voluble person, who chattered away to him about her prowess. But all the same, Mrs. Lycett, with her vivid account of her feats in so many departments of sport, could not make up to him for Gloria. She was an athletic girl too, but she had not that slight touch of the masculine which rather disfigured Mrs. Lycett, and, above all, Gloria did not boast about her achievements. She was so distinctly feminine and lovable. Long before the protracted meal was over, Leonard found himself growing more than a little weary. He had not bargained for being thrust so suddenly into a crowd of absolute strangers. He looked back with pleasure on his two *sub-rosa* meetings with the beautiful girl, whose glance he only occasionally met across the big dinner-table.

After dinner the men sat for a little time to smoke a cigarette and then joined the ladies. Soon the large party split up into groups. Some went to the billiard-room, most sat down to bridge. A few clustered round the piano, where Gloria sang some very charming songs in a well-trained voice. Lydon joined this particular group, not because he was so keen on music, but from a desire to be as near to Gloria as possible.

At a fairly early hour in the evening, carriages were announced, and the neighbours departed, almost in a body. Only the house party was left, and after a little while the ladies took their candles, and the men adjourned to the smoking-room, a handsome apartment decorated in the Moorish style, for a final chat. The two visitors from London were elderly men, contemporaries of the host, and their conversation was chiefly about general topics in which the three were interested.

The next day, Sunday, was, on the whole, quite enjoyable. Everybody except one of the London men went to church in the morning. In the afternoon, Leonard, to his great delight, got Gloria to himself, and they went for a long walk from after lunch till close upon tea-time. No other guests were present at dinner, for which the young man was very grateful. The elderly people gravitated naturally to each other, and left the young couple very much to themselves.

They carried on a low-toned conversation at the far end of the big drawing-room. In the course of it, Leonard suggested they should soon have another lunch in town, Gloria was quite willing. "I think you can suggest it quite openly now," she said. "As a matter of fact, you can include auntie if you like, but she will be quite certain to refuse. She has so many interests at Effington and she so loves the place, that it is difficult to drag her up to London except when she wants new clothes. And really you might pay Uncle Howard the compliment also, and, ten to one, the result would be the same. He takes a good many holidays, but when he does go to his business he works like a horse, so at least he tells us, and has no time for frivolity."

"Works hard and plays hard," remarked Lydon. "So far as I can judge from my short stay here, he seems to revel in the good things of life."

Miss Stormont smiled. "You have judged him quite accurately. My dear old uncle is a perfect sybarite, a crumpled rose-leaf in his bed would disturb him acutely. He likes the best of everything, 'the best that money can buy,' as he puts it in his rather blunt fashion. The most perfect food, the choicest cigars, the rarest wines. Of course he has to dine out here a good deal, as he cannot affront his neighbours by refusing. But the dear man really prefers entertaining to being entertained."

"When he entertains, he is sure of the quality, eh? He knows he won't be put off with the second best," laughed Lydon. "Away from home he might get an inferior vintage or an inferior cigar."

"I am afraid he has that idea at the back of his mind," admitted his niece.

"Well, if he should accept my invitation to lunch, I will take him to my best club and allow him to order the luncheon," said Lydon, speaking in the same light spirit. "Well, what about Mrs. Barnard? Is she a sybarite like her brother?"

"Not in the least. Like me, her individual tastes are very simple, she likes moderate comfort, but she has no hankering after luxury. She is a frightfully energetic woman, busies herself in everything going on in the neighbourhood, local charities and so forth, and writes letters by the score. She would die of *ennui* if her hands were not fully occupied. And, of course, at her time of life, sport has no attraction for her. She is rather devoted to bridge, but she never plays it till the evening."

Lydon was very pleased to hear that Gloria had simple tastes, that luxury was not essential to her. Presently he said to her: "Do you know, I have got a little whim that I should like to have just another of those quiet little

29

meetings before we take the others into our confidence. I wonder if you would very much mind?"

Miss Stormont had one very delightful feminine trait, she was always ready to admit the supremacy of the sterner sex, and give way to them wherever it was consistent with her own dignity.

"If you very much wish it, I don't mind in the least," she answered sweetly. "But I would like to know the reason of this whim."

"I am afraid I cannot give a very lucid explanation," said the young man rather lamely. "Somehow, I seem to like you in a somewhat less gorgeous setting than this. You are housed like a Princess."

She looked at him with comprehending eyes. "Does it oppress you just a little bit, this—this magnificence?" she asked.

"A tiny bit, I must confess," he admitted, admiring her quickness.

She looked thoughtful. "I had rather the same feeling when I first came to live with my uncle. My father has a good position in China, but he is not of course a rich man, and our life out there was quite simple compared to this. I am rather surprised though about you. From what I am told, your father was quite a wealthy man, uncle says, much richer than himself. You must have been used to it all your life."

"Not quite. All the time we children were at school—and my dear father gave us the best of educations, he thought that was the most priceless asset a man could bestow upon his offspring—our home was conducted upon a comfortable but perfectly modest scale. It was not till after I left Oxford that he launched out into something like this. And during those very fat years I was seldom at home. So I had really no time to grow in love with luxury."

"I don't know that I am really in love with it. I mean it would cause me no pain to descend to a much lower standard of living. But to uncle all this is the breath of his nostrils; he is naturally one of the most reckless and extravagant of men. He scatters money with an absolutely lavish hand. I am sure that auntie, who, of course, knows more about his affairs than I do, is often frightfully worried about it. She has often tried to dissuade him from some contemplated extravagance, but to no purpose."

These remarks gave rise to a new train of thought in Lydon's mind. Were things quite satisfactory at Effington? Was this army of servants of all descriptions, footmen, gardeners and chauffeurs, perfectly justifiable? If Howard Stormont was living within his income, why should his sister be worried? Was the man one of those you so often meet with, who can make money but cannot hold it? Was he living up to the hilt, and might some sudden turn of fortune's wheel bring him headlong to the ground? He would have liked to question Gloria a little closely on the subject, but their acquaintance was too recent for him to take such a liberty. No doubt he would learn more later on.

But if it was the fact that, in his selfish desire for luxury, he was spending money as fast as he made it, and putting by nothing for a rainy day, something that had puzzled Lydon became easily capable of explanation. In this case, Gloria would not be an heiress, and her uncle had not formed any grandiose plans for her future. He would be content if she could marry a man who would keep her comfortably, and not expect any fortune with her.

And, as a result of this hypothesis, Howard Stormont fell distinctly in his estimation. He was simply living for his own gratification, oblivious of those he left behind; in Lydon's opinion, the most contemptible conduct any man could be capable of.

On Monday morning the two elderly couples departed. The young man would have gone also, but on the Sunday night Stormont took him on one side and pressed him to stop another day, if his business engagements would permit.

"I very rarely go up on a Monday myself, unless there is something very urgent," he had said. "And, at my age, I think I may be permitted to allow myself a little latitude. I simply love pottering about this dear old place; although I have had it for some time now, it is still a new toy to me, after being pent up in cities nearly the whole of my working life. Stop till Tuesday morning, and we will go up together."

Lydon, nothing loath, agreed to the pleasing proposition. The Monday was the happiest day of his visit. Soon after breakfast Stormont went off on his own. Mrs. Barnard was fully occupied during the morning and afternoon, and he had Gloria practically to himself until it was time to dress for dinner.

That evening in the smoking-room Lydon told his host what Hugh had disclosed in that letter which the solicitor, Shelford, had handed to him. He fancied that Stormont did not take very much interest in the matter. This, however, was hardly to be wondered at, as Hugh had always treated the man with a certain *hauteur* which he could not have helped observing, had he been a much less intelligent person than he was. When the story was finished, Lydon learned a piece of the Clandon family history that was unknown to him.

"A very remarkable family, the Clandons; I know a little about them," he remarked.

It was by no means the first time the young man had noticed that Stormont always seemed to know a good deal about everybody who was of any importance in the world. According to what Gloria had let drop, he knew that Lydon's father had been a man of considerable wealth. He rather wondered where this information was procured. Stormont of course knew a great many people about Effington, but so much gossip of the big world would hardly filter there. He had never heard him speak of numerous acquaintances in London, and so far as Leonard knew, he did not belong to any London club, a circumstance which in a man of his apparent wealth seemed rather peculiar.

"A very remarkable family, the Clandons," repeated the genial, rubicund man. "Remarkable in this respect, that for some generations they have transmitted to their descendants a very high order of intelligence. They have never produced any first-class brains, it is true. They have never boasted a Prime Minister, a great general, a distinguished lawyer, but several of them have filled second and third-rate posts with some distinction. This poor chap who killed himself after trying to murder the girl, for example. I don't suppose he would have been a Stratford de Redcliffe, or a von Bieberstein, but he would no doubt have developed into a quite respectable diplomatist of the average order."

It hurt Lydon to hear him speak of his old friend in such a slighting manner. But Hugh had certainly taken no pains to conceal his dislike of "the aggressive profiteer," and Stormont was human. The next words startled him greatly.

"Well, as I told you, I know some things about the Clandon family, one a fact not at all generally known. By the light of that knowledge, your friend's act can be accounted for. There was insanity on both sides, the mother's and the father's."

"You astound me," cried Lydon in genuine amazement. "I never had a suspicion of this. But then how should I have? Even if Hugh was acquainted with the fact, which it is more than likely he was, he would scarcely reveal it even to his best friend."

"Quite so," assented Stormont. "Men don't speak of these painful things as a rule. But you can rest assured that what I have told you is quite true. The uncle of the present holder of the title, Hugh Craig's father, a man of good fortune, endowed with all the blessings of life, cut his throat in his bath one morning without any apparent reason or motive; this man's sister, Lord Clandon's aunt, died a raving lunatic. On the mother's side, Lady Clandon has a younger brother who has been in a private asylum for the last twenty-five years. It is not generally known outside the family. My sources of information happened to be rather exclusive. So you see the taint suddenly developed in this poor chap as soon as he got an overpowering shock."

So the family history accounted for poor Hugh's sudden aberration. The mysterious malady of madness that sometimes passes a whole generation, to break out with virulence in the next one!

On the Tuesday morning Leonard travelled up with his host. They parted at Waterloo Station, as Stormont said his offices were in the City, while those of Leonard were in Victoria Street. The young man was warmly pressed to pay another visit to Effington at an early date.

Obviously this genial uncle was not going to put any obstacle in the way of increased intimacy between the young people. The very significant facts admitted by Gloria seemed to solve what might otherwise have proved a puzzling problem. Mr. Howard Stormont had apparently made up his mind to live for the day, and to say with the French monarch, "Après moi le déluge."

A few days later he met Gloria at the luncheon which she had agreed should be a secret one. She was very sweet and amiable, but evidently her conscience pricked her, for when they parted she told him firmly it must be the last under such conditions.

"There is really no longer any necessity for it," she said. "Uncle likes you very much, and he has now made you free of Effington. If he disapproved of our friendship, he would not ask you to his home."

"You are quite right," admitted Lydon. "It was a foolish sort of whim of mine. I could not quite get it out of my mind that if I took such a liberty with the niece of the owner of such a splendid place as Effington Hall, he would send me to the right-about."

Gloria laughed, told him that he seemed an exceedingly modest young man, and hoped he would always remain so. It was evident that Stormont desired his friendship, for on the following Friday he rang him up, and inquired if he would go down with him to Effington the next day.

Of course, the young man was only too pleased to go. He had not ventured to hope that he would see Gloria again so soon. Stormont was at the station awaiting him, and with him was a tall, thin man of about the same age as himself, whom he introduced as Mr. Whitehouse. This gentleman was a quiet, reserved sort of person, and Lydon did not feel particularly attracted to him. Stormont added an explanation that they were very old friends, and did a good deal of business together. As he said this, Leonard remembered that he had never heard the nature of Stormont's business either from himself or his niece.

This visit was quite a different one from the last. No big dinner party at night with the army of well-trained servants in attendance; just a cosy meal in a smaller apartment, half morning-room, half dining-room. Mr. Whitehouse seemed well known to the household, but he was not by any means a great talker. Probably he had come down to discuss business matters with his host.

After dinner the two elder men retired to Stormont's study. Lydon went with the ladies into the drawing-room, Stormont excusing his absence with the genial remark that they were treating him as one of the family.

After Gloria had played and sung a little, she proposed that they should adjourn for billiards, a game at which she was no mean performer. The billiard-room was next to Stormont's study, the door of which was open, and as they went in Lydon heard these words uttered in Whitehouse's rather deep voice:

"Yes, it is most unfortunate that the thing should have happened at the moment it did. She is absolutely essential to this particular scheme. We can't start it without her."

These words made the young man wonder a good deal. What possible business could it be, to the prosecution of which a certain woman was essential?

CHAPTER FIVE

HE had always felt curious on the subject of Stormont's business, one which evidently brought him in a large income, for how otherwise could he have maintained the upkeep of such an expensive place as Effington. It was strange, too, that the man had never made any allusion to it himself, more especially as he did not appear to be of a reticent or secretive nature. With the majority of persons it is not necessary to know them for very long before they let drop something that proclaims their occupation.

He had told the Stormonts all about himself on the occasion of his second meeting with them at Brighton, without any reserve. If he had foregathered more intimately with them at Nice, he would have told them then. Even with such a very reticent man as Craig, you could not have been in his society for a few hours without learning that he was a member of the diplomatic corps. It certainly was odd that Stormont never dropped a remark that enabled you to fix his occupation. He occasionally spoke of himself as a business man, and that was all.

To carry on any sort of business, he must have an office or offices somewhere, and presumably they were in London. But Stormont had never given him the address. Only once, when they had travelled together up to London and parted at Waterloo, he had mentioned that he was bound for the City, a sufficiently vague definition.

Those words he had overheard uttered by the man Whitehouse aggravated the curiosity he had for long felt on the subject since he had become so intimately acquainted with the family.

Very delicately he questioned Gloria as they proceeded with their game in the billiard-room.

"I suppose business does not take up all your uncle's time? He spends a good deal of it in this delightful place," he said.

There was not the slightest hesitation in the girl's reply. He had long ago made up his mind that everything about Gloria Stormont was open and above-board. How frank she had been about herself, and her youthful days in China with her father and mother.

"I shouldn't say he went up to London more than three days a week on an average; his heart has been wrapt up in Effington ever since he bought it from young Sedgemere a few years ago. When we lived in London itself, he used to work much harder."

35

"Oh, you lived in London before you came here," said Leonard, who learned this fact for the first time. Certainly Stormont was a very reticent fellow about strictly personal matters. He had never made any allusion to a previous home which, from his intense fondness for rural life, the young man fancied might have been in the country.

"Yes, we had a dear old eighteenth-century house in Curzon Street. It was very comfortable and convenient, but my aunt and I welcomed the change as much as he did. I should hate to go back to town life again after this sweet Effington."

"I suppose you had a very large circle of acquaintances in town?" asked Lydon, still pursuing his questioning.

"Not large at all, considering the fact that my uncle seemed so well off," was the frank answer. "He honestly owns that he is not very fond of general society. He has a few friends who come down here now and again. There were some of them with us on your first visit. Of course we know a lot of people round about here, in fact a great many more than in London."

"You travel a great deal, don't you? Mr. Stormont seems well acquainted with all the principal places in Europe." This was one of the subjects on which her uncle had not been reticent. His knowledge of the Continent, of the customs and habits of the different foreign nations, was extensive and exhaustive, and he always seemed pleased to air it.

"Oh, uncle is a tremendous traveller; he has been everywhere and seen everything; but he has not travelled so much since we have been here, a matter of some five years. Before that he used to be away the greater part of the year. Sometimes my aunt and I went with him, but usually he went alone. His business took him a good deal abroad, you know."

Here was the opportunity he had been waiting for, and he hastened to seize it. "It seems rather funny, one learns these things so soon, as a rule. But I have never heard what your uncle's business is."

Gloria's reply was perfectly free from embarrassment. "It is connected with finance; I suppose he is what you call a financier."

So the secret was out: the owner of Effington Hall was a financier. Well, there were a good many people belonging to that profession, some of them quite reputable, controlling vast interests, some of them quite the reverse, addicted to very shady doings. No doubt the rubicund Stormont was one of the respectable ones, but why the deuce had he been so reticent about it? The proper pursuit of finance was quite a respectable calling. When a man does not openly mention his occupation, his silence rather gives you the idea he is secretly ashamed of it.

It was quite within the bounds of possibility that Stormont was not amongst the high spirits of the financial world, that his activities inclined a little to the shady side of the profession. But if that were so, would he have had the hardihood to buy Effington, and run the gauntlet of the respectable people of the neighbourhood?

On the Sunday morning Stormont absented himself from church, contrary to his usual custom. Mr. Whitehouse remained at home to keep him company. All the others went as they had done on the previous occasion. Lydon had a shrewd suspicion that the two men wanted to be alone to discuss business affairs. Evidently matters were settled during the morning, for the two men did not shut themselves up again during the rest of the day.

Whitehouse might possibly be an excellent man of business, but he was not a lively or inspiring person. Grave and taciturn to a degree, he spoke very little, and only when addressed directly by his host or some other member of the party. He did not volunteer conversation. From a few hints dropped by Gloria, Leonard gathered that the women rather disliked him, and looked upon him as a wet blanket.

In reply to further questioning, Miss Stormont said that he used to be a frequent visitor to Curzon Street; but since they had taken up their residence at Effington, he came somewhat infrequently, not more than three or four times in the year, and then only for a stay of a day or two. She understood that he and her uncle had been connected in business for many years and that they had a very great regard for each other.

Whitehouse left directly after breakfast on the Monday morning, and Lydon hailed his departure with pleasure. There was something rather repellent about the man, with his taciturnity, his unsmiling gravity, his deep-set eyes and sombre gaze. For himself, he accepted Stormont's cordial invitation to stay another day, during which he enjoyed the society of the charming Gloria to the full.

He had expected that his host would accompany him to town on the Tuesday morning, but Stormont announced that, as the weather was so fine, he had made up his mind to take a week's holiday. Lydon thought it must be a very accommodating business that allowed him so much leisure, more especially in view of the fact, inadvertently dropped by Gloria, that he was in a certain sense living from hand to mouth, at any rate spending money as fast as he made it.

Mrs. Barnard said good-bye to him in the dining-room after breakfast. Stormont and his niece went with him into the hall. When he had shaken hands with them, rather a lingering process in the case of Gloria, Stormont detained him with a gesture, and went out to tell the chauffeur to drive down to the lodge gates and await them there. "Just a word with you, my boy, before you go," he said, linking his arm in that of the young man and conducting him slowly down the avenue, leaving a rather surprised Gloria behind.

When they were well out of earshot, he spoke. "Look here, my dear Leonard, I hope you don't mind me calling you by your Christian name, but I think we are now intimate enough to excuse the liberty."

"Not in the least," answered Lydon, who wondered what was coming.

"Thanks. I want to tell you that I'm not blind, neither is my sister. You are in love with Gloria, aren't you?"

Leonard was rather taken aback by the direct question. In his confusion he could not make any coherent reply. "I am," he stammered, "But, of course, I—I—I——" He could not finish the sentence.

"I quite understand, my dear fellow," said Stormont, his broad rubicund face relaxing into a smile. "You admit you love Gloria. I wanted you to be quite frank and open with me in the matter. I don't wonder at it, for she is a sweet girl, one out of a thousand, charming, honest, open as the day. Well, I will let you into a little secret. If my observations are correct, I believe she returns your affection. My sister thinks so too, and women can read each other pretty well as a rule."

He spoke in his hearty, breezy way. In spite of Craig's caustic criticism of him, there was something engaging about the personality of the homely-looking man. Lydon could not help flushing. "It makes me inexpressibly happy, sir, to hear you say that. I take it, from your telling me so much, that you do not disapprove. Have I your permission to speak to Miss Stormont?"

"When and as soon as you please," was the hearty response, "I had half made up my mind to tell you yesterday. I wish I had; I dare say by now I should have been congratulating you and my niece. Personally I am very pleased that you have fixed your affections on Gloria. So is Mrs. Barnard, who is a shrewd judge of character. In common with myself, she likes you very much and thinks you would make an excellent husband. Well, I can't say more, can I? Run down here again next week, and fix it up. Come as often as you like. My sister and I love young people about the house."

Lydon thanked him in warm terms for having made his wooing so easy. True, Gloria had not yet revealed her feelings, but in his heart he had not much doubt as to what they were.

But Stormont had not yet said all he wanted. As they drew near to the lodge gates, where the car was waiting, he motioned the young man to a halt.

"Just a little something more, to make everything plain and clear. Very possibly you have thought that Gloria is the niece of a rich man and will come into a tidy sum when I die?"

The young man interrupted him hastily. "I assure you, on my word of honour, Mr. Stormont, I never speculated on such a contingency. If I gave it a thought, I was rather depressed by the circumstance than otherwise. I felt

38

a natural reluctance to ask a girl brought up so luxuriously to share a very modest fortune."

"You're not the sort of which fortune-hunters are made. I could see that at a glance, or I should not have been so open with you," was the generous reply. He sank his voice very low when he continued: "Well, I must let you into a little secret which I think nobody suspects. I am not in the true sense of the term a rich man. I make plenty of money and I believe I shall continue to do, if my luck holds, as long as I live. But I am an incurable spendthrift; I fritter as fast as I make. Of course, you are a totally different temperament from me. At such an admission you will shrug your shoulders and think I am an insensate fool."

Lydon preserved an embarrassed silence. Had he expressed in words what he really felt, they would have been far from palatable to the hearer.

After a short pause, Stormont spoke in a tone of considerable emotion, as if he were voicing his real remorse. "You cannot blame me any more than I blame myself. But this love of spending for spending's sake, when it once gets hold of a man, is as deadly as any other form of vice, as drink or gambling. Dozens of times I have tried to check myself, to act prudently, but to no purpose."

Again there was a pause, and again Lydon could find nothing to say, since if he had spoken he would have been compelled to condemn, in no measured terms, the man's contemptible and selfish weakness.

And Stormont went on in that half-apologetic, wholly shamed voice. "So when I do die, I shall have lived my life to the full, but I shall leave next to nothing behind. Mrs. Barnard is provided for; she will always be able to live in comfort, and luxury makes little appeal to her. It is on Gloria's account that I feel remorse, the selfishness of my conduct."

And then at last the young man found something to say: "There is one thing I should like to tell you, Mr. Stormont, without attempting to criticize you in any way, a thing I have no right to do. So far as Gloria is concerned, I am glad she is not likely to be an heiress. I love her for herself. I want no dowry with her."

"It is just what I should have expected from you," replied the rubicund financier with a rather melancholy smile. "Well, things may not turn out so badly for Gloria after all. My brother, her father, is the exact opposite of myself, a prudent, evenly-balanced man who counts the cost of everything, looks long before he leaps, and I should say out of every pound he earns, saves ten shillings. He has a splendid position, and only another child, a son. He is one of the justest men I know, and whatever he leaves—I'll wager it will be no mean sum—will be divided equitably between his family. So my dear Gloria may be an heiress in a small way, in the end. Now I have kept you talking too long, you have got your train to catch. Good-bye for the present. We shall expect you next week."

The two men shook hands and Lydon drove to the station, thinking very much over Stormont's somewhat humiliating confession. How deceitful are appearances! In the eyes of the local circle round Effington, the man with his lavish expenditure must have passed as a person of considerable wealth. And yet the real truth was that he was living, in a sense, from hand to mouth, and that any day might see him stripped of his fair possessions.

Well, the way was perfectly clear to him now. He would run down again next week and ask Gloria to marry him. He would make a lucid statement of his position to her uncle, if he were not already aware of it. Stormont was a weak man, a foolish man in most important respects, but he was certainly not simple-minded, and he seemed to possess an amazing amount of information about other people. He had probably seen a report of the elder Lydon's will in the papers soon after his death, and knew the exact extent of Leonard's fortune.

The next week, availing himself of Stormont's general invitation, he went down on the Friday, having written his host to that effect. The car met him as usual at the station, and to his great delight Gloria was on the platform to meet him. This was, of course, the first time she had ever done such a thing, as on the previous occasions he had travelled down with her uncle.

When they reached the lodge gates, Lydon halted the car and suggested to the girl that they should walk up the avenue. She agreed, not without blushing slightly. He had been unusually quiet during the journey, as if he were pondering very deeply. No doubt with womanly intuition she guessed what was in his mind.

Having resolved upon the step he was taking, he lost no time; as soon as the chauffeur was out of earshot, he spoke:

"I was delighted to see you on the platform; somehow it seemed so intimate. The last time I was at Effington, your uncle brought me along here, and we had a very serious talk together. Perhaps he has told you something of this?"

With a deep blush, the girl admitted that he was correct in his surmise, and this answer encouraged him to proceed.

"I love you very much, Gloria. I wonder if you can care for me a little."

Her bosom heaved, there was a tender light in the deep blue eyes, her lips trembled slightly as she gave him her answer: "I think I can care for you more than a little."

The car by now had reached the stables: a bend in the avenue hid the lodge gates: there was nobody in sight. He did what any lover worthy of the name would do under such circumstances. He bent down and pressed his first kiss upon the sweet lips that made a tremulous response to his. He and this charming girl, whom he knew he had fallen in love with at first sight, were now betrothed lovers.

They walked up to the entrance to the picturesque Tudor house, both perhaps a little shy from their new-found happiness, the great event that had happened in their young lives. The door was wide open. Stormont and his sister stood in the hall to greet them; there was no white-haired butler, no inconvenient servants to extend a silent welcoming. Lydon shook hands with his host and hostess, and then turned with a radiant face to his fiancée.

"Gloria has made me very happy," he said simply, by way of announcing the tremendous fact.

Mrs. Barnard first kissed her niece, and then bestowed an affectionate salute upon Leonard. Stormont literally hugged Gloria and wrung the young man's hand heartily. "We must celebrate this at once," he cried in his loud, ringing voice. "Come along. There is only one wine worthy of the occasion. I have still left in the cellar a few bottles of a matchless Krug. We will open one."

And, as they went along to the dining-room, Stormont and his sister leading the way, the young couple following them, Gloria laid her slender hand on her lover's arm and whispered, "You have made me very happy too, dear."

CHAPTER SIX

THE week-end was a very quiet one, Lydon being the only guest. The young man thought this might be due to Stormont's delicacy, that he felt it was only kind to allow the lovers to pursue their courtship in comparative seclusion. But in the following week the phenomenon was repeated. Nobody came down from London; none of the neighbours were asked to luncheon or dinner.

Stormont occupied his time in pottering about the grounds and taking long walks. But there was a certain restlessness about him, an air of boredom which showed that this somewhat unusual isolation was not agreeing with him. Leonard commented on it to his sweetheart.

Gloria shrugged her shoulders. "He's always like that when he leads a quiet life; he is never really happy unless he is surrounded by plenty of people. He loves crowds."

"Perhaps he is sacrificing himself for our sakes," suggested Leonard.

The girl's smile was good-humoured but sceptical. "Uncle Howard has a heap of good qualities, but I don't think self-sacrifice is conspicuous amongst them. To tell you the truth, I think he is going a bit slow because he is compelled to."

They were walking in the beautifully-kept gardens which required a small army of gardeners to keep in order, and must have cost a pretty penny to maintain in such perfection.

Only one interpretation could be put upon her words. "You mean to infer that he is a bit hard up," said Lydon bluntly.

She nodded her pretty head. "Yes, from what auntie told me, he has been spending a lot more than he ought, and has got to pull up for a time. These sorts of crises occur now and again. We have had about a dozen of them at least since we came here, and at such times entertaining has to be cut down with a ruthless hand. In Curzon Street I don't suppose the outgoings were a quarter what they are here. Auntie says he ought never to have bought the place, considering the expense it entails. He gets a lot of enjoyment out of it, of course, but he also gets a lot of worry."

"And yet I suppose he is a shrewd business man?"

"He must be, or he could not make the money he does. But you see he has got the spendthrift temperament. If he takes a fancy to a thing, he will have it, whether he can afford it or not. And the fatal thing about him, and it is that which worries my aunt more, he has no hesitation about going into debt, if he hasn't got ready money to pay for his whims."

"Your aunt does not share his extravagant ideas, then?"

"Oh, dear no. She has a nice little income of her own which she lives up to, but I am sure she never exceeds it. And she has a most wholesome horror of debt. I know she is awfully worried now because some of the tradespeople's accounts are overdue; they are getting a bit pressing."

Delightful as Effington was, and perfectly satisfying to the lover of natural beauty, Lydon thought residence there was dearly purchased by these crises to which she had alluded. So Mr. Stormont was behindhand with the local tradespeople! What a horrible situation! They would begin to gossip presently, and then the bubble would be burst amongst the neighbours.

"There was a perfect orgy of spending for a couple of months just before you paid us your first visit," said Gloria after a short pause during which her lover was ruminating on the hollowness of the position at this splendid country residence. "A big dinner party nearly every day in the week, on the usual lavish scale, and all this time he was giving liberally, not to say ostentatiously, to all the local charities. I suppose it was then he overran the constable. You came in at the fag end of it. Since then the motto seems to have been retrenchment all round, with a disastrous effect on my uncle's spirits."

"These crises worry you a good bit, don't they?" queried her lover.

"To tell the truth, they do. Much as I love the place—and nobody could live at Effington without loving it—I often wish that we could have a place that entailed smaller outgoings. And, of course, one is always haunted by the fear that one day he will get himself into a terrible mess from which he cannot extricate himself."

Lydon thought this very possible. It was very likely the spendthrift himself had some premonition of such a catastrophe, and that was the reason he had almost thrown his niece at the young man's head. In spite of her fondness for Effington, perhaps Gloria herself would not be sorry to exchange all this for a position of less magnificence and greater security.

Had he not been convinced of her frank, open nature he might have thought that the girl had been in league with her uncle to secure him. But he was sure of her good faith and honesty of purpose. He remembered her agitation when he had proposed to her in the avenue, the love-light that had shone in her beautiful eyes. No woman, not even the most practised coquette, can summon that light at will.

He did not see his sweetheart at all the following week. The stern exigencies of his profession called him abroad. At Ryder Street, on his return, he found a letter from Stormont awaiting him, asking him to lunch the following day at the *Piccadilly*, as he wished to consult him on a matter of some urgency.

43

Very curious as to what this matter of some urgency could be, Lydon presented himself at the *Piccadilly* at the hour appointed. He noticed a decided change in Stormont in the short time he had parted from him at his splendid country house. The man's manner was restless and jerky, and he looked anxious and worried.

He ordered a very sumptuous lunch, the most expensive food and wine on the list. Lydon found it far too sumptuous; he was not accustomed to a heavy meal in the middle of the day, in fact, was not very keen on the pleasures of the table at any time. Stormont drank by far the greater portion of the champagne, and finished up with a couple of liqueurs of the finest brandy. During the progress of the meal he talked fitfully, and it was easy to see he had something weighing on his mind; but he made no allusion to the subject on which he wanted the young man's advice. It rather looked as if he were justifying himself before he could approach it.

When they had finished, he led the way into the smoking-room, where he selected a quiet corner suitable for private conversation, and ordered refreshment. Lydon would take nothing but a cup of coffee. For himself he ordered a large whisky and soda. When he had taken a deep draught, he unburdened himself, not without a considerable tinge of embarrassment in his manner.

"I am afraid you will think I am taking an infernal liberty, Leonard, so early in our acquaintance. But the fact is, at the moment I am in a bit of a hole, and hardly know where to turn."

Lydon had an idea of what was coming, by the man's fidgetiness and embarrassment, which had been patent from the moment they met. He murmured some conventional words of condolence, and waited for further details.

"I'm expecting a sum of five thousand pounds in a week at the latest, in fact I may receive it any day between now and then. In the meantime there are some pressing things I ought to pay. Would it be possible for you to lend me a thousand pounds for a week, at a fair interest, of course?"

It was rather a cool request, even to a man who was about to enter his family. Leonard was by no means a parsimonious man, but he rather resented it. Why the deuce did he not manage his finances properly, curb his extravagance, instead of sponging upon somebody apparently much poorer than himself?

He spoke rather coldly; he thought that if he made it too easy, Mr. Stormont would be encouraged to fall back upon him at any time he thought fit. "It's a bit inconvenient, but if you can't get it anywhere else, I must do it. Won't your bank do it?"

Stormont shook his head. "The manager is a very cross-grained chap, puts every obstacle in the way of doing you a favour. And, to tell you the

44

truth, I am just a trifle overdrawn. It is not the most propitious time to ask for even a short loan."

This admission revealed a terrible state of things, thought Lydon. Just a trifle overdrawn! He had probably drawn his last cheque to pay for the unnecessarily expensive lunch, unless he had borrowed the money from his sister. The solid fact emerged that Howard Stormont, who had driven up to the *Piccadilly* in his Rolls-Royce, the supposed man of wealth, the owner of that lordly pleasure-house, Effington Hall, was at the present moment as hard up as anybody could be. And he appeared to have no credit, no husbanded resources. He was awaiting that five thousand which was to come not later than a week, which might come earlier, which, for all the young man knew, might never come at all. That request for a thousand pounds might be the last throw of a desperate gambler.

Still, if he was going to run the risk, he might as well do the thing gracefully. "Can you deposit anything in the way of security, in case of unforeseen accidents?" he inquired casually. He was fairly certain of what the answer would be, but he wanted to make quite sure as to whether or not Stormont had any resources.

Again the financier shook his head. "Nothing that you could call absolute security," he replied, his rubicund face growing a shade redder as he made the damaging admission. "I could, of course, show you papers proving there is a lot of money coming to me. But as the accommodation is for so short a time, I should suggest my note of hand for the amount, plus interest."

"I don't want any interest," said the young man hastily. "I am not a money-lender. I am doing this in a friendly way. Well, I've a busy afternoon before me, so, if you don't mind, we'll settle this affair as soon as possible. Drive me round to my rooms in Ryder Street and I will give you my cheque; I have as much lying at the bank which I was intending to invest. We can get a bill at the nearest post-office as we go along."

But there was no necessity for this; Stormont had a bill of the required amount in his case. He explained that he always carried bill stamps with him, as they were so frequently used in his business dealings. Lydon did not quite believe this. He thought the man had taken his acquiescence for granted, and had come prepared.

They drove to Ryder Street, and in five minutes the transaction was completed. The rubicund Stormont put the cheque in his pocket, it being too late in the afternoon to pay it in, and drove back to Effington in his opulent-looking car, leaving Lydon wondering whether he should ever see his money back, whether that five thousand pounds was a myth invented for the occasion.

It was on the Tuesday that this affair took place, and it was understood that Lydon would go down to Effington on the following Friday. His confidence in Stormont was now so rudely shaken that he was prepared for anything unexpected to happen in the meantime. He would not have been surprised to receive a frantic letter from him to the effect that he was flying the country, that Mrs. Barnard and Gloria were seeking refuge in some suburb round London, and that Effington Hall was up for sale.

Lydon rather wondered what was his position with regard to this splendid mansion. Originally he must have been able to put his hands on a considerable sum of money for its purchase. In all probability it was now mortgaged up to the hilt.

Happily, nothing of such a disturbing nature happened. On his arrival at Guildford Station, Gloria met him in the car. She was, of course, delighted to see him again after his brief absence; but her lover fancied there was just a shade of embarrassment in her manner, the reason of which he presently learned as they drove along.

"There is a renewal of festivities which are such an abiding joy to my uncle's soul," she said, speaking in a hard voice. "To-night we've a dinner-party of a dozen people, all neighbours; nobody is staying in the house but you."

So the rubicund Stormont had resumed his extravagant habits the moment he found himself in possession of a bit of money. He had no doubt paid off some pressing old debts, and was feverishly incurring new ones. The young man had no desire to face a lot of strangers, but perhaps this dinner-party was, in a way, a healthy sign. Even Stormont would not have been so rash as to fritter away his last shilling if he were not sure that salvation was close at hand. Lydon was relieved to think that this five thousand pounds was not a myth, but a solid fact.

Gloria went on in low and embarrassed tones: "I cannot say how ashamed and humiliated I am that he should have come to you. I only heard it this morning from my aunt, who thought I ought to be told. When he mentioned to her that he was going to apply to you, she did all in her power to dissuade him from making such a request, but all to no purpose. The fact of it is, he is not a man who feels any shame in borrowing."

He could see plainly that she was very much distressed, and he hastened to console her. "My darling, there is really nothing for you to worry about. I am sorry your uncle was put about, but he made it clear to me it was quite a temporary embarrassment, and I was very pleased to be of service to him. Such a thing might happen to anybody—might have happened to myself."

The girl spoke with some heat. "It is very sweet of you to try and restore my self-respect, but it would never have happened to you. You are the last man in the world to spend your money on riotous living and then go with a

46

pitiful tale to a friend. Why did he not go to one of his business friends, if he was forced to borrow, or, better still, sell some of the valuable things he has got at Effington?"

She was evidently stung to the quick that her happy-go-lucky uncle had exploited the young man's affection for herself in order to replenish his exhausted exchequer. Lydon himself could not help thinking it was a mean thing to do, in spite of his making light of it to her.

The dinner-party was a great success. Stormont beamed on his guests as genially as ever, and was in the highest spirits. As he sat at the table he gave the impression of a man who had not a care in the world. Lydon could hardly understand such a swift alteration of mood, of the change from the haggard, harassed man of a few days ago to this jovial creature who laughed and joked with the greatest ease. But then he did not comprehend the mercurial temperament of the incurable spendthrift.

The Saturday was to be a comparatively quiet day, Gloria told him, there being only two guests expected. The taciturn Mr. Whitehouse was bringing down his niece, Zillah Mayhew, to lunch. But their visit would not be a very long one. They were returning to London by an afternoon train.

The words that he had overheard that night when he had passed the door of Stormont's study recurred to him at the mention of Miss Mayhew's name. Was this the woman whose co-operation was essential to some business there was on hand? "What sort of a girl is she?" asked the young man. "Not as gloomy as her uncle, I trust?"

Gloria smiled. "She is the exact opposite, most bright and vivacious, really quite charming. I haven't seen her more than half a dozen times in my life, but I took a great fancy to her."

"Does she live with the solemn Whitehouse?"

"Not permanently. Uncle has never told me much about her history, but I know that her parents are dead, that she has a little income of her own, and lives now with one relative, now with another. She passes a great deal of her time abroad, where she has several friends and connections."

Lydon began to feel rather interested in the young woman. When the time came for them to be met at the station, he noticed a rather peculiar thing. Stormont dispensed with the services of the chauffeur and drove the car to Guildford himself, a most unusual proceeding on his part. The young man was convinced by this circumstance that his suspicions were correct. Stormont wanted to be alone to have a quiet chat with Whitehouse and his niece.

The lovers went for a walk, and on their return a few minutes before luncheon the visitors had arrived. Lydon shook hands with Whitehouse, and was introduced to Miss Mayhew, a tall, dark, handsome girl, with splendid eyes, and the complexion of the brunette. She spoke English without the faintest trace of accent, but there was a foreign air about her.

He looked at her very attentively, and his scrutiny revealed two very strange things. On the back of her neck was a blemish partially concealed by powder, and she wore as a pendant a magnificent sapphire carved in the shape of a closed lotus flower.

His memory flew back to that day when he had stood in the drawing-room of the Villa des Cyclamens, and called the attention of Madame Makris to a similar jewel which was lying unheeded on the table.

CHAPTER SEVEN

LIKE a man in a dream, he heard the pleasant, contralto voice of Miss Mayhew asking him if he did not think Mr. Stormont looked wonderfully well, and then, without awaiting his answer, go on to remark that country life evidently agreed with him.

Having broken the ice with Lydon in the easy manner that showed she was endowed with plenty of self-confidence, she turned to the rubicund gentleman himself, whom she addressed familiarly as Uncle Howard. "I'm afraid since you took possession of this lovely place, you don't work half as hard as you used to do."

Whatever her relations with the other two members of the family, she was apparently on very close terms with the head of it, as was apparent from the way she addressed him. Gloria had said that they had seen very little of each other, Stormont then must have had additional opportunities of intimacy. Unless she knew him very well, she would not have called him uncle in the presence of his real niece.

He wondered whether Gloria quite relished the familiarity. In spite of her obvious recognition of Stormont's failings, and her resentment of what had just taken place between himself and her fiancé, he was sure that she had a very soft spot in her heart for her uncle, whom she always declared to be one of the kindest and most generous of men.

But Gloria did not seem piqued in any way, and she had told him that Miss Mayhew was not only very bright and vivacious, but especially charming also. One of his sweetheart's best traits was that she was not a jealous or an envious girl.

Whitehouse was always taciturn; he ate heartily and drank a fair amount, but neither of these processes ever seemed to exhilarate him. Mrs. Barnard was naturally a quiet woman, of a disposition rather reserved than otherwise. The conversation at lunch was carried on mainly between the host and the dark, handsome girl. Miss Mayhew appeared to have travelled a great deal abroad, for she was constantly making references to places where apparently she and "Uncle Howard" had been in each other's company. It was no doubt owing to these meetings that they seemed so intimate with each other.

The visitors did not stay very long after lunch, although Stormont, in his hospitable way, pressed them to reconsider their decision, and postpone their departure till at least the following day. But Whitehouse shook his head and replied briefly it was impossible, as he and his niece had an engagement on Sunday.

Stormont drove them alone from the house, as he had driven them alone to it. There must be some reason, for Lydon knew he was not fond of acting as chauffeur. Probably he wanted a few last words with the girl who was necessary to the prosecution of some business scheme hatched between the two men.

After they had left, Mrs. Barnard retired to her usual task of writing letters, and the engaged couple went into the billiard-room.

"Well, what do you think of the handsome Zillah?" asked Gloria as they chose their cues. "Uncle says she breaks hearts wherever she goes. Did you find her very fascinating?"

Lydon had certainly been greatly fascinated by her, but not for the reasons Gloria had in her mind when she put the question. What had fascinated him was that brilliant sapphire pendant and the blemish on her neck, only partially concealed by the liberal use of powder.

He answered her question lightly: "I expect most men would find her more than ordinarily attractive. But you know, darling, I have never had any great admiration for dark women."

Gloria no doubt was quite satisfied with the answer, for she did not pursue the subject. She had been rather eclipsed at lunch by the vivacious and brilliant Miss Mayhew, but now she was alone with her lover she chatted away merrily enough as they played their game.

And, as she talked, Lydon found himself speculating on the recent visitor and the strange position of affairs at Effington. There was plenty of unreality about the whole thing. Was there also perhaps more than a mere suspicion of mystery? Why did Stormont maintain that persistent reticence about his business, a man usually of a most garrulous disposition? Even now Lydon did not know precisely where his offices were situated. On the bill of exchange it was necessary for him to put an address, but he had simply described himself as of Effington Hall, Surrey.

Whitehouse, seemingly his most intimate friend, seemed more than a little mysterious too. He always gave Leonard the impression of a man who was constantly keeping close watch upon himself lest he should drop something that he did not wish known.

And who was this independent, self-assured young woman, Zillah Mayhew, with the blemish on her neck and that striking pendant, who seemed to spend her life in rushing hither and thither, and was on such intimate terms with Uncle Howard?

He led the conversation presently round to the same subject, for all the time he was making his strokes the dark, handsome Zillah, with her foreign look, was in his thoughts.

"What a lovely sapphire that is she wears! You noticed it, of course?"

"One could not very well avoid noticing it," was the reply. "As I have told you, I haven't seen her many times, but on every occasion she has had it on. Uncle says it is her mascot."

"And did you also notice that peculiar blemish on her neck which, cleverly as she tries to hide it, peeps through the powder?"

"Yes, I did," answered Gloria, "for the first time to-day. I am certain it was not there the last time I saw her."

"And how long ago might that be?" was her lover's next question.

The girl considered. "Let me see. I am not very good at remembering dates. But I do recollect this much. She came over here a few weeks before we went on that visit to Nice where we met you and your friend, Mr. Craig."

Lydon was thinking rapidly: "You didn't happen to meet her at Nice?"

Gloria looked at him in surprise at the question. "No, I am sure I did not. What makes you suggest it?"

The young man laughed a little awkwardly. It was too early to tell his sweetheart the strange suspicions which had formed in his mind. "Oh, no particular reason. But from what she said at luncheon, she seems to be always on the travel. It just struck me she might have been there at that particular time."

He left on the Monday morning this time, having on a great pressure of work. He would not be able to ask Gloria to lunch in town during the week, as he was so uncertain of his engagements, but he would be sure to be down on the following Friday.

He went back to his business, very much obsessed with his thoughts of the dark, handsome girl known as Zillah Mayhew. Was it only a queer fancy of his that had led him to connect her with the woman who had been the cause of his friend's death?

When he got back to his rooms in Ryder Street, he hunted up the portrait in the illustrated paper which he had brought with him from Nice. It was a blurred and wretched thing. One moment he fancied he could detect a resemblance between Elise Makris and Zillah Mayhew, the next he was bound to confess he could see not the slightest resemblance.

It happened that he did see his sweetheart during the week. On the Wednesday morning he had to carry out some tests of wireless telephony at one of his Company's experimental stations at Esher. He was testing a newly-invented thermionic valve, and during the morning he got into communication with Aberdeen and Rotterdam and was gratified to learn they reported his speech and gramophone music as strong and clear.

He lunched at the *Bear Hotel*, and a happy thought struck him. He would pay a surprise visit to Effington. So he drove away down the Portsmouth Road, passing through Guildford and over the Hog's Back, and early in the afternoon swung into the big lodge gates of Effington.

His unexpected visit was a most delightful surprise to Gloria. He would remain to tea, of course; and Mrs. Barnard, who was as hospitable as her brother, insisted upon his stopping to dinner. She regretted that Stormont would be absent, as he had motored to London to a directors' meeting, and would not be back till late.

Mrs. Barnard served them tea from the old silver pot in the great oak-panelled hall where high stained-glass windows bore the *rose-en-soleil* badge of the dead and gone Sedgemeres.

Duncan, the white-haired, grave-faced butler who never permitted himself the luxury of a smile, except when some guest bestowed upon him a more than usually generous tip, officiated with his customary dignity, handing round the cake-basket of pierced Georgian silver. Duncan had served the greater part of his life in noble families. Stormont, on the look-out for a dignified major-domo, had tempted him from his last place by the offer of a salary about double what he was getting.

Duncan, in a way, had fallen from his high estate in accepting service under a man about whom nobody seemed to know very much. But, like the mercenaries of old, he was content to enlist under any banner where the pay was good.

In the waning light, the big, high-pitched hall looked ghostly and cavernous, with its floor of polished oak over which high-born dames of the days of Charles the Second had danced merrily. There was the great stone fireplace with the wrought-iron fire-back, bearing upon it the date of 1621. There were the Caroline day-bed with spindle legs and fragile canework, the high carved arm-chairs upholstered in faded crimson, and the big oak gate table, loaded with game books, and visitors' books mixed with modern novels.

Around, upon the dark panelled walls, hung several portraits of women and men in wigs, one being a portrait by Kneller of Hugh, sixth Earl of Sedgemere, and another by Reynolds of Anne, wife of the great Lord Sedgemere who had fought in the Peninsular War.

While they gossiped and sipped their tea, the sun slanted across the oak flooring, tinted by the antique escutcheons in the long coloured glass windows of the lofty hall.

At dinner Lydon casually referred to Miss Mayhew. Had they heard anything of her since he had met her at luncheon?

Mrs. Barnard answered the question: "No, nothing. Isn't she a splendid girl? I wish we saw more of her. She is so amusing and vivacious. No wonder men are always attracted by her!"

"Does she live in London?" Lydon asked.

"When she is in England, she stays with her uncle, Mr. Whitehouse. But I believe she is a great deal with her brother in Paris."

So this cosmopolitan young lady had a brother in Paris. Lydon would very much have liked to ask something about the brother, and also in what part of London Whitehouse resided, but his delicacy kept him back. Somehow, personal details never seemed forthcoming in the Stormont family, with perhaps the exception of Gloria, who was frankness itself. You always had to dig for them.

After dinner they went as usual into the billiard-room. Mrs. Barnard, contrary to her usual habit, accompanied them and took upon herself the office of marker.

After the game was over she very considerately left them to themselves for a few moments. No doubt, she had a recollection of her own courting days. A little while before the young man was preparing to take his leave, she came in with a bundle of letters in her hand.

"Leonard, I found these on my brother's table just now. He had intended to take them along with him, and forgot them in the hurry of leaving. Will you please post them at Guildford or somewhere as you drive along?"

Lydon promised that he would. He said good-bye to the amiable Mrs. Barnard. Gloria accompanied him to his car, and here the farewell was a somewhat protracted one, as is usual with newly-engaged couples.

He drove away over the Hog's Back, and stopped before the Guildford Post Office. For the first time he looked at the letters as he dropped them into the box. He came to the last, and read the superscription in Stormont's bold handwriting. It was addressed to Miss Mayhew, 18 Ashstead Mansions, Sloane Square.

A little time ago he had been longing to ask at dinner where Mr. Whitehouse lived, and had refrained from feelings of delicacy. By the merest accident, the forgetfulness of Stormont, he had found out what he wanted. This was a piece of luck.

His first natural impulse was to scribble the address upon his shirt-cuff and send the letter into the box with the others. He never quite knew why he changed his mind. Probably his strong conviction that there was a great element of mystery about Stormont himself, and, secondly, his equally strong obsession that Elise Makris and Zillah Mayhew were one and the same person.

Second thoughts gained the day. Instead of posting the letter, as he knew he ought to have done, he put it back in his wallet, jumped back into the car, and drove along the London Road through Ripley, Cobham, Esher and Kingston to the garage close to Ryder Street.

He was determined to pluck at the heart of the mystery. Two hours after it had been given to him by Mrs. Barnard, he stood in his rooms in Ryder Street, and the letter from Howard Stormont to Zillah Mayhew was lying open in his hand. This is what he read:

"My very clever Zillah.—I have seen Edwards and arranged everything. You will leave for Paris to-morrow and wait at the *Hôtel Terminus* for further instructions. Edwards will bring or write them. Show this to Whitehouse and then destroy.—UNCLE."

He read it through a dozen times, and then he carefully resealed the flap, for the gum was still wet from the steam he had applied. When it had dried under the weight of some heavy body, he went out and posted it in the nearest pillar-box. In all probability, Miss Mayhew would not glance at the postmark.

What did it all mean? Zillah Mayhew was intimately connected with Stormont's business, whatever it might be. Of what nature was this peculiar business that required a female partner?

On the face of it, that brief epistle might refer to a perfectly legitimate transaction. A woman's subtle influence might be necessary to secure some special concession, some particular contract.

But the more he thought it over, the more he rejected this explanation. The predominant thought in his mind about Howard Stormont, the country gentleman who played his rôle with such absolute enjoyment of it, was that he was a very different person from what he appeared to his neighbours at Effington.

And this suspicion would become a certainty if he could prove that Elise Makris, the decoy of swindlers and blackmailers, was none other than Zillah Mayhew, the niece, or pretended niece, of the taciturn Whitehouse.

But would it become a certainty without further corroborative evidence? Going into the question a little more deeply, he was bound to admit it would not. After all, he had nothing but undefined suspicions with regard to Stormont. He would be bound to give him the benefit of the doubt.

If the girl were found to be Elise Makris, it did not follow that Stormont was aware of her criminal activities. It was not an absolute certainty that even Whitehouse, if he were her uncle, knew of them. She was obviously a very clever, resourceful young woman; she would not go about proclaiming her nefarious profession from the housetops.

Stormont might have originally made her acquaintance in a quite simple and ordinary way, and found her talents useful to him in a peculiar line of business that entailed the exercise of a considerable amount of diplomacy.

In fair-mindedness he felt bound to reason on these lines. But, all the same, his instincts loudly confuted his reasoning. And those instincts told him that the rubicund financier was very different from what he appeared to be.

CHAPTER EIGHT

LYDON might not be able to lay claim to any remarkable brilliance of intellect. At Harrow and Oxford his progress had been steady and respectable, but he had not distinguished himself like his friend Craig, for instance, to whom the acquisition of knowledge was an easy task, whose mental alertness was the delight of his masters and tutors.

But he was a shrewd young fellow, and endowed with a considerable fund of common-sense. He also possessed a dogged spirit of determination. When he once took a thing up he persevered with it, and was not easily daunted by obstacles. There were, at the present moment, two things he was resolved to find out by some means or other—the precise nature of Stormont's business and the life history of the dark, handsome girl known as Zillah Mayhew.

He thought the best thing he would do as a start was to go and consult Shelford, the solicitor in Lincoln's Inn. As he was pretty well master of his own time, he paid him an early morning visit before he went to his business in Victoria Street. That genial gentleman was disengaged and saw him at once.

To him the young man related his accidental meeting with Miss Mayhew at the house of a mutual friend, and the two remarkable facts that she had a blemish on the neck, and was wearing a rather original piece of jewellery, similar in design to one he had seen in the drawing-room of the Villa des Cyclamens when he had called there to condole with Madame Makris on the tragedy.

Mr. Shelford was very much impressed, as Lydon was sure he would be: "One or other of the facts, taken singly, would not lead one very far," he observed. "There are no doubt heaps of girls who may have a mark of this kind, and I suppose there is no piece of jewellery which is absolutely unique, which has not several replicas. But taken in conjunction, the evidence is very remarkable. Well, I suppose you want to go further into it. What you have learned about this young lady in the ordinary course does not satisfy you?"

Lydon answered that it certainly did not, that he wanted to have his suspicions disproved or confirmed. What did Shelford advise?

The solicitor was quite ready with an answer. "If you or I were to undertake the task of tracing the history of Miss Mayhew, I expect we should find out next to nothing. Such a business is not the least in our line. But there is, fortunately, a class of men who are experts in this kind of thing, and perform wonders if you give them something to go on. You have heard of course of private inquiry agents, perhaps may have employed one in your time?"

"I have heard of them, naturally. Some of them advertise their skill in tracking faithless wives and erring husbands. But I have never had occasion to avail myself of their services."

"Then, if you want to get at the bottom of this, you had better go to one at once, while the scent is hot," advised Mr. Shelford, speaking in a brisk tone. "Like every other profession, there are all sorts in it, some very smart, some the reverse. I can recommend you to a particularly good man, as keen as mustard. Whenever we have any of this sort of work, we give it to him, and he has always served us well. His name is Grewgus, and his office is in Craven Street, Strand. I will give you a note of introduction to him, and as he is a busy man, you had better ring him up for an appointment. Stay, as it is pretty early, he'll be at his office. I'll ring him up now and make an appointment for you."

In a few minutes the affair was settled. Mr. Grewgus would be engaged practically the whole of the day, but he could see Mr. Lydon at six o'clock that evening, if convenient. If not, at ten o'clock the following morning. As the young man was anxious to get on with the matter as quickly as possible, he chose the evening.

"By the way, I have a little bit of news for you," said Shelford as they shook hands at parting. "Poor Hugh Craig's private fortune is sadly depleted. As far as we are able to make out, he has either parted voluntarily or been forced to part with something like twelve thousand pounds in the last eighteen months. You remember, of course, there were some vague allusions to blackmail in that letter he sent to you from Nice, under cover to us?"

"Yes, there was certainly reference to blackmail. But how could he have laid himself open to it? I knew Hugh the best part of my life—he was the soul of honour and probity. He could never have done anything that he would have been ashamed to come to light."

The experienced man of the world shook his head. "The lives of a great many of us are a sealed book, Mr. Lydon. The poor fellow was no doubt distraught when he wrote that letter, and may have used the word without strict regard to its meaning. This harpy may have inveigled it out of him on some plausible pretext or another. All the cheques were drawn to himself, and paid in cash, so we have no means of knowing to whom the money actually went. But, as you can see, he was bled to a pretty good amount."

Later on, about twelve o'clock, Lydon was rung up in his business room where he was hard at work. Stormont's well-known voice came through the instrument. He was speaking from the *Cecil*, he said. Would Leonard lunch with him at one?

He wanted to settle up that little matter with him.

But for the concluding words, the young man might have declined the invitation, making some polite excuse. At the present moment he was too much disturbed in his mind about Mr. Stormont to hold any unnecessary intercourse with him. Repayment of the thousand pounds loan was evidently meant. The expected remittance was not a myth, as he had fancied more than once, but had actually arrived.

He, therefore, accepted. He did not consider Stormont was a safe enough man to have money left in his possession for too long. If he waited, he might only get a part of the debt, some more pressing creditor might be beforehand with him.

Besides, after all, he need not be so squeamish about meeting him. He had no intention of breaking with Gloria just because he had some strong suspicions of her uncle. He would be going to Effington on Friday for his usual weekly visit, and must perforce be the rubicund financier's guest as before.

Stormont seemed more hearty and genial than ever when they met in the entrance hall. As on the previous occasion, he ordered a most lavish lunch and the most expensive wine. Before going into the restaurant, he slipped into his guest's hand a rather bulky envelope. "I have brought it in cash," he whispered, "ten one hundred notes. I should have liked to add something substantial for the accommodation, but you were so emphatic on that point that I didn't dare."

Well, Stormont, so far, had kept faith with him; that should certainly be accounted to him for righteousness. But Lydon could not help thinking how strangely the financier managed his affairs for a man of business. Why did he not give him a cheque instead of these bulky notes which he might not have time to pay in to-day? He hated carrying big money about with him.

Then his suspicions, which had become chronic since he had read that letter, leading him to put an unfavourable construction upon every action, recurred to him. Perhaps he owed his bank, not a trifling sum as he had pretended, but a very considerable amount, and had only partially settled with them. Hence his reason for not drawing a cheque.

Lydon was not in a very talkative mood; he was thinking of his forthcoming interview with the private inquiry agent. The host, however, was in the best possible spirits and conversed enough for the pair.

Towards the close of the meal, the young man roused himself from his reveries, and inquired casually whether he was likely to meet Miss Mayhew on his next visit to Effington.

Stormont answered in the negative, adding: "I understood she was going away almost directly on a visit to her brother in Paris."

After a pause he added: "Splendid girl that, so clever, so accomplished. She's a first-class linguist too. Gloria often says she wishes she could speak foreign languages like her. A capital woman of business too. She has been of some use to me and her uncle in that way on more than one occasion."

"She has helped you in your business," cried Lydon, rather surprised at such a frank admission from a man so reserved on the subject.

Mr. Stormont winked knowingly. In addition to the greater portion of the champagne, he had imbibed two glasses of very fine liqueur brandy. They had perhaps made him unusually communicative.

"In my line of business we often have to deal with persons in high places, some of whom are very susceptible, not to say inflammable. When you come across a person of this description—and there are plenty of them abroad—it is astonishing what influence a pretty and clever woman can wield. And her worst enemy must admit that Zillah is both."

It seemed quite a straightforward sort of statement. Lydon, in spite of his suspicions, was bound to admit as much. He tried to lead the financier to talk further on the topic, but obviously he did not wish to pursue it. Perhaps he felt he had said enough.

At half-past two they separated. There was just time enough to walk briskly to Coutts, and pay in the thousand pounds. Leonard was busy at the office till it was time for him to keep his appointment in Craven Street with Mr. Grewgus.

He reached the offices of the private inquiry agent a few minutes past the hour. Mr. Grewgus himself was standing in the outer room apparently used by his staff. But there was nobody there except himself, a fact which he explained to his new client.

"I am alone, Mr. Lydon; I never keep my staff after the stroke of six. Of course I don't restrict myself to the time-table. I am at the disposal of a client at almost any hour."

Lydon rather liked the look of him. He was a tall, thin-faced man with rather hatchet features, clean-shaven. His manners were suave and courteous, his eyes keen, his expression was indicative of alert mentality.

He led the way into his own apartment, and, after placing a chair for the young man, invited him to state his business. Leonard told him the story as the reader already knows it. Grewgus listened without making any comment or interruption, but it was easy to see his trained intelligence grasped every detail. When Lydon was finished, he spoke:

"I understand that you wish me to find out all I can about this man, Howard Stormont, the nature of his business, etcetera, etcetera. Secondly, you want me to do the same thing with regard to the young woman, Zillah Mayhew, and this will necessarily involve her uncle, John Whitehouse, whom you say lives at 18 Ashstead Mansions, Sloane Square."

Leonard intimated that the detective had accurately comprehended his requirements.

"You do not know the address of Stormont's offices, only that they are somewhere in London. You have looked him up in the directory, as a matter of course? You have, and can't locate him. Trading no doubt under another name. Nothing actually suspicious in that by itself, of course, but it is a little peculiar he should be so exceedingly reticent on the subject."

He paused a minute or two to digest things before resuming: "Well, Mr. Lydon, I can leave Stormont to one of my lieutenants; I have no doubt he can soon be run to earth. The young lady will, I am sure, prove the more difficult job of the two. You say she is starting or has started for Paris?"

"The letter was written yesterday; I posted it last night. Therefore, if she obeys the instructions, she will leave to-day."

"Quite so," assented Mr. Grewgus. "I will, as I said, leave Stormont and the man Whitehouse to a deputy; we shall learn something about them in a very short time. I shall take Miss Mayhew in hand myself, and I ought to follow her to-morrow at the latest. But there is a little difficulty. I don't know her by sight, although I dare say you can give me a pretty accurate description of her. Still, if she registers at the *Hôtel Terminus* under another name, which is quite likely, time may be lost. Would it be possible for you to accompany me?"

"But wouldn't our objects be defeated if I did? Remember, we have met at Effington Hall, and if she is the woman I believe her to be, she would be naturally interested in me as the friend of Hugh Craig. She would recognize me the moment she saw me."

Mr. Grewgus smiled genially. "Quite right, Mr. Lydon, but I shouldn't manage things as clumsily as that. If you will come round to the office an hour before we start, I will disguise you so effectually that your nearest and dearest will never suspect your real identity. You will enter it Leonard Lydon, you will leave it anything you decide upon. We are used to make-up here, I can assure you."

There was something that appealed to him in the suggestion; it would be a decidedly novel experience to spy upon Miss Mayhew under an impenetrable disguise. He could easily spare a few days; there was some business in Paris he could attend to at the same time.

The weekly visit to Gloria was the only drawback. But for the moment the prospect of tracking Miss Mayhew outweighed the disappointment of not seeing his sweetheart. He would write her to-night, explaining that he had suddenly been summoned to Glasgow on important business which could not be delayed.

It was arranged, therefore, that Lydon should be round at the office early the next morning, and after he had assumed his disguise, the two men should proceed at once to Paris.

But Mr. Grewgus, who certainly did not spare himself in the interests of his clients, had something more to propose. A bright idea had suddenly occurred to him. He asked his client if he had any important engagements for that evening, and on receiving an answer in the negative, unfolded his plan.

"Well, as you can spare the time, I suggest that we take a peep at Ashstead Mansions and see if we can get anything useful out of the porter at the flats. Most of these fellows will talk if they can see money is about."

"But, the same objection," began the young man, and Mr. Grewgus interrupted him with uplifted hand and a quizzical smile.

"Of course, I foresee that. You might meet the Mayhew girl or Whitehouse, or both coming down the staircase, and they would at once smell a rat. What about having a rehearsal of that excellent disguise which you are going to assume to-morrow? I can rig you out comfortably in a quarter of an hour."

Lydon agreed. There was an element of sport in the whole thing which the hatchet-faced detective seemed to enjoy as much as his client. Disguised in a heavy beard and moustache, the young man walked out of the detective's office. They took a taxi and dismounted within a few yards of Ashstead Mansions.

The porter, a young military-looking man, was standing outside the particular block they entered. Grewgus whispered in his companion's ear. "I've reckoned him up in a single glance. I know the type. He will talk till doomsday after the first ten-shilling note is slipped in his hand. Of course, you won't mind a bit of expense over the job?"

Lydon whispered back that, under the circumstances, expense was no object. He was prepared to spend a considerable amount of money to confirm or disprove his suspicions of Zillah Mayhew.

They went into the hall, and scrutinized the board containing the names of the particular block in which Number 18 was situated. The name of Whitehouse did not figure on it.

The detective rubbed his thin face. "This is 18 Ashstead Mansions, right enough, but nobody of the name of Whitehouse resides here. You are quite sure of the number?"

The young man smiled. Detectives perhaps resembled solicitors; they did not credit the average person with ordinary intelligence.

"Impossible for me to make a mistake," he answered. "I was far too interested not to make sure. I only learned it last night."

Seeing they were obviously perplexed, the porter strolled up to them. "Are you looking for somebody, sir?" he asked, addressing Grewgus, whom he evidently regarded as the more dominant personality of the two. "Perhaps I can assist you."

Grewgus spoke in his rather precise, formal way. "Am I correct in saying that a Mr. Whitehouse occupies one of these flats?"

The military-looking man shook his head. "Nobody of that name in this block, sir, or any of the others."

Grewgus turned to his companion with a finely simulated air of surprise. "Either we have been misinformed as to the precise locality or the name itself," he said.

Lydon, not used to the subtle processes of the detective mind, thought it best to say as little as possible. He just muttered the safe words, "It certainly looks like it, doesn't it?" playing up to the lead given him by the astute Grewgus.

That gentleman extracted with a great air of deliberation a ten-shilling note from his waistcoat pocket and pressed it into the receptive hand of the porter.

"I may as well tell you we are here to make a few inquiries about a certain party," he said. "You say there is no Mr. Whitehouse here. Does a young lady named Mayhew reside in this or any of the other blocks?"

The porter, stimulated by the *douceur* so promptly and adroitly administered, became voluble at once, thus justifying the detective's hasty diagnosis of his temperament.

"Miss Mayhew, sir, lives with her uncle and aunt, Mr. and Mrs. Glenthorne, in this block, Number 18. I believe she is their niece; I have heard her call him uncle."

Grewgus turned to the disguised young man and addressed him with the utmost coolness and suavity. "Of course, we were given the wrong name. I suspected it after I searched that board."

He turned to the porter, who, by the knowing smile that showed itself upon his good-looking face, appeared to be awaiting developments of an interesting character.

"Now can you tell us something about this Mr. Glenthorne? Do you know his profession, his business, his occupation?"

The smile on the porter's face deepened, as he saw Grewgus' hand steal ostentatiously to his pocket, and withdraw another note. It had evidently dawned on his mind by now that they were detectives, and were prepared to pay liberally for information.

"I could tell you about almost anybody in this block, sir, but not Mr. Glenthorne. When he is in London, he seems to go out every day, and returns at all sorts of hours, sometimes to lunch, sometimes to dinner, sometimes not till close upon midnight."

"A gentleman apparently of quite irregular habits?" interjected the detective.

"Quite so, sir. Whatever his business is, it takes him away a good deal. He spends more than half the year abroad."

"And what about Miss Mayhew? Is she as erratic?"

"Never stays here very long, sir. She was off to-day. From something I heard, I think she was bound for Paris."

A second note found its way into the porter's ready palm, and Grewgus was prepared to admit that he had earned it.

The two men were turning away, when the porter said in a low voice: "Here is Mr. Glenthorne, sir. Do you know him?"

Grewgus motioned him to silence. A well-remembered figure entered the hall and ascended the staircase. He cast a sharp glance at the two men, but it was evident he did not penetrate Lydon's disguise.

When he was safely out of earshot, Leonard whispered to his companion: "It is the man whom I know as John Whitehouse."

They went out into the street, and then the detective spoke. "Glenthorne in Ashstead Mansions, and Whitehouse when he visits his friends at Effington. The beginning of a very pretty mystery, Mr. Lydon. Perhaps our trip to Paris will help us to solve it."

CHAPTER NINE

WHEN they had left Ashstead Mansions safely behind, the detective turned down a side street, and, leading the young man under a convenient archway, dexterously whipped off the disguising beard and moustache and put them in a small bag he had brought with him.

"Now Richard is himself again, and can face the world in his own proper person," he observed in a jocular tone. "I suppose we will separate here. I am going on to Hammersmith to see one of my smartest men and put him at once on the job of finding out what he can about Stormont and the man whom you originally knew as Whitehouse. Better be at my office about eight o'clock to-morrow. As soon as I have made you up, we will start."

As they parted, Grewgus observed that he had better pay out all the out-goings, and Lydon could give him a cheque from time to time. "I expect it will run you into a pretty penny," he said, "but from what you have said, I gather you don't mind that. The thing certainly seems worth investigating. The fact of this fellow having two names is very suspicious. And whatever is going on, I have little doubt we shall be able to connect Stormont with it. It is impossible he can be ignorant of the fact that Whitehouse calls himself Glenthorne when he is away from Effington."

Lydon went back to his rooms, and in the evening dined at the *Berkeley* with a friend. The more he thought over the matter the more he congratulated himself on having gone to the solicitor, and through him to Grewgus, who impressed him as a man of remarkable capacity. What they had learned at Ashstead Mansions was enough to prove that there was some deep mystery about the occupants of Number 18, a mystery in which the owner of Effington Hall was obviously involved.

Whatever that mystery was, did Gloria and Mrs. Barnard know anything about it, or were they as ignorant as he was when he had first set foot in the fine old Tudor mansion where the rubicund profiteer posed as a man of business who had lately taken up the rôle of country gentleman?

Of Mrs. Barnard, he could not, of course, be sure. She was a singularly quiet, self-contained woman, not much given to general conversation. Considering the hours he had spent down at Effington, he had really seen very little of her. She seemed to play a very subordinate part in the life led there, her brother taking the lead in everything, impressing himself upon his guests, in his bluff, genial way, while she remained in the background.

She seemed, so far as he could judge, to be interested in two things—clothes and the local charities. And no doubt Stormont had put her on to the latter, in order to make a good impression in the neighbourhood, and disarm the critical attitude which is so often assumed against a new-comer.

Gloria he was convinced knew nothing and suspected nothing. He loved the girl with his whole heart and soul, with every pulse of his being, but even his great love would not have blinded him if he had observed anything suspicious or evasive about her. In all their intercourse together, she had been so perfectly frank, even with regard to the uncle whose kindness she so greatly appreciated. When she told him that Stormont was a financier, it was evident she was telling what she believed to be the truth. And about her early life with her parents in China she had been as open as a book. Whatever mystery there might be about Stormont himself, there was none about the brother who held a high position in one of the biggest banks in that far-off country.

She had shown him more than one letter from her parents, who kept up a constant correspondence with her, and he could see from what he read there was nothing suspicious about them. In the last one he read, there was an intimation that at any moment they might make up their minds to come to England for a brief holiday. Yes, there was no doubt everything was open and above-board with Jasper Stormont, her father.

The young man found himself wishing that visit would be paid soon. He could question a man more closely than he could a woman.

He was at Grewgus' office at the appointed hour next morning. As before, there was nobody there but the detective himself. The staff did not put in an appearance till nine. In a very few minutes the disguise was effected, with a few additional touches which made it more complete.

When he had finished, Grewgus drew back and surveyed his handiwork with an air of pardonable pride. "If Miss Mayhew meets you face to face, she will never suspect you are the young man she met at Effington Hall. There was no recognition in Whitehouse's glance last night, although I have no doubt he was suspicious of what we were doing there. I bet you he will have asked the porter a question or two by now. But that chap is no fool; he will know how to put him off."

When Leonard looked in the glass which Grewgus handed him, he was bound to confess that a complete metamorphosis had been effected. There was no resemblance between this heavy-bearded creature and the good-looking lover of Gloria Stormont.

"Now I think we will be off," observed Grewgus. "I have written a letter to my head clerk telling him I'm off to Paris, and giving him the address of the hotel we shall stay at. Of course it will not be the *Terminus*, that would hamper us too much. I shall only take you there for the purpose of identifying her; I shall watch her from elsewhere. To stay there would be fatal to our plans. If she is the person you believe her to be, she is naturally as sharp as a needle, and she would soon tumble to the fact that we were taking a suspicious interest in her."

A short time later they had left London behind them and were on their way to Paris and Zillah Mayhew. It was a fairly empty train and they had a first-class compartment to themselves.

Grewgus proved himself a most entertaining companion, and told Lydon many interesting things in connection with himself and his profession, in the pursuit of which he took the keenest delight.

He was about fifty-five, he told the young man, who was surprised at the statement, for, with his clean-shaven face and keen, alert expression, he looked a good ten years younger. He had been fifteen years at Scotland Yard, and ten years on his own.

While at the Yard he had acquired a considerable experience of the underworld. He told him some wonderful stories of the wide ramifications of crookdom of all classes from the lowest to the most aristocratic, of high-class gangs directed by men who presented a most respectable appearance to the outside world, mixing in decent society, and adopting some well-known business or profession as a blind. He regaled him with some thrilling tales of how diamond had cut diamond, of the marvellous ingenuity with which certain professional detectives had got the better of their natural enemies, the criminals.

Since he had been in private practice, his experiences had been less thrilling. He did a good deal in divorce business, and he was applied to in many cases of blackmail.

"If this young woman turns out to be Elise Makris, as you suspect, we are likely to be up against a blackmailing gang here," he observed. "And I should gather they pursue their activities chiefly abroad. You will remember the porter dropped the fact that Glenthorne was frequently out of England."

They snatched a light meal at Boulogne and they got out at Amiens for a very welcome whisky and soda. The Paris train was pretty full, and there was no opportunity for further disclosures of a confidential nature. Just before they rolled into the station, Grewgus whispered in his companion's ear:

"As you said I was to spare no expense, I sent a wire to an old ally of mine to meet the train. We have worked together very often, and he is a most useful fellow, being a splendid linguist. He can speak French like a native, even to its slang. It may be I shall have to watch more than one person, and he will come in handy for the other."

Evidently Mr. Grewgus was going to do the thing thoroughly, and the young man was pleased that he had got hold of such a painstaking fellow. The man with whom he had made the appointment was waiting on the platform, a clean-shaven, smart-looking individual rather like Grewgus himself. He was introduced to Lydon by the name of Simmons.

"I think you and I, Mr. Lydon, will stay at the *Palace Hotel*; it is pretty handy to the other one. We will go there first and book our rooms, and then proceed to the *Terminus*. If we wait a bit in the great hall there, we shall be pretty certain to spot our quarry. We'll take Simmons with us, as he will want to know her as well, in case he has to be put on the job later."

They secured their rooms and then went on to the *Terminus*. The hall was very full, but they found room in a corner, an admirable situation where they could survey everybody at their leisure without attracting too much attention themselves.

They sat there a long time, and Lydon was beginning to fear that Miss Mayhew had changed her plans, gone to some other hotel than the one given in Stormont's letter of instructions. But presently a familiar figure, dressed in the height of fashion, passed through the hall, and when near the exit, lingered as if she was waiting for some one. Lydon spoke to the detective in a low voice: "That is she, waiting at the end."

The two men took stock of her. "Singularly handsome young woman," commented Grewgus in the same cautious tones. "I suppose she is waiting for the man Edwards."

But she was not. To Lydon's surprise and relief, another familiar figure crossed the hall, joined her, and the two went out together. It was that of the woman he had known as Madame Makris, the tenant of the Villa des Cyclamens.

There was no mistaking her. He remembered too well that stout form, the still handsome face with its traces of youthful good looks, the Jewish cast of countenance. He imparted the information to Grewgus.

A satisfied smile stole over the detective's countenance. "Well, this is a bit of the most splendid luck at the very start," he said. "The mother, the blemish which I could not see from here, the pendant which I could see, I think we have found one of the most important things we wanted, at once. There can be no doubt, in face of those three things, that she is Elise Makris, or at any rate that that is one of possibly numerous aliases. Anyway, she is the woman who drove your friend to frenzy. I expect mother and daughter are devoted to each other, and hunt in couples wherever they can. The next thing is to find out what game they are after here."

He whispered a few words to his colleague, Simmons, who rose and left the hall. "I have sent him to make an inquiry," Grewgus explained. "He knows a few of the servants here, and, as I told you, he speaks French like a Frenchman."

Simmons returned presently and related the result of his visit. "They give out they are Englishwomen, and are known as Mrs. and Miss Glenthorne.

No man of the name of Edwards is staying here."

"Ah, I thought she wouldn't register as Miss Mayhew," was the detective's comment. "I suppose a different name for each job. Well, gentlemen, we've got as much here as we can for the present. I don't think we'll stay any longer. I propose we adjourn to a café, have a drink and discuss our future plan of action."

They agreed with his suggestion. In their walk to a café close at hand, Grewgus did not speak much. His mind was no doubt busily working on the situation, and the best way of tackling it.

When they were half-way through their drinks, he spoke. "We can't hope to do very much this evening. Now what I propose is this, Mr. Lydon. I know Paris rather thoroughly, although I daresay my friend Simmons knows it better. This isn't exactly a pleasure trip you've come on, and you won't want to spend more money than is absolutely necessary. We must have something to eat, for that light meal at Boulogne wasn't very satisfactory."

Lydon laughed. "I am in hearty agreement with you. The long journey has made me feel frightfully hungry."

"Well, if we go to one of the swagger places, you'll be charged through the nose. This is the city *par excellence* of good cooking, and I can take you to a capital little restaurant close by where everything is excellent, and you'll pay about a third of the price. Their wines are good and reasonable too."

"I'm in your hands," said the young man. "I should like you to take me along as soon as possible." He noticed that Simmons did not appear to be included in the suggestion. The reason was explained when Grewgus turned to his colleague.

"It's not likely we shall be fortunate enough to do much to-night, as I said just now. We have had one big bit of luck to start with which has saved us a lot of time and trouble. All the same we won't let our vigilance sleep. I want you to start on the watch at once, Simmons, if this woman and her mother come back. We shall be at the *Restaurant Grice* for at least a couple of hours. If in the meantime there is anything to report, come to us there. If we have gone, come to the hotel."

The obedient Simmons finished his drink, rose up and went forth at once to obey his leader's commands. After a final *apéritif*, Grewgus led his companion to the *Restaurant Grice*.

Here they had a most excellent meal, consisting of a good soup, a sole worthy of the *Café Royal*, followed by some tender veal. They drank with it a white wine recommended by Grewgus.

While they were eating, the detective dwelt regretfully on the vast difference between now and before the war. "If you knew the ropes, it was one of the cheapest places in the world to live in, and whatever you paid, you got splendid value for your money. Of course, very few of the English who came here *did* know the ropes. I shouldn't have known them but for a young fellow I met, a student in the Latin Quarter. Gad! What he didn't know about Paris wasn't worth knowing."

After their dinner was over, they sat and smoked to the accompaniment of another bottle of white wine. Grewgus was not keen on spirits. They had promised to wait a couple of hours there in case Simmons had anything to report, and they were as comfortable here as they would have been in their hotel, more so perhaps.

During this period of waiting, Grewgus entertained his host with some more thrilling stories of crooks and crookdom. Lydon found himself much interested. Before he met this reminiscent person he had no idea that there was so much rascality in the world. According to Grewgus, every big city was teeming with it. On the whole, for what he called aristocratic crookdom he was inclined to give the palm to Nice, "where our friend Miss Mayhew appears to hail from," he observed with a sardonic chuckle.

"She's a member of some foreign gang, I suppose?" suggested Lydon. "She has a foreign look about her, although I heard her mother was an Englishwoman, apparently an English Jewess."

Grewgus shook his head. "I should rather fancy an international one. Whitehouse is mixed up with her; we can't assume him to be ignorant of his niece's activities, if she is really his niece. Then there is the man Edwards, and of course Stormont, upon whose business she is here, according to that letter. Three Englishmen, you see. Decidedly an international gang by that."

"What is your reading of it so far, Mr. Grewgus?"

"Well, we can't say positively till I've found out what her game is here. But I should say she is one of the working members of the gang, and Edwards is another. Whitehouse and his friend are probably the controlling spirits who plan and engineer but never come into the open, never execute the dirty work."

A few minutes before the two hours had expired, Simmons bustled in with an air of importance that told he had something of interest to communicate.

It was briefly this. Mother and daughter had returned to the hotel alone, an hour after they left it. The mother had gone upstairs; Miss Glenthorne had sat in the hall, evidently waiting for somebody. That somebody presently turned up in the shape of an opulent-looking Frenchman, thickly bearded and of middle age. The couple left together and drove to one of the most expensive restaurants in Paris.

Simmons followed them into the expensive restaurant, and had his dinner there, conceiving it to be his duty to spend money in order to watch them. From the waiter who attended on him, he learned that the Frenchman was an old customer, and a wealthy man. He was a partner in the big firm of jewellers, Dubost Frères, located in Marseilles. Every three months he made a trip to Paris to have dealings with firms in the same line of business. On these occasions, the waiter had been told, he brought with him several samples worth thousands of pounds. His name was Monsieur Léon Calliard.

With regard to the young woman, the waiter knew nothing about her. He fancied he recognized her as having been in the restaurant before during his period of service, but he could not say with whom. This was certainly the first time he had seen Monsieur Calliard in her company.

From the restaurant, where they quickly got through their dinner, Simmons followed them to a music-hall, where he had left them when he came to make his report.

"Nobody joined them in the music-hall, no Englishman who might be the man Edwards?" queried Grewgus when his colleague had finished his recital.

"No, so far, Edwards has not appeared upon the scene," was the answer.

The detective looked at his client. "Looks like a case of blackmail, or perhaps robbery and blackmail," was his comment. "Anyway the old game."

"I didn't know whether you would like to go and have a look at them yourself?" hazarded Simmons.

But Grewgus thought not. He would wait till to-morrow to get on the track of the man Edwards, that is, if he were taking an active part in the affair and still in Paris.

CHAPTER TEN

AFTER breakfast the next morning, Grewgus inquired if Lydon had any intention of making a long stay in Paris.

The young man replied in the negative. His business claimed him, his sweetheart claimed him, although he did not communicate the latter item to the detective. He had, up to the present, said nothing about her, or her relationship to Stormont. Naturally, he shrank from doing so.

"I take it, if I stayed, I could be of little use to you in your proceedings, Mr. Grewgus?" he queried.

The reply was polite, but quite emphatic. "Well, Mr. Lydon, I think not. If I detailed you off on the watching business, you might find it a very difficult job. Shadowing people is an art—of course Simmons and I are quite used to it."

"I am sure I understand. If I attempted to follow Miss Mayhew about, she would soon spot it. You do it in some mysterious way, so that while observing, you contrive to escape observation."

Grewgus was pleased to find his client took such a sensible view of the situation. He bestowed on him a cordial smile.

"Everybody to his job, Mr. Lydon. I may say to you that, speaking from a professional point of view, this promises to be an exceedingly interesting case, more especially when we succeed in getting on to the track of the man Edwards who is no doubt about. I don't fancy the young woman is doing it all off her own bat."

There was a certain air of satisfaction about Grewgus as he spoke which convinced his client he was engaged in a business after his own heart. There had been aroused in him those sleuth-like instincts, lacking which no man makes a good hunter of criminals.

Grewgus was away all the morning, and Lydon took advantage of his absence to stroll about and renew his rather slight acquaintance with the beautiful city. They met for *déjeuner* at the same place where they had dined the previous evening.

There was news of some importance to communicate. Simmons had seen Miss Mayhew with a tall, elegant-looking young man in the Bois de Boulogne. They had separated very soon, and, surmising the man to be Edwards, he had followed him to his quarters in an hotel in a different part of the city, close to the Gare du Nord. Discreet inquiries elicited that the young man was registered under his proper name; he had not thought it necessary to change it like Miss Mayhew.

"It looks as he if were in charge of the job, and that the girl is playing her usual rôle of decoy," remarked Grewgus, when he had imparted this information. "The two meet while this silly old Calliard is doing his business in Paris. No doubt Miss Mayhew and her elderly admirer will spend this evening and other evenings together till it is time to pluck him. The waiter told Simmons he is a married man. If he were not, we might give the young woman the benefit of the doubt, and credit her with the intention of pulling off an advantageous marriage."

"In that case, the man Edwards wouldn't be wanted," observed Lydon, who was quite shrewd in his way. "He will probably appear upon the scene presently as the injured husband, or outraged brother, or something equally terrifying to this poor enamoured old man."

Later on, Grewgus saw his client off at the station and wished him *bon voyage*. "I instructed my man in London to send a report of his discoveries with regard to Stormont and Whitehouse, not only to me here, but to you at your private address, as it will save time. I shall keep you posted at this end. Of course, for a day or two I may have nothing to communicate, as so far we have found out a good bit in the short time. We have located Edwards, we have proved beyond the smallest possibility of doubt that Zillah Mayhew and Elise Makris are one, by the presence of the mother. And, of course, our friend at Effington Hall stands revealed by his letter as the prime mover in the affair."

Lydon arrived in London the same night, and early on the following morning sent a wire to Gloria asking her to meet him at the *Savoy* for luncheon. On his breakfast table had lain an envelope addressed in an unfamiliar handwriting. It contained a long memorandum headed—"Copy of a report forwarded to Mr. Grewgus in Paris." Obviously the detective's agent had lost no time, he must have worked at top speed, as he could only have devoted two days to the inquiries.

The report read as follows: "I could not start as soon as I should have liked, as I had no personal knowledge of Stormont and had to travel down to Effington and hang about there till I had spotted the man, and learned something of his habits. On the next morning I shadowed him at Waterloo, and followed him to Hornby Square in the City. He went into a small suite of offices, on the entrance door of which were marked the names of Robinson & Company, financiers. Further inquiries elicited that his firm kept no staff, that only two men were there, sometimes together, sometimes alone, Stormont and a taciturn, rather unpleasant-looking man whom the porter knew by the name of White-house.

"I shadowed Whitehouse when he left in the afternoon about four o'clock and found he occupies a flat Number 18 in Ashstead Mansions, off Sloane Square. The family consists of himself, his wife and a niece, Miss Mayhew. Both uncle and niece frequently take journeys abroad. He is known there as Glenthorne."

Leonard smiled as he read this part. It was evident that the hall-porter at Ashstead Mansions had again been a source of information.

"There seems little or no business doing at Hornby Square, so far as I could gather. There are a very few occasional callers, and a fair amount of correspondence. Taking the aspect of things in a general conjunction, and remembering the suspicious circumstance that the man Whitehouse calls himself Glenthorne in private life, I should say the office in Hornby Square is used as a blind, and that no legitimate business is carried on there."

There was a letter to Lydon accompanying the report signed John Ross, in which the writer stated that he was forwarding it in compliance with the instructions of his principal, Mr. Grewgus.

Lydon laid the report down, thinking that it fully confirmed his suspicions, and marvelling what an immense amount had come to light in consequence of his sudden determination to open the letter to Zillah Mayhew. If Stormont only knew, how he would curse his sister's officiousness in getting those letters posted.

As he expected might be the case, he found Gloria very hurt that her sweetheart had not written to her during his brief absence. It was very unkind, she told him: if the positions had been reversed, she would have sent him a long letter every day.

He hated lying to the charming girl, she was always so frank and open herself. But what was he to do under the circumstances? He could not admit that the journey to Glasgow was a myth, that he had really gone to Paris to get evidence against her uncle.

The day might come when he would have to open her eyes as to Stormont's real character, but it had not arrived yet. He must have stronger evidence than he possessed at the moment.

"My darling, you can't imagine how busy I was," he pleaded in excuse of his neglect. "I was rushing about from place to place; when I had a spare second I was 'phoning somebody or writing telegrams."

Being a very sweet-tempered girl, she was soon placated, and made no further allusion to the distasteful subject. Nothing of any moment had happened at Effington; there had been one dinner party during his absence, and there was to be another one on his next weekly visit, on the Saturday.

"I think uncle is drawing in his horns a bit," she observed. "He seems to be cutting it down to one dinner party a week instead of two or three. He has been up to London a good deal more lately; he says he has a great deal of business on. So that I daresay consoles him for the comparative lack of gaiety. But, of course, he's never really happy unless he is entertaining."

"And I suppose he doesn't really care twopence for the people on whom he lavishes so much of his money?" queried Lydon.

"I'm sure he doesn't," was the answer. "It's just a form of excitement. That's the pity of it. I am fond enough of company in a reasonable sort of way, but then I would choose people I really liked for themselves, for their qualities, not because they lived in a big house and were important people in the neighbourhood."

He rather looked forward with distaste to his next visit to Effington. It would be so difficult to avoid showing a change of manner to Stormont. He knew that a dozen times in the day an almost irresistible impulse would overtake him, prompting him to tell the rubicund hypocrite that he knew him for what he was, the friend and abettor of Elise Makris, the decoy of a gang of blackmailers. The day would come when he must tell him, but for the present he must practise patience.

He must wait till his case was strengthened, so as to leave Stormont no loophole for plausible explanation. If confronted now, how easy for him to say that he knew nothing of the girl's criminal activities, that he could not be supposed to be aware she was leading a double life. He could hear him rolling out in an unctuous voice some such words as these:

"My dear Leonard, do be reasonable. I made her acquaintance through Whitehouse, a most respectable man with whom I have been associated in business for years. I found she had great aptitude. She is useful to me, with her charm of manner, in many delicate and difficult financial negotiations with important people. The man Edwards is one of my trusted agents. I often send him when I cannot go myself, confident that he will look after my interests faithfully. Your suspicions are the merest moonshine."

He might even be able to wriggle his way out, with regard to the man John Whitehouse. He would say that he carried on two businesses under two different names for the sake of distinguishing them. That at Hornby Court he was Whitehouse, at his other offices Glenthorne.

No, he must not yet show in his manner that he was on his track. But he would avoid him as much as possible, see as little of him as he could, take long walks and drives with Gloria. To do him justice, the so-called financier did leave the lovers pretty much to themselves; so did Mrs. Barnard, who might or might not be in the secret of her brother's double life.

Still, he would have to sit through a good many meals with his host, and he would find it trying. He was not very fond of those lavish dinner parties which gave Stormont such keen pleasure, but he felt rather grateful for this particular one which would keep them very much apart for that evening.

On that same Saturday afternoon, a very strange thing occurred. Mrs. Barnard had gone out to luncheon that day, and the three sat chatting together for some little time after the meal was concluded, Lydon being the most silent member of the party.

Presently they went out into the hall together, the young man having suggested to his sweetheart that they should take a stroll in the grounds. A peculiar spectacle met their view.

A bronzed-looking, elderly man, with a shaggy beard and moustache, rather shabbily dressed, was standing inside close by the door. A smart-looking young footman stood near to him, with rather the air of mounting guard. Duncan, the butler, was advancing in the direction of the dining-room, but halted when he saw the party approaching.

He spoke in his grave, respectful voice, in which there seemed just a tinge of surprise. "A—a—person wishes to see you, sir. He declines to give his name, says he wants to surprise you."

Stormont started for a second, then advanced towards the new-comer whom he could not see very distinctly, as he was afflicted with short-sight. Then, when he got close to him, his face went pale under its tan, and the words dropped from his lips slowly, as if they were forced from him. "Tom Newcombe, by all that's wonderful."

The shabby-looking man burst into a loud laugh and extended a hand. Lydon noticed it was not over-clean, and the other took it with evident embarrassment.

"Tom Newcombe it is, your old pal. Glad to see you again, Howard, and to find things are so well with you. That gentleman is quite right, I wouldn't give my name, I wanted to give you a surprise." He glanced at the footman. "I think this young fellow has got an idea I'm a burglar or something of the sort; he's been looking at me suspiciously ever since I came in."

There was an awkward pause. Stormont's agitated countenance showed that he was very much upset by this unexpected arrival of his "old pal." The footman disappeared rapidly. Duncan retreated with his slow, majestic step, his grave face looking graver than ever. Before he came to Effington, he had lived all his life in refined and aristocratic families. Never had he known, in his respectable experience, such an occurrence as this—a shabby-looking stranger entering the house and greeting the owner as "your old pal." There is no doubt the dignified butler was thoroughly shaken.

Lydon was very generous-hearted, and in spite of the altered feelings with which he now regarded Stormont, he could not but feel a wave of pity for the man, subjected to such a rude shock in the very midst of his splendour, before the eyes of his astonished servants. Thinking the most tactful course was to withdraw, he touched Gloria lightly on the arm.

"Let us go for our stroll," he said, and she, understanding his object, nodded her head. They went out and left the agitated Stormont to deal with Mr. Tom Newcombe.

When they were in the grounds, she turned to him, a look of surprise, Lydon fancied a faint hint of trouble, in her clear, candid blue eyes. "What can it mean, Leonard? Such a common fellow too, his way of talking! Not a broken-down gentleman. You heard him speak of uncle as his 'old pal.' Where in the name of wonder could he have known him?"

"Do you know anything of your uncle's past, of his life as a young man?" As her sweetheart put the question, his thought was that she probably knew as little of the past as she did of the present.

The girl answered him with her usual frankness. "Nothing. From some little things father dropped, I gathered that he was rather wild in his youth. I don't fancy they had ever been very good friends as young men. I am sure you have noticed how little Uncle Howard ever talks about himself, about his business or his past. I know nothing about these things. Auntie may know more about them than I do, but I don't fancy very much. He is so strangely reticent. He certainly told her he was going to borrow money from you, but I expect he did so because he thought you might let it out to one of us. If he had been sure of your silence, she would never have heard a word about it, I am convinced."

After a short pause, she resumed the subject. "I cannot understand it, the man is obviously of such a common class. The Stormonts come from very homely stock, I know, but they are miles above this. I don't think I have ever told you much about the family history, which I learned from my father, not my uncle. I don't think I have ever heard him allude to his family. He is as reticent about them as he is about himself."

She proceeded to tell him about the past Stormonts. Her grandfather was a small tradesman in a Midland town, his family consisted of two sons, Howard and Jasper. Although not ambitious for himself, he was for his children, and he stinted and screwed to give them a good education to enable them to do better in the world than their father.

That education had stood them in good stead and developed their native brains. Jasper, the elder of the two, was a very clever fellow, although he had made nothing like the money his brother had done. This, in Gloria's opinion, was simply due to lack of opportunity, to that absence of luck which plays such a large part in human affairs. And what money Jasper did make he took good care of.

"But although he has never tried to make any show, father's career has been one of steady success," she concluded with an air of pardonable pride.

"And he is one of the most upright men, with high ideals of duty. He has not got Uncle Howard's robust geniality, but he has most lovable qualities. I should be so pleased for you to meet him."

They strolled about for a long time before they returned to the house. Before they went in, Gloria had confided to her lover her perplexity as to what Stormont would do with his unwelcome guest. Mr. Newcombe certainly could not join the ultra-respectable dinner party that would assemble in the evening.

This problem was presently solved by Stormont himself, who later on came into the billiard-room to find them.

He had recovered a good deal from the shock, but it was easy to see by his nervous, jerky manner, that he was still very ill at ease over this disconcerting experience, and the necessity of furnishing some explanation of it.

He tried to carry it off in his usual hearty bluff way, but Lydon knew that he would have given a big sum of money for it not to have happened.

"Strange after all these years, very strange! Poor old Tom Newcombe to have come down so; he was fairly prosperous at one time. A rough diamond, but one of the best, one of the very best." It was obvious to both there was no real heartiness in his voice as he pronounced these warm eulogies on the shabby-looking man.

He went on in the same jerky, unconvincing manner, addressing himself rather more directly to his niece. "I suppose you are wondering how I came to know him?"

"I think we are," said Gloria, speaking with her usual directness. "He spoke as if you had been on very intimate terms."

"So we were, so we were," was the reply. "I must reveal a little bit of my life that I have said nothing to you about before. Even your aunt and father know very little of it. When I was quite a youngster, I was a bit inclined to kick over the traces. And, in one of my wild moods, I went out to Australia in the hope of making my fortune quickly. It was there I met Tom Newcombe, who had been lucky and made quite a respectable pile. In that land of democratic equality we chummed up together. After a few years I left, having made no headway. But during that trying time Newcombe was a splendid pal to me, let me share with him when I was wanting a meal. I have never set eyes on him since. And now poor old Tom has turned up, broke to the world. One of the saddest things I know."

Lydon was firmly convinced the man was lying, that he had invented this explanation of his acquaintance with the rough-looking stranger. Even Gloria looked somewhat doubtful.

"What are you going to do with him, uncle? Will he stay here?" she asked quickly.

"Of course. Could I turn out a man who befriended me as he did?" answered Stormont with a fine show of virtuous rectitude. "A pity we have got that party on to-night. I should have been proud to have such a fine fellow at my table, in spite of the fact that he is not quite of our—er—class. But he is a sensible chap and sees things clearly. He has no evening clothes, and none of mine would fit him. He will have his dinner in my study, and I shall instruct the servants to show him the greatest respect. There will be nobody here to-morrow, and he can then join us."

He was carrying it out very bravely, as well as anybody could, turning the rough Tom Newcombe into almost a hero. But Lydon disbelieved every word he said, as he naturally would, and Gloria did not seem very convinced.

"You are going to help him, of course?" she said in the same quiet tone.

A generous glow seemed to animate Stormont's whole manner as he replied to her. And Lydon was more than ever convinced that the man was acting for all he was worth.

"I should think so. I have heaps of faults, but want of humanity, thank Heaven, is not one of them. I shall help poor old Tom as long as he wants help, as he helped me when I was in need."

With the utterance of these noble sentiments, the conversation ended. Stormont went away to shut up with his guest till dinner-time. The respectable people of the neighbourhood came to the banquet and did full justice to it, in ignorance that not far from them, in the host's study, a shabby-looking man, waited upon by a rather supercilious footman, was partaking in solitude of the same rich viands and choice wines.

When the last carriage had rolled away, Mrs. Barnard went to bed, explaining that she was tired with her long day. Was it because she wished to avoid any conversation with her niece about the unexpected guest?

Stormont went to look after Newcombe. He promised to join them shortly in the billiard-room, as the night was still young.

He came in looking rather relieved, and proposed a three-handed game. "I've set the poor chap in front of a bottle of whisky; it will do him good after his privations," he said genially. "I hope, though, he won't take too much; he has a little weakness in that direction."

They had not played more than half an hour when the door opened, and the shabby figure of Mr. Newcombe appeared. His face was very flushed, there was no doubt about his condition. His gait was uncertain, and his voice was decidedly thick.

Advancing towards the billiard-table, he looked at his host with a very unfriendly expression, in which Lydon saw, or perhaps fancied he saw, a hint of menace.

"Look here, Stormont, my boy. Old pal as you may have been, I'm not going to stand much more of this sort of thing. I'm being treated in a way I don't like. It's devilish unhandsome, to say the least of it."

The more than half-drunken man was meditating a scene in revenge for some real or fancied grievance. Gloria paled and reddened by turns and looked apprehensively at her uncle.

Lydon waited developments. Would this fellow in his cups, and without the least control over his faculties, blurt out something that would give the lie to Stormont's hastily concocted story?

CHAPTER ELEVEN

STORMONT himself seemed quite taken aback by this almost savage on-slaught, almost as deprived of self-control as Newcombe himself. "What are you complaining of?" he asked, in a voice that was scarcely audible.

The man whom his accent declared to be a Colonial, answered in his thick utterance: "I don't say anything about not being asked to dine with your swell friends, they're not my kidney, and I'd rather have their room than their company. But after they'd all gone, you might have introduced me to your family."

He pointed a shaking forefinger at the shrinking Gloria, who was immensely afraid of a drunken man. Stormont was pretty liberal in his potations, but he never got into anything approaching this condition.

"This pretty girl, I take it, is your niece. And this, I suppose, is her young man you told me about. Looks a bit stuck-up, I fancy, like the young feller who brought me my dinner. But I daresay I shall find him a good sort when we're better acquainted."

He walked with his unsteady gait towards the table on which the ever-thoughtful butler had placed refreshments.

The action seemed to rouse Stormont from his trance. "Stop it," he shouted in a voice of thunder. "Stop it. You've had more than you can carry already."

But he was too late, Newcombe had already filled a tumbler half-full of raw whisky and tossed it down his throat as if it had been water. Having done this, his manner seemed to change. From a mood very nearly approaching ferocity, he lapsed into one of maudlin sentimentality. A weak smile overspread his bearded countenance.

"Well, my boy, we mustn't quarrel, we've been too dear old pals for that." He laughed with the disconcerting hilarity of a drunken man. "Lord, what fine games we've had in our day, Howard, haven't we? Do you remember that glorious day we followed up old Billy Stiles——?"

Again Stormont's voice rang out, and there was a note of almost agony in it. "Stop, Newcombe, for Heaven's sake stop. You forget there is a woman present."

The appeal seemed momentarily to sober the wretched man. He turned his bleary eyes in the direction of Gloria. "Sorry, miss, I'm sure; I forgot you were here. No offence meant, Howard, my dear old pal. I haven't said anything; you've noticed that."

It was time to end the disgusting scene. Stormont turned to the young man. "Very sorry, but you'd better take Gloria away. I'll deal with this drunken creature and get him to bed."

As he spoke, he turned a very malevolent glance on the huddled-up Newcombe, who had closed his eyes after his last speech, and appeared to be falling asleep. There was positive hatred in that glance, Lydon felt assured. And yet a few hours ago he had spoken of the man as a splendid fellow, as one of the very best. The young man doubted if there was much love lost on either side, in spite of Newcombe's reference to his friend as a dear old pal.

The lovers went into the drawing-room. Gloria still looked pale, and not a little indignant. "What a perfect brute!" she cried. "Why has uncle put up with him for five minutes? You could see the sort he was at the first glance, a rough savage. Why did he not give him some money, and make him go?"

Almost before he was aware of it, the words slipped out of her sweetheart's mouth, words that voiced his inmost thoughts.

"Depend upon it, dear, Mr. Stormont has some good reasons for not wishing to offend this uncouth fellow."

The girl looked up with a startled glance, one which had fear in it as well as surprise. "Leonard, what is in your mind? Do you suggest"—her voice faltered for a second—"that he knows anything to Uncle Howard's discredit?"

Lydon felt he had gone a bit too far at the present juncture. He shrugged his shoulders and spoke in indifferent tones.

"I don't suppose young men who go out to Australia and mix with a rough crowd lead very saintly lives. I daresay Newcombe is acquainted with a few episodes that would be better suppressed in your uncle's family circle. Don't worry, darling."

"But I can't help it," replied the ever-frank Gloria. "The whole thing is so mysterious, and somehow uncle's explanation seemed to me lame and halting. Did it strike you in the same way?"

Leonard hesitated for a moment. It would be easy to say that he had accepted that statement in perfect good faith, in short, to tell an absolute lie. But he thought it better on the whole that Gloria should be allowed to nurse her suspicions. The blow would fall lighter on her when it had to come. He told her, therefore, that the same impression had been made on him.

"I wonder what he was going to say when he was stopped!" she remarked, after a brief pause. "When he was going to tell something about a man they had followed up. Uncle seemed in an agony of apprehension. I almost wish it had come out; I shall only be speculating what it was. I do hope he is not making an indefinite stay here."

But on this point Lydon thought he could see his way to give her some comfort. Stormont was much too clever a man to allow Newcombe to exhibit himself to his neighbours; he had been disturbed quite enough by the fact that he had been seen by the family and servants.

"Your uncle is a resourceful man, Gloria, I am sure he will soon see a way of getting rid of him without hurting his feelings. And when the fellow gets sober again I daresay he will have the sense to perceive that Effington Hall is hardly a fit *milieu* for him."

The next morning the Colonial did not come down to breakfast; probably it was too severe a task after the potations of the previous evening. He appeared in Stormont's study about twelve o'clock, Lydon and the ladies having gone to church. What passed between the pair, they had no means of knowing. Newcombe lunched with them, and his demeanour was very chastened. He ate heartily, but drank very sparingly. Perhaps his host had given him a lecture on the fatal effects of intemperance. And during the meal he scarcely opened his lips.

Gloria and her sweetheart went out for their afternoon walk. When they came back to tea, neither Stormont nor Newcombe was visible. Mrs. Barnard said that her brother had driven the visitor up to London, where he intended to find a lodging.

Lydon drew a breath of relief: had the Colonial stayed, there might have been another disagreeable scene. Gloria openly expressed her satisfaction. "Loathsome creature, I hope he has gone for good," she ejaculated fervently. "Have you ever seen him before, aunt?"

"Never, my dear, nor do I want to see him again. It must have amazed your uncle very greatly. Of course in a wild place such as he went to as a young man, you cannot pick and choose the people you are forced to associate with. But it is distinctly unpleasant when they turn up in after life and remind you of the old acquaintance."

Had Stormont told her the same tale he had told to them, or did she know more about that sinister visitor than they did? Nothing in her demeanour enabled Lydon to determine the point.

Stormont returned in time for dinner, having deposited his visitor somewhere. No further allusion was made to him by any member of the party, but his advent had created an uncomfortable feeling which was not wholly allayed by his departure.

Leonard guessed that Mr. Newcombe had taken away with him either a good sum in cash or a substantial cheque. He had no doubt in his own mind that the Colonial knew something damaging about Stormont, and that his visit had been made for the purpose of extorting hush-money. If so, there was a grim irony in the situation. The man who, according to all the present evidence, was a blackmailer, was being blackmailed himself, and maintaining his position as the opulent owner of Effington by the grace of this rough and down-at-heel Colonial.

After dinner Stormont shut himself up in his study. During dinner he had been very quiet, quite unlike his usual genial, rather boisterous self; it was evident that Newcombe had left a disturbing influence behind him. Mrs. Barnard went to her own particular sanctum, and the young people had the drawing-room to themselves.

"It may have been my fancy," remarked Gloria, "but I thought I detected a subtle difference in Duncan's manner to-day. I saw his face drop in the hall when that creature spoke of himself as being an old pal of uncle's. I shouldn't wonder if he has made up his mind that it is no longer a respectable establishment to remain in and intends to give notice."

She had diagnosed the state of the dignified butler's feelings correctly, for the next day Duncan intimated his wish to leave. When pressed for a reason, he murmured something evasive about his desire for a change. It was a decided shock to his employer, as it showed him what an unfavourable impression had been created by the unwelcome visit of this rough stranger.

Lydon did not know this when he left. Duncan had not delivered his bombshell till later in the morning. There had been considerable excitement at the breakfast-table. Something had happened which temporarily drove Mr. Newcombe out of the minds of every member of the family. Stormont had received a letter from his brother Jasper, dated from the *Hotel Cecil*.

Gloria's father and mother were staying there, having arrived in London early on the Sunday. They had given no previous intimation of their intended visit, as they wanted it to come as a complete surprise to their relatives. Would they come and see them on the Monday if they had no previous engagement which it was impossible to put off? Of course they would dine with them, and in this invitation Leonard was included. Gloria must stay with them at least a week if not longer.

The unpleasant atmosphere created by the late happenings seemed very much cleared by this pleasant news. Stormont and his sister seemed quite pleased, in spite of the fact that the brothers had not been very great friends in their youth. He remarked with a touch of his former geniality that it would be very pleasant to see good old Jasper again, a sentiment fully endorsed by Mrs. Barnard. Gloria clapped her hands together in her frank delight.

"How lovely!" she cried. "It was on the tip of my tongue to say I wish they had let us know beforehand. But I think I am rather glad they have taken us by surprise. It is such a sensation."

She turned impetuously towards her sweetheart. "I am sure you will like my father very much, Leonard. He is one of the dearest men, and very fond of young people, who all take to him. He is awfully liked out there by everybody, and he has the highest reputation for integrity and highmindedness."

Did Howard Stormont look just a little glum as he listened to this sincere praise of his elder brother, or was it Lydon's fancy? Had the man's conscience, deadened as it must be, suddenly awakened to fresh life and pricked at him as he thought of the difference between Gloria's father and himself?

Lydon was pleasurably excited at the prospect of meeting with Jasper Stormont, of whom his daughter had always spoken with love and the greatest respect. She had often told him how attached to him she had been as a child, and what grief she had suffered at parting from her parents. And time and the generous treatment of her aunt and uncle had never weakened that early affection.

When the young man met them in the hall of the *Cecil*, a few minutes before the time fixed for dinner, he was very favourably impressed by the appearance of both mother and father. Mrs. Stormont was a very handsome woman, and her slim elegant figure made her look remarkably young. She had preserved herself wonderfully, and might have passed for her daughter's elder sister. It was easy to see the husband was very proud of his youthful-looking wife.

In appearance, Jasper Stormont was quite unlike his younger brother, his junior by two years. He was tall and spare, with an aristocratic bearing. His face, if not exactly handsome, was pleasant to look upon and his features were refined. His manner was quietly genial, without that bluff boisterousness which distinguished the so-called financier. It exhaled an air of old-world courtesy which stood out in marked contrast to some modern manners.

He welcomed the young man with a cordiality that was perfect under the circumstances, not too effusive or overdone. Lydon was prepared to think that everything about the man was genuine; he seemed a perfect type of the commercial aristocracy.

"Delighted to see you, Mr. Lydon; later on I shall come to the more familiar Christian name. But to such a long exile—we have been over only once before since I left England—everything seems strange, and in some cases I must confess, of course not in the present one, a little out of tune. I am glad to see my little girlie looking so well; certainly her uncle and aunt have taken great care of her and made her very happy. She is staying here with us for a week, and at the end of that my brother Howard insists that we must shift our quarters to Effington."

There was something a little formal in his words, in his diction, that Lydon rather liked. There was also about the man an ease, an unconscious air

84

of authority that pleased him. Beside him his brother, Howard Stormont, with his supposed great wealth, appeared plebeian.

He learned afterwards from Gloria that the elder brother was much the superior in mentality. He might not have the money-making instinct so strongly developed, but he had taken far greater advantage of the good education their father had bestowed upon them. He was a very cultivated man, passionately fond of art and music and an omnivorous reader. Howard was essentially a man of the world and nothing more; the arts did not interest him, and the daily newspapers were almost his sole literature.

It was a very pleasant dinner. Jasper Stormont was an exceedingly good talker, but he led the conversation without any attempt to monopolize it, giving everybody a chance to contribute to the common fund of entertainment.

Howard Stormont and his sister were staying the night at the hotel, returning to Effington on the morrow. Leonard left early, good taste suggesting that he should not intrude himself too long on what was a family conclave. There must be many things they would wish to discuss alone.

The liking between the two men seemed mutual. Jasper Stormont shook Leonard's hand very warmly when they parted. "As I told you, Gloria is going to give herself to us for a week, and I should like you to come very often. To dinner every night if you can."

He gave him a very charming smile when the young men protested that this was taking undue advantage of his position. "Not at all, my dear young friend. I am afraid my motive is a rather selfish one. I want to become well acquainted with my future son-in-law."

Gloria saw him off; the others with commendable tact did not intrude upon the tender farewell of the lovers.

"You like my dear old dad, don't you, Leonard? He has a heart of gold," asked Gloria as they said good night.

And Leonard was able to say honestly that he had taken a great liking to Jasper Stormont. He was quite convinced, even on this short acquaintance, he was a white man through and through.

It followed that, being so pressed, the young man did dine at the *Cecil* every evening of that week. The Stormonts had a small private sitting-room, but Jasper often took Lydon down into the smoking-room for a private chat. He had openly avowed his wish to become better acquainted with his future son-in-law, and these informal intimate conversations would help him quickly to that knowledge.

He told Leonard first of his future plans. He expected to retire in about five years from now and would come back to spend his declining years in England. He was nothing like so rich a man as his brother Howard, so he said, but he would be able to live comfortably on the interest of what he had saved.

He went on to speak of Gloria's childhood, and the unhappy time when they had to part with her.

"It was one of the greatest griefs of our life," he said in his simple, straightforward way. "But there was no help for it. We had the best medical advice, and the verdict was unanimous, she could not live in the East. My other child, a son, has thrived there—difference of constitution, of course."

He paused a moment, before resuming this portion of his daughter's history, a good deal of which the young man had gathered from his sweetheart.

"Just to go back a moment. Howard and I had not been very attached brothers in our youth, I should hesitate to say with whom the fault lay. Enough that with regard to most things we did not see eye to eye."

Jasper Stormont did not say what those things were. And Lydon, dearly as he would have liked to know, did not think it seemly to ask him.

"But we kept up a rather desultory, if brief correspondence. When this trouble came upon us, I wrote to him in an agony of spirit as it were, telling him that we had to part with one of our beloved children. In writing that letter, I had no ulterior motive in my mind. From what I knew of my brother's character, I should have considered him the last man in the world to consider anything but his own comfort, to disturb the mode of life which he had mapped out for himself."

Lydon gathered this much from those words: namely, that Howard Stormont was judged to be, in reality, a selfish creature, who lived for himself, who only studied himself.

"To my intense surprise, I received an answer which caused me to take a totally different view of him. He wrote me that having remained a bachelor so long, there was practically no chance of his exchanging his estate. He had prospered greatly in the world; he lived with our widowed sister, Maud Barnard, who had a small income of her own. The house was at times a bit dull; he thought it would be brightened by the presence of a child, in whom they could take an interest and find an object of affection. He offered to adopt Gloria, and make her welfare his solemn charge. Anyway, let the experiment be tried, for say a couple of years. If, at the end of that time, Gloria found she was not happy, her father could make other arrangements."

Jasper Stormont paused a little time before he resumed. "But, fortunately, that did not happen. They spoiled the girl from the day she went into her new home, and the spoiling has gone on, but I think I can say my dear girl is none the worse for it. And now, my dear Leonard, I come to a somewhat delicate topic."

"I think I can guess the nature of it," interjected Lydon.

"Ah, of course Gloria has told you. I gathered as much from her. Naturally, grateful as she is to her uncle for his care of her, his kindness and generosity, she would conceal nothing from us. She has told me of that loan of a thousand pounds, which of course throws a very clear light upon my brother's financial position. We are both men of business; it tells the same story to both. I know nothing of the nature of Howard's business, but it must be a very precarious one, since he is up to-day and down to-morrow. I don't suppose he will leave anything behind him."

"I feel quite certain he will not," Lydon agreed. "But when I asked Gloria to be my wife, I never took any expectations of that sort into account."

"I quite believe you; you loved my dear daughter for herself. Well, Leonard, I should like to tell you this. When I and her mother die, whatever I may have to leave will be divided equally between my children. Gloria will not be an heiress, but neither will she be a pauper."

Leonard bowed his head in acknowledgment of this intimation, conveyed with such delicacy and courtesy.

Howard Stormont might be a scoundrel, a mover in crooked ways, as his connection with Elise Makris proved, but his brother was certainly an honest man.

CHAPTER TWELVE

AT the end of the week, the Jasper Stormonts moved to the fine old Tudor house at Effington. And, shortly before they did so, there came for Lydon an invitation from his future uncle-in-law which the young man fancied had been instigated by the banker. If it did not interfere with his business arrangements, would Leonard make the Hall his headquarters for the next week, going up to London in the morning and returning when the duties of the day were done? Jasper Stormont's holiday was to be only a brief one, and shortly he would return to China for another long period of exile. Perhaps in this brief time he wished to see as much as possible of the man who was to marry his daughter, in order to prove if further acquaintance would increase or diminish his first favourable impressions of him.

For Gloria had told him that her father had formed an exceedingly good opinion of him, and expressed his satisfaction that she had made such a wise choice.

"And dear dad's opinion is worth having," said the girl proudly. She was fond of her uncle, very grateful to him for all he had done for her, for the happiness he had brought into her life. But it was easy to see that for her father she had a great respect almost amounting to reverence, in addition to her filial love. No doubt, so far as character was concerned, she put the two men on totally different planes. And Lydon knew that her instinct was right. Even if he had never opened that letter to Zillah Mayhew, and still believed Howard Stormont to be what he had originally thought him—a shrewd, blunt, genial fellow—he would have soon discovered that Jasper was made of the sounder metal.

The young man laughingly told his sweetheart that he thought her father had been at the bottom of this unusual invitation, and she admitted it.

"He's a very keen judge of character," she said. "In his responsible position he is bound to be. And he says you never thoroughly know a man till you have stayed in the same house with him. No doubt that is why he wanted you here daily for a time."

"Till he had completed his investigations, eh?" observed Lydon, with an amused smile, although at the same time he had every sympathy with regard to Jasper's anxiety on behalf of his child. "Well, dear, I shall have to mind my P's and Q's, shan't I? I must take care not to come down grumpy in the morning, or show any of the latent villainy that is hidden somewhere in my disposition."

The girl laughed happily. She had inherited her father's capacity for reading character, and she had not much fear of this open, honest, even-tempered young fellow, whose moods hardly ever seemed to vary.

It occurred to Lydon that, on this visit, Stormont was devoting himself much more closely to his business, whatever it might be, than was usual with him. He went up pretty early to London every day, and on two occasions he missed dinner, and did not return till late in the evening. Evidently something of importance was going on.

There were, strange to relate, no dinner parties during that week. Lydon could hardly believe there was so much affection between the two men that Howard wanted to enjoy his brother's company without interruption. He thought it was rather a matter of policy.

Howard knew that, if questioned, Gloria would not be able to conceal the fact of his extravagance. She might even let out that there were periods when he was obviously short of money, and in view of these possible confidences he did not wish to give Jasper the elder brother's privilege of lecturing him. In the eyes of such a financial purist as the banker, his happy-go-lucky methods would savour of nothing short of criminal folly.

Lydon listened to his sentiments one night when the two men were together in the smoking-room, on the second occasion on which Howard had not returned to dinner. The banker's face was very grim as he delivered his criticism on what he knew and had observed.

"I have known next to nothing of my brother's affairs since he left England. I knew he went to Australia for a while and that things did not prosper greatly with him there. When his letter arrived, offering to adopt Gloria, and stating that he was firmly on his feet, I accepted what he said in good faith. Her letters showed they were all leading a very luxurious life, and that money seemed to be spent like water. Of course, I was terribly disillusioned when, such a short time ago, I learned the actual truth. Without mincing words, I can tell you I was not only surprised but intensely disgusted, especially when I heard of that thousand pounds borrowed from you. It hit Gloria very hard, that transaction. She is a girl of extremely delicate feeling, and under the peculiar circumstances it was in the very worst taste. Drowning men, we know, catch at straws; it showed how very near to drowning he must have been. He is no fool; he must know how ugly it would look to a third party."

Lydon made no comment. Had things not been as they were, he might have put up some defence for Howard Stormont, out of his natural kindness of heart. But he could not do so now. The man was unscrupulous to the core.

"When my brother was a young man, he was always very headstrong, also fearfully extravagant, if only in a small way," went on Jasper in the same severe tone. "He never seemed able to curb his desires, to restrain any momentary impulse. If he wanted a thing and hadn't the money to pay for it, he would go into debt to get it, trusting that luck would enable him to avoid the disagreeable consequences. I know this fatal weakness was a great anxiety to our parents, honest and God-fearing people, and made them tremble for his future.

"This big house, with its staff of indoor and outdoor servants eating him up, is a piece of the most colossal folly I have ever come across, and in my business we meet with very many specimens of the spendthrift. Everybody in the banking world does. I have no hesitation in discussing it with you; as Gloria's future husband you have a right to know how matters stand. And further, in the distress which he brought on himself, he showed his hand plainly to you."

As Jasper Stormont elected to be so confidential with him, he thought he might continue the conversation on the same lines.

"It seems to me that his business is evidently a very precarious one. It is rather a strange thing that I have never known what that business really is; it is not a thing on which you can put a quite straight question to a man, but it usually leaks out pretty soon. You know that I am a consulting engineer; I know that you hold a high post in the banking world. I have never even heard from your brother where his offices are. Gloria does not seem to know much about it. She thought he was what you call a financier. Well, we must admit that is rather a vague term."

"And I can assure you, Leonard, I know almost as little as you do; my sister appears equally ignorant. When I have talked about the subject, about which there should be no mystery, there is an obvious attempt to sheer off it. So far as I can gather from random statements, he might be described as a financier. He gets concessions from foreign countries; he negotiates big loans for all sorts of things, does a bit of company promoting, etc. But he avoids details and gives no names. Of course, some men are very reticent about their private affairs, but reticence so pronounced savours greatly of mystery."

There was a long pause and then the banker waved his hand round the room, decorated and furnished in such a costly fashion, with a gesture that was contemptuous.

"But one thing I am certain of, I have often been told that I possess second sight in matters like these. This cannot go on for long, in the light that has been thrown upon it by his borrowing from you what was, after all, a trifling sum for a man in a good way of business to find. A year or two of bad trade will bring him to the ground. Perhaps another year's reprieve in which he will be struggling to tide over. You and I will then, I expect, be invited to put money into the sinking ship. If so, take my advice and sternly refuse. With a man of my brother's headstrong nature and extravagant proclivities, you might as well throw it in the sea."

Lydon thanked his future father-in-law for his advice, thinking, as he did so, that Howard Stormont would never get another loan out of him. Did this honourable, straightforward man of business only know what he knew, he would be overwhelmed with grief and shame at possessing such a brother.

"You can see it is a subject on which I have necessarily to hold my tongue," exclaimed Jasper Stormont. "For all I ought to know to the contrary, he may be conducting his affairs with the greatest prudence, is making enough to enable him to run this place and accumulate a fair fortune besides. What I know about the true state of affairs comes from Gloria, from whom I have drawn it with the greatest reluctance. My lips are sealed; she would hate him to find that she has been telling tales out of school; for whatever faults he may have, he has taken the place of a second father to her, and she cannot but appreciate him for that."

Yes, scoundrel as he might be, Howard Stormont no doubt had his good points, and his kindness to his niece was not the least amongst them.

"I forgot to tell you one thing, not that I am very greatly impressed by it," said the banker as they parted for the evening. "The other day, in a fit of confidence, he imparted to me that he was on a very big thing which he expected to mature shortly, something out of which he would make enough to secure a handsome competence for life. If this came off, he said he would retire from business, and lead this life of a country gentleman which appears to have such great fascinations for him."

Leonard pricked up his ears at this information. If Howard Stormont was on some big enterprise, it would be of a nefarious kind.

"He didn't disclose the nature of this great *coup*, of course?" he asked.

The banker shook his head. "He didn't give me the slightest hint. But, as I said, I attach very little importance to it. All these speculators are sanguine creatures, and follow wills-o'-the-wisp with a blind devotion worthy of a better cause. They have always got some grand scheme on which is to make them rich beyond the dreams of avarice."

Lydon was much impressed by that conversation with Jasper Stormont. Like himself, at an earlier stage, he had sensed a certain mystery surrounding his brother. He wondered whether bankruptcy and poverty would be the only doom that might fall upon the owner of Effington Hall? He thought he might escape that, in spite of the banker's gloomy predictions. After all, he had kept up opulent state for a great many years. According to Gloria's statement, he had been wealthy ever since she had taken up her residence with them. He was a cunning and resourceful man; although he lacked the solid qualities of his brother, probably he would never come quite down to the ground. But the young man was not sure a darker doom might not descend upon him in spite of his cleverness.

He wondered if his sweetheart had told her father of the visit of that shabby Colonial, and the scene in the billiard-room when the drunken creature had been on the point of blurting out something, and had been stopped by his host, who was in a perfect agony of apprehension. He asked her the next day, and she assured him she had kept silence.

"I have really let out more about Uncle Howard than I ought," she explained, in a contrite voice. "But dad has a very persuasive way with him; he would have made a splendid cross-examiner. I expect his business has developed his faculties in that direction; he says that people wanting favours come to him with all sorts of ingenious lies. He leads you on in a quiet, suave sort of way to all kinds of admissions. And you know I haven't the gift of reticence, I am far too outspoken. I could see that uncle was terribly upset by that visit. I have noticed a great change in him since. He gives me the impression of a man who has received a great shock, and can't recover from it."

Lydon had himself noticed a certain change in the man. He was less bluff and genial than he used to be, and at times he caught a brooding expression, an air of abstraction, as if he were thinking deeply over something. At first he imagined Howard was nerving himself to make a confession to his brother, similar to the one he had made to himself, that he was living up to his income and that Gloria could expect very little from him when he died. But on thinking more over it he came to the conclusion that his sweetheart was right, that the change in his demeanour was due to the visit of Tom Newcombe, his "old pal."

In the meantime Lydon had received reports from Grewgus, the first arriving a few days after he had left Paris. From these he learned that the detective and his colleague were keeping a close watch upon the man Edwards and Miss Glenthorne, to call her by her latest alias. They watched them from about eleven o'clock in the morning—the woman did not stir out till then—till late at night.

The programme was much the same every day. In the morning Zillah met the man Edwards, and they walked about together in the outskirts of Paris. They steered clear of the well-known portions, as no doubt Calliard was pursuing his business there, and they might run across him at any moment. In the afternoon they usually took a car and drove out to Versailles or some other suburb.

In the evening Zillah invariably met the opulent jeweller, Calliard, and they dined together at one of the numerous expensive restaurants that abound in the gay city. Monsieur Calliard was evidently a rich man and begrudged nothing in the pursuit of his pleasures.

Then one day came a brief telegram from Grewgus: "The birds have flown, slipped away. All news when we meet. Leaving to-day. Be at my office to-morrow morning as early as you like."

On the face of it, it looked as if the detective had failed in his mission, that the two schemers had outwitted him, and stolen a march on him.

CHAPTER THIRTEEN

LYDON thought that Grewgus looked somewhat crestfallen when they met the following morning in the offices in Craven Street.

He opened the conversation in a rather apologetic tone. "Well, Mr. Lydon, the primary object for which we went to Paris was the establishment of the fact that Zillah Mayhew was the same person as Elise Makris. But that fact we established on the first day we arrived there. I stayed on in order to find something more than that. I am sorry to tell you I have found nothing, except one little thing that makes the affair more mysterious."

"You say they contrived to give you the slip. How was that done when you were keeping such a close watch on them?" asked the young man in a tone that plainly showed his disappointment.

Grewgus hastened to explain. "I am afraid I must plead guilty to a little want of foresight. After watching very carefully for three days, we became pretty sure that neither the woman nor her friend Edwards were what you would call early birds. They did not stir out before a fairly late hour in the morning."

Having, as they thought, established this fact, the two men did not begin their watch till a certain hour themselves. Had they not been so confident, it would have been easy to take it in turns to watch one of them, since, if one of them went out, it was for the purpose of ultimately meeting the other. As a fact, to carry out the thing thoroughly, a third, perhaps a fourth, man was wanted.

"That of course would have entailed a great deal more expense than I felt myself justified in putting you to," said Grewgus in exculpating himself. "The last time I saw Zillah Mayhew, she was dining as usual with her elderly cavalier. Edwards, according to custom, was spending his evenings at one of the music-halls. My colleague Simmons never observed him with anybody, and he never met Miss Mayhew at night. And it is pretty certain that he never came into contact with Calliard. Whatever business was to be carried on with the Frenchman seemed to be left entirely in her hands. No doubt she talked things over with Edwards in their daily meetings."

"You have not even proved conclusively that her object was what we all thought it to be, blackmail?" interjected Lydon.

"If you don't mind, I will just leave that question unanswered for a moment or two while I relate how they gave us the slip. On that particular morning, no Zillah Mayhew issued forth from the hotel. I waited about for a very long time till Simmons joined me. His news was startling. Edwards, who, as I told you, had put up in another part of the town, did not turn out either. After a decent interval, Simmons, who knows somebody in pretty nearly every hotel in Paris, went in and made inquiries.

"He learned that Edwards had left some two hours before, carrying his luggage, a very light portmanteau, with him. He had told them he was returning to England. Of course I smelt a rat at once, and instructed Simmons to go into the *Terminus* and inquire if Mrs. and Miss Glenthorne were still there. The answer was in the negative. They had also made an early departure, and had driven to the Gare du Nord; presumably they were returning to England too."

"It seems pretty clear they found out they were being watched, and judged it prudent to leave," was Lydon's natural comment.

"It looks very like it," admitted Grewgus. "Now comes the surprising part of the story. I should have come away at once, but that I had a fancy to interview Calliard to ascertain if our suspicions were correct—our suspicions, I mean, as to the object of her acquaintance with a man so much her senior."

Grewgus then proceeded to narrate how, on the following evening, he had run the jeweller to earth, while dining at one of his favourite restaurants. He was alone at a rather big table, and the detective seated himself at it, after a polite apology to the Frenchman for disturbing him, which was accepted with the habitual courtesy of his country. Presently they got into general conversation, and when he judged the time was ripe, Grewgus produced his card and handed it to him.

When Monsieur Calliard, who, by the way, spoke English very passably, ascertained from the card the occupation of the man who had seated himself at the table, he turned pale and showed considerable signs of embarrassment. Grewgus easily guessed the reasons for his disturbance. This opulent jeweller was no doubt a good bit of a philanderer, and easily attracted by women. His first thought was that his wife suspected him and had put a private inquiry agent on his track.

Of course, this notion had to be quickly dispelled. Grewgus explained that he was not at all concerned with the way in which Monsieur Calliard chose to spend his leisure hours, but he was greatly interested in the lady with whom he had dined so frequently.

At this reassuring statement, Monsieur Calliard recovered his composure and insisted upon helping his companion to a glass of the very excellent champagne he was drinking with his dinner. It was easy to diagnose him as a free liver, a man of considerable *bonhomie*, and by no means inclined to take a puritan view of life. He answered the questions put to him in the frankest manner. How had he made the acquaintance of the lady, and had he always known her by the name of Glenthorne, as she went sometimes by others?

The genial jeweller raised his eyebrows at the second of the two questions. He was evidently going to learn something.

"Listen, and I will tell you all about it. I suppose it goes without saying you know who I am?" began Monsieur Calliard.

"Certainly," replied Grewgus, with an amiable smile, "you are a partner in the well-known firm of Dubost Frères of Marseilles."

"Of course it would be easy for you to find out. I suppose I am known to a large circle of waiters in the hotels and restaurants of Paris. I met this young lady first at Trouville last year, where we formed a slight acquaintance. I met her later on in Rome, the acquaintance progressed a little further, and I have only known her under the name of Glenthorne. At both these places she was in the company of her mother, a rather good-looking Jewess."

"She was not formally introduced to you by anybody, I suppose?"

Monsieur Calliard shrugged his shoulders with the wealth of gesture typical of his countrymen. "Ah, no. At Trouville I stayed in the same hotel, at Rome I met her casually in the street, and she and her mother dined two or three times with me. She struck me as a very chic and charming young person who had every wish to make herself friendly. But I could not quite place her, and her mother was perhaps just a little in the way at Rome, so that I could not get to know very much about her. She was exceedingly quiet and ladylike, well educated, and the mother seemed a most respectable person."

"At Rome, I take it, you began to get a bit more fascinated, Monsieur Calliard?" suggested the detective.

Again that shrug of the shoulders. "At Marseilles, where one is so well known and, to a certain extent, looked up to, Monsieur Grewgus, one has to lead a very staid life. I will confess frankly I am not quite as good a boy as I should be. I travel about a great deal in the course of my business, and when I find myself in a place where I have no intimate friends, I admit to a little flutter now and then. I am too old to be a gay Lothario, but I am naturally fond of women's society," he added with a roguish smile, "especially the society of pretty and attractive women."

He paused to pour out a second glass of champagne for the interested Grewgus. Certainly there was no sullen reserve about the genial and opulent-looking jeweller. He alluded in the frankest fashion to his little weaknesses, even his peccadilloes.

"This happened last year," he resumed. "Charming and chic as she is, she had almost faded from my mind. Behold, walking down the Boulevard des

Italiens, I come upon her alone. I was very pleased to see her, for I was getting a bit bored with my own society, and she appeared pleased to see me. She told me she and her mother were staying at the *Hôtel Terminus*. Ah, that excellent mother, she had spoiled the Rome visit. I did not require any more of the good mother. I plucked up my courage, and asked her point-blank if she could see her way to dine with me without a chaperone. I should not have been surprised if she had declined, but she accepted, explaining that things were very much altered in her own English country since the war, and that for herself she had always paid little heed to convention."

With another expressive gesture, Monsieur Calliard lifted his hands. "Since then she has dined with me every evening up till last night."

"Do you know she has left Paris this morning?" queried Grewgus.

"She informed me of her intention as we sat at dinner. I was a little amazed because, having a slack time to-day, we had half made an appointment to go to Versailles. She excused herself on the plea that her mother had to return to London on urgent business. I suggested she should follow Madame Glenthorne later on, but she smiled when I did so. 'I am pretty unconventional, Monsieur Calliard,' she said, 'but not quite bold enough for that.' I think, my friend, that is all I have to tell you, and now, perhaps, as you seem to know a good deal about this young lady, you will tell me something that interests me."

"With the greatest pleasure, Monsieur Calliard. I will presently tell you all I do know. But first I should like to put another question. What sort of an account did the young lady give of herself to you?"

The jeweller considered: "I cannot remember that she was very communicative. I gathered that her mother had private means, that they travelled about a good deal, and were very familiar with the Continent. She also told me her father was dead, and that they had hardly any relatives."

"Did she tell you where she lived when in England?"

"They did not stay very much in England, according to her account. When they did they stopped with an uncle—ah—what is the name of the place, where your King has a fine Castle?"

"Windsor," suggested Grewgus.

"That is it, Windsor. I did notice one thing about her, that she was very reserved about her own affairs."

"She had every reason to be," said the detective grimly. "Well, Monsieur Calliard, you have been very obliging. It is now my turn to give you some information. I have every reason to believe that this agreeable-mannered young woman is one of the decoys of a firm of blackmailers; that she gets hold of men with the ultimate object of fleecing them."

The Frenchman looked intensely astonished. "The decoy of a blackmailing gang," he remarked. "A handsome, brilliant young woman like that! She ought to have made a good marriage. I cannot help feeling for her more pity than disgust. And that respectable-looking old Jewess, the mother. Is she a criminal also?"

Grewgus looked at him sharply. "You had no suspicion, then, of this, I take it? Now, Monsieur Calliard, whatever you say to me on this subject will pass out of my mind; I promise you I will not make use of it. Can you assure me that she has not attempted to blackmail you?"

It occurred to Grewgus that she had made the attempt, and that her sudden flight was due to the fact that she had been foiled, that the Frenchman had taken a bold attitude and defied her. The next words undeceived him.

"Upon my word of honour, Monsieur Grewgus, no."

Grewgus was fairly convinced that the jeweller was speaking the truth, that he was not actuated by a feeling of shame which led him to deny he had been the victim of an artful adventuress.

"Upon my word of honour, no," he repeated emphatically. "The opinion I formed of her was that she was an unconventional girl, leading a roving sort of existence with a careless and not very interesting mother, that she was pleased to come across anybody who would take her about and give her a good time. In spite of her gaiety and enjoyment of life, I judged her to be of a rather cold temperament. She never seemed to crave for admiration, although, like all women, she liked a compliment when you paid it to her."

"But surely you made her handsome presents from time to time," persisted Grewgus. Monsieur Calliard was a genial old fellow enough, but not likely to attract a handsome young woman by his personal gifts.

But the Frenchman shook his head very decidedly. "Monsieur Grewgus, I come of thrifty forbears. I like my little flutter now and again, as I have admitted to you, but I never care to pay too dear for my weaknesses. What did I give Miss Glenthorne during this visit? Bah! it is not worth thinking of. A few flowers sent to the hotel, some boxes of chocolates, once I think half a dozen pairs of gloves. It was not that which made her dine with me whenever I asked her. It is a bit of a riddle, I confess. Do you think there is any possibility of your being mistaken, of your having received wrong information about her? I am a man of the world, and I could detect no sign of the greedy adventuress."

Grewgus replied that his evidence was too strong to admit of such a supposition. But still what Calliard had told him imparted a fresh air of mystery to the affair.

"If blackmail was not her game, she must have had some other object in view," said the detective to Lydon when he had finished the story. "I cannot think those meetings in Rome and Paris were the result of accident. I should say that by some means she or her friends had obtained information of Calliard's movements, and she had followed him for the purpose of insinuating herself into his good graces. She, no doubt, read him at a glance, a weak, susceptible man, a bit thrifty perhaps, and garrulous to a fault."

"You did not, of course, mention anything of Stormont or Whitehouse to the Frenchman?" asked Lydon, who had been thinking very deeply as he listened to the story.

"I gave him no indication that there was anybody else concerned in my investigations," was Grewgus' reply.

"Is it possible that we have suspected Stormont wrongly, after all?" said the young man presently, who was profoundly astonished that there had been no blackmail. "Is it possible that he sent her and the man Edwards on some peculiar and special business errand, and that he, and perhaps Whitehouse, knew nothing of the double life she is leading, this combination of business woman and adventuress?"

But the experienced detective shook his head. "They have both been closely watched, Mr. Lydon, except in those few particular hours when they made off. If they were engaged on legitimate business in Paris, with whom were they doing it? They would have called on people; people would have called on them. She was never with anybody but Calliard and Edwards. Edwards had not got even a second string to his bow; he was never seen with anybody but her."

"What is your reading of it, then?"

"I incline to the idea they found out they were watched, and gave up the game in the middle, before the woman could formulate her plans for fleecing Calliard."

"Have you any other theory?"

"Only that a further mystery is developing, which we may or may not discover. By the way, there is something I forgot to tell you. They left, as you have learned, a day before me. I wired at once to one of my men in London in code to find out if Zillah Mayhew had returned to Ashstead Mansions."

"And the reply?"

"She had, and also the mother. They left Paris as Mrs. and Miss Glenthorne. They have returned to London as Mrs. and Miss Mayhew."

It was all very puzzling, very baffling. Lydon owned frankly he could not see his way through the maze.

After a pause, the detective spoke. "Now the question is, Mr. Lydon, do you feel disposed to spend any more money?"

"What is your advice?" asked the young man.

"To go on," answered the detective in a decided voice. "I am convinced that we are only at the beginning of the mystery."

"So be it, then. What are the next steps?"

"Simmons only awaits a message from me to take them. In the course of conversation, Calliard told me he was only staying three days longer in Paris. He is going on to Brussels, where he does a big business. Now you have decided, I shall instruct him to follow Calliard. If there is a further mystery, as I strongly suspect, it is round him that it will centre. Here in London I shall keep observation upon Miss Mayhew, and if I can possibly come across him, upon Edwards."

With that the interview ended. At the end of another week, Jasper Stormont and his wife came back to the *Cecil*, bringing Gloria with them. Lydon had a shrewd suspicion that the banker, who, according to his daughter's account, was a man of simple tastes and habits, was not a little oppressed by the opulence and splendour of Effington.

CHAPTER FOURTEEN

IT was not long before Grewgus' prophecy that they were only at the beginning of the mystery came true. What is now about to be narrated is gleaned from the letters sent to his chief from Brussels by Simmons. Later on he came to England, and amplified the various details of the whole affair.

Monsieur Calliard went to Brussels in due course from Paris and took up his quarters at one of the well-known hotels in that delightful city. Simmons, obeying his chief's telegraphed instructions, followed him, and was always at his heels.

On this visit the gay old Frenchman was apparently devoting himself whole-heartedly to his business, and not indulging in any little flutters. His habits were exceedingly regular. He devoted his mornings, and frequently his afternoons, to visits to his various customers. The rest of his time he spent at the hotel. No ladies, young or middle-aged, relieved the monotony of his leisure moments.

Needless to say that Simmons kept open a wary eye for the reappearance of Zillah Mayhew and the man Edwards. To his surprise neither turned up. In the meantime Grewgus was keeping a watch on the women at Ashstead Mansions, and convinced himself, with the aid of the friendly hall-porter, that she was in London during the whole of the time that Léon Calliard was in Brussels. Therefore, a certain theory of his was shattered, when he found she was staying on from day to day.

His idea was that, having discovered she was being shadowed in Paris, her plans had been suddenly nipped in the bud by that fact, and she had headed for the shelter of the flat. This did not mean that she had given up her original designs against the wealthy jeweller, only postponed them. After a brief interval, during which she judged the scent would have become cold, she would follow him to Brussels, and there add him to her no doubt very numerous list of victims. It followed from this, then, that blackmail had not been her ultimate object.

But it was obvious that she had some object in sticking so closely to the Frenchman. And so far as it was possible to reason, the instructions given by Stormont to Edwards were concerned with the wealthy jeweller, as neither the man nor the woman had associated with anybody else during their stay in Paris. Edwards had been seen about with nobody except the girl who called herself Miss Glenthorne.

For three days Simmons kept a pretty close watch on Calliard. On the fourth he relaxed his vigilance a little, having made up his mind by now that nothing more was to be feared from the pair of confederates. And on this day something unusual happened. Calliard did not return to the hotel for lunch, and he did not return for dinner. Simmons did not attach very great importance to this; he might have gone somewhere else for the day on business. To-morrow he would see him pursuing his ordinary routine, without a doubt. But when the morrow came, and no Calliard appeared in his usual haunts, Simmons became alarmed.

That evening he went to the director of the *Palace Hotel*, with whom he had a slight acquaintance, and who knew the nature of his occupation, and inquired for news. He explained that, unknown to Calliard himself, he was watching his movements in connection with a certain couple who might have evil designs upon him.

The director, a most voluble person, was quite ready to talk to a man whom he knew he could trust.

"I have known Monsieur Calliard for years, ever since I have been connected with the *Palace Hotel*; his connection with us is a long one and dates before the time I came here. I suppose you know that he is a man of considerable wealth, a partner in a very flourishing firm in Marseilles. He came here about every few months to do business with the leading jewellers in Brussels, and he carried in that brown bag his samples, worth some hundreds of thousands of francs. When he had finished his rounds for the day, it was his invariable custom to deposit that very valuable bag in our safe."

Simmons noticed that the director had been speaking all along in the past tense. He had a very sure premonition of what was coming.

"He went out as usual after breakfast to make his customary morning calls, taking his bag with him. As I take it, you have been watching him, probably you know that as well as I do?"

Simmons had to admit that on this particular morning his vigilance had been relaxed. Having made up his mind that neither of the pair he suspected was in the vicinity, he was prepared to take it easy till Monsieur Calliard left Brussels, when he would follow him to his next stopping place.

The director shrugged his shoulders: "That is most unfortunate, for then we might know more than we do. He said especially that he would return to luncheon—as a matter of fact he has lunched and dined here every day during his visit—but he happened to make particular mention of it. Luncheon time arrived, and he did not turn up. We didn't attach very great importance to the fact. He might have been detained, or been invited by one of his customers. When dinner-time came and he was again absent, I began to feel a bit uneasy. Remember he was carrying in that bag a small fortune."

"Monsieur Calliard is just a little bit—what shall we say—frisky for a man of his age, is he not?" queried Simmons.

The director smiled: "A wee bit, perhaps. I fancy he is rather susceptible where the other sex is concerned. On previous occasions he has sometimes brought here to lunch and dinner some fascinating members of it. But this time nothing of the sort happened. Not a soul has been to see him since he first set foot in the hotel."

Simmons thought there might be a good reason for this. No doubt the volatile Frenchman had received a rude shock when Grewgus told him the real character of the young woman to whom he was so hospitable in Paris. He had resolved to walk more warily for a little time.

"When I came down this morning and found he was still absent, I came to the conclusion it was time to act. I notified the police at once. I despatched a long wire to his firm in Marseilles, acquainting them with the suspicious circumstances. I have had one in reply."

"And they are, of course, very alarmed?" said Simmons.

"Not so much as you would imagine. It is a very long wire, and in it they suggest he may have gone to Ostend to see a certain client, and will return in due course. But I am very doubtful of this. Monsieur Calliard was a very methodical man, not likely to do anything on the spur of the moment. If he had intended to pay this visit to Ostend, he would have had it in his mind for some little time, and notified us of his intention. Well, the affair is now in the hands of the police."

It was not till five days later that the dénouement came. It was evening, and Simmons sat on the terrace of the *Café Metropole*, sipping his *apéritif*. While doing so, he opened the *Petit Bleu* and read a long account of the recovery of the body of an elderly, well-dressed man from the river Meuse, at a bend about a mile behind the little village of Godime. The doctors declared that it had been in the river since about the date corresponding with the disappearance of the wealthy jeweller.

Upon him was found a sum of about three thousand francs, and papers which conclusively proved that he was a Monsieur Léon Calliard, member of a well-known firm, and residing in the Rue Lenon at Marseilles. In his pocket was found a half-obliterated letter written in indelible pencil, stating his intention of committing suicide in consequence of an unfortunate love affair.

Simmons hastened round to his friend the director of the hotel, whom he found acquainted with the news. This gentleman threw scorn upon the suggestion of suicide.

"Bah, my friend," he cried excitedly, "Calliard was not that sort of man; he was a most devout Catholic. A love affair that would drive him off his head at his age. The idea is preposterous. He was fond of the society of attractive women, granted, but his was not the sort of nature capable of a great passion. I should like to see that letter, Monsieur Simmons. I will wager it is a forgery, put there by the assassin who killed him in order to get hold of that bag with its valuable contents."

And so, later on, it was proved to be the case. When the letter was shown to some of his intimate friends they unanimously declared it was a clumsy imitation of Calliard's handwriting.

"So all along it was robbery and murder, not simply blackmail that was intended," said Grewgus, as he and his client sat discussing the whole facts of the case. "Simmons, of course, committed a blunder in not following Calliard that particular morning. He might have averted a tragedy. On the other hand, he might not. This is the work of a very cunning gang, and so long as Calliard had that bag in his possession, they were determined to have it. They would not have been satisfied with a first rebuff or a second. They would have followed him till they got it. Depend upon it, they had their plans laid with devilish precision. I don't suppose we shall ever know how they got him into their clutches."

"It is strange that Edwards and the woman should have so suddenly effaced themselves," commented Lydon. "If they had a hand in it, you would think they would have been in at the closing act. Is it possible, do you think, that this tragedy is simply a coincidence? That he was done to death by people who had no connection with them?"

Grewgus shook his head. "There is no evidence against them, certainly. Miss Mayhew has been at Ashstead Mansions every day since she came back from Paris, that I have ascertained. In her case she has a perfect alibi. Of Edwards I can speak with no positiveness. Simmons took a snapshot of him in Paris, and I have had two men scouring London for him with no success, as we are unacquainted with his haunts. Of course, for all we know to the contrary, he might have been lurking in the neighbourhood of that little village of Godime. But, all the same, I believe Miss Mayhew played a big part in this affair."

Lydon looked at the detective inquiringly. "I should like to know in what way you connect her with the case," he said. "Of course, in a thing of this sort, I feel myself utterly helpless, so far as my reasoning faculties are concerned."

Grewgus smiled. "One would hardly expect otherwise, Mr. Lydon. Up to the present, you can have had no experience of criminal methods, which I can assure you are very subtle. Robbery was intended from the beginning, supplemented by murder, if that was absolutely necessary. In this case I assume the existence of a cleverly organized gang of international crooks, with spies everywhere. They find out that the unfortunate Calliard, member of a wealthy firm, is accustomed to make periodical visits to the various important capitals, carrying with him in that small bag an immense amount of valuable property.

"They already know a good deal, but they want to know more, be better versed in details. They set Miss Mayhew on him, one of their cleverest decoys. No doubt, the beginnings of the plot were hatched at Trouville, where he first made her acquaintance and, unfortunately for himself, was attracted by her. Their meeting was not accidental. They knew he would be there and dispatched her to the same hotel, to find out all she could, to make herself acquainted with his movements, to insinuate herself into his confidence.

"She found him very easy to deal with. Calliard no doubt was a good business man in many ways, or he would not have been entrusted with such important missions, but for one of his age he struck me as singularly simple. And he was garrulous and communicative in the extreme. He blurted out a lot of things to me which he would have shown wisdom in keeping to himself. He took me on trust, as it were, on my production of a card stating my name and profession. That card might easily have been prepared for the purpose. I give this as an illustration of his simplicity, of his tendency to take things at their face value. A clever woman would twist him round her little finger, easily get out of him what she wanted to know. Neither in Rome nor Trouville did they find things fall out quite in accordance with their plans. It was not till they got him to Paris that they were able to set to work in grim earnest, with the result we know."

"None of the jewellery has been traced, I suppose?"

"Not that I have heard of," was the detective's answer. "They had their plans cut and dried, you may depend. A few hours after they had got hold of the stuff you can be sure the valuable stones were out of their settings and on the way to a safe market."

After a little while, Lydon spoke. "You have reconstructed the whole thing very cleverly, and in my own mind I feel you are right. But we have really no tangible evidence against Stormont, have we?"

Grewgus shrugged his shoulders. "Nothing that would convince a jury, I fear. It is all intensely circumstantial. Still, that letter of his to Zillah which you intercepted is a very important link. Would you like me to go to Scotland Yard and put them in possession of all we know, so that they could join forces with the Paris police?"

But Leonard could not bring himself to consent to this step. The thought of his beloved Gloria, of her father, a man of the highest probity and honour, forbade it. Much as he would have rejoiced, for his dead friend's sake, that Elise Makris should be punished, he shrank from bringing disgrace upon Howard Stormont's innocent relatives.

It was finally arranged between the two men that Grewgus should still keep a watch upon the flat in Ashstead Mansions, and note the further movements of Whitehouse and his supposed niece. It was evident that this taciturn individual had taken no active part in the Calliard affair, was not even so much implicated in it as Stormont appeared to be by that letter to his "clever Zillah." But Grewgus had a very strong suspicion that the couple worked very closely together.

They did find something out about Whitehouse a little later on which added to the general mystery. Hornby Court did not absorb the whole of his activities. He had a small set of offices near Bedford Row, where he attended three days a week. His staff consisted of a senior and junior clerk, and he practised as a solicitor under the name of Glenthorne. So far they had not been able to discover what sort of a business it was, or what class of clients patronized him. It certainly had not the air of a particularly flourishing concern.

From the *Cecil Hotel*, the Jasper Stormonts, accompanied by Gloria, soon moved further afield. It had been cordially acquiesced in by Howard Stormont that during their stay in England they should have their daughter to themselves. For his own part, Jasper would have liked to make a tour in Scotland, but he was a very unselfish man, and he could not bear the idea of parting the two young people. He felt that he had come too little into the girl's life to permit him to think only of himself. He therefore chose Brighton; it was so easy for Lydon to run down and return by a fast train.

Although a man rather inclined to frugality than extravagance, Leonard was surprised to find that he had elected to stay at one of the most expensive hotels in the place. And not content with the public apartments, he had taken a private sitting-room. He explained matters to his future son-in-law with his usual kindly smile.

"You must not think, my dear boy, I am trying to rival my spendthrift brother. The simple truth is this. At home I conduct my affairs in a very steady and prudent manner. But when I take a holiday, I like to do things well and have every comfort. A thoroughly economical holiday is worse than none."

They intended to stay at Brighton till it was time to return to China, and Lydon was very pleased with the arrangement. All that he had learned recently had made Effington exceedingly distasteful to him. As for Howard Stormont, he could hardly bear to shake hands with him, in view of his grave suspicions.

It was about three weeks after the interview between himself and Grewgus that he received an important message from the detective to come round to his office at the earliest moment, as he had the most surprising news to communicate. He did not want to blurt them out over the telephone.

Lydon was round as soon as possible, and found the detective looking quite excited for a man of his usually calm temperament.

"You will be as surprised as I was, I expect," he said as soon as his client was seated. "Our friend Miss Makris, alias Mayhew, alias Glenthorne, has left Ashstead Mansions. She has taken one of the smaller houses in Curzon Street, has furnished it splendidly in a few days, and is living there under the name of Mrs. Edwards with her husband, the good-looking fellow who was over in Paris when she was playing her game with poor old Calliard. The mother is not with them. I should say they are after something very big this time."

And as Grewgus spoke, there flashed across the young man's mind what Jasper Stormont had told him a little while ago. His brother was looking forward to a great *coup* which might enable him to give up business altogether. Was the owner of Effington at the back of this sudden metamorphosis of the "clever Zillah" into Mrs. Edwards, the tenant of the house in Curzon Street?

CHAPTER FIFTEEN

ABOUT a fortnight later, Lydon had the news confirmed from another quarter. Gloria received a letter from her uncle, in which was the following paragraph: "I have got some news for you. Zillah Mayhew is married to a very charming young man, named Edwards. She has been a very sly little puss about it all. It appears from a somewhat belated confession to her uncle, my dear old friend John Whitehouse, they have known each other for some four or five years. They met again during her recent visit to Paris and were married there. Edwards is a man possessed of considerable means and moves in good society. They kept the marriage secret for a little time on account of family reasons connected with the husband. I am very glad that Zillah has done so well."

The letter then proceeded to state other things, some of which Lydon, to whom his sweetheart read the epistle, had already heard from Grewgus. The married couple had taken and furnished a house in Curzon Street, where Zillah proposed to entertain. Zillah had led a retired life when in England, did not know many people. But her husband had heaps of friends and acquaintances, and would soon fill the house. They proposed to give a big reception shortly. Stormont and his sister would attend it. And Zillah insisted that Gloria, her father and mother, and her fiancé should be her guests on such a special occasion.

Innocent Gloria read out all this to her fiancé, and the young man made certain inward comments as she went along. It was very unlikely the couple had been married on Zillah's last visit to Paris. Grewgus had been watching the woman, Simmons the man till the eve of their disappearance. If there had been any marriage ceremony, they would have known of it. If they were husband and wife, they had been married long ere now, and had lived apart, the better to pursue their nefarious ends.

Gloria, woman-like, was interested in what appeared to be a real romance. "I am so glad," she said enthusiastically. "Zillah is such a delightful, charming girl, she deserves a good husband. I am surprised that she has not been married long before this. Uncle Howard speaks well of him, doesn't he? And I think he is a very shrewd judge of character. We must certainly go to that party to see for ourselves. You agree, I am sure."

Yes, Lydon certainly agreed. Of course, he could not as yet give a hint to the unsuspecting girl of his reasons. He would dearly like to observe the adventuress and Edwards at close quarters.

In London the next day, he found time to run round to Grewgus and inform him of what Howard Stormont had written.

"Well, you will keep your eyes open when you are there," said the detective. "I wish you could take me with you, but that, I suppose, is impossible. I'm a master of disguise, you know; I could go as something quite different from Grewgus. I might spot something that would escape you. I am very curious as to the game they have got on; it must be something big, or else they wouldn't go to this considerable expense. Of course, that account of the recent marriage in Paris is all bunkum."

Lydon would dearly have liked to take the detective with him as an old friend, to obtain a card for him through Stormont. But he saw it was too risky. Stormont was a man of diabolical ingenuity and cunning. He would smell a rat at once. Later on, he might be able to work him into the Curzon Street ménage.

"By the way, I have never shown you the snapshot of Edwards that Simmons took in Paris, have I?" asked the detective presently.

He opened a drawer in his writing-table, extracted a photograph and handed it to his client. Lydon gave a cry of astonishment as he looked at it. "Well, of all the strange things that have ever happened! This man is a member of my own club, the Excelsior."

"What do you know about him?" asked Grewgus in an excited voice.

"Well, almost next to nothing. The Excelsior is a big club, as you know, and there are dozens of different sets. He mixes rather amongst the fast lot. I have heard that he is a man of good family, a public school and Cambridge man, and has considerable private means."

"Do you know him to speak to?" asked Grewgus eagerly.

"I may have exchanged a dozen words with him since I have belonged to the club. We both joined it about the same time, three years ago. I should rather say I knew him to nod to."

"I think we might classify him as a typical specimen of the aristocratic crook," remarked Grewgus. "Well-born, well-educated, gifted with brains of the wrong sort, who has taken to evil courses either from natural inclination, or because he dislikes honest work. Well, Mr. Lydon, this is very interesting and I may say very fortunate. To think we have been scouring London for him, and not hit upon the Excelsior Club. You must certainly go to that party, take diligent notes, and report to me what you have observed."

In due course, formal cards arrived for the big reception, an afternoon one from four to seven, to the Jasper Stormonts, Gloria and Lydon. The banker and his wife sent their excuses. They were a stay-at-home couple and had no desire to rub shoulders with a lot of strangers who knew nothing about them and about whom they knew nothing.

"Except Gloria and yourself, and my brother and sister, there would not be a soul we knew," said Gloria's father. "The hostess is a most delightful young woman, my daughter tells me; but she will be much too busy to pay any attention to a couple of old fogies like ourselves. Of course, Howard will be in his element amongst a crowd; in a lesser degree, it is possible my sister will also be happy. I and my wife will remain here while you young people are disporting yourselves in society."

Howard Stormont had written to say that Gloria had better spend the rest of the day with them, driving down to Effington after the reception was over. If Lydon wished, he could drive down with them, have dinner and stay the night. But the young man got out of this. He would meet Gloria in London and take her back to Brighton the day after instead. He wished to be in Howard Stormont's company as little as possible.

The day after he had received the card, he strolled into the club of which both he and Edwards were members. It was a big establishment, situated in Piccadilly, and had a large clientèle—stockbrokers, barristers, a few actors, artists and authors, and several wealthy business men. Almost the first person he saw was an elderly barrister named Joyce, a member of the committee, who had recently retired from practice. This gentleman was a very gregarious person, a great gossip, and supposed to know more about the private history of his fellow-members than anybody else in the club. To Mr. Joyce he at once addressed himself:

"I've had a card for a big reception from Mrs. Edwards, the wife of our member. Although a common name, he is the only Edwards in the club. I don't think I owe it to him, for we are hardly on more than nodding terms, but his wife is a great friend of a man I know, Stormont, to whose niece I am engaged. Of course, they were bound to ask my fiancée, and they have very kindly included me."

The elderly barrister rose to the bait at once. He was quite ready to talk about Edwards; he was always ready to talk about anybody with whom he was acquainted. "I have had a card too; going to be a rather big thing, I am told. About half a dozen of us here have been asked. Edwards doesn't mix very freely with the members, rather keeps himself to himself. As a matter of fact, he doesn't come here very often, travels abroad a lot."

"No, I haven't often met him," said Lydon in a careless tone. "Who is he, and what is he? I suppose you know?"

Mr. Joyce smiled; he was very proud of his general knowledge, which he acquired by his assiduous attendance at the club.

"I know as much as anybody else, I think, but there doesn't seem very much to know about him. He talks very little about himself. He is a Cambridge man, comes, I believe, of a good old Sussex family, follows no profession or occupation, has private means."

The information was decidedly meagre; but it was certain that if this was all Mr. Joyce knew, nobody knew any more.

"Rather a surprise this marriage, isn't it?" asked Lydon after a pause. "I learn from Stormont that they were married a very short time ago abroad, I think he said in Paris."

"Quite right," confirmed the barrister. "We knew nothing about it here till quite lately. But you see that is not to be wondered at. Nobody of the half-dozen who have received invitations is more than just a club acquaintance. I suppose they really want to fill the rooms. He rushed in here about a week ago, told me what you know, that he was recently married, had taken a house in Curzon Street, and they were going to hold a reception, sort of house warming. He was going to send cards to a few of the members. Would I pass on to them what he had told me, as he might not be in the club again before the party came off?"

After lunch, Lydon took a taxi down to Craven Street, and imparted to Grewgus the result of his interview with Joyce, both men agreeing that what he had learned from that gentleman was practically no more than what they knew already.

The party was a week hence. Grewgus was still very bent upon going, but he recognized the impossibility of getting there.

"If I could get a chance, I would go as a waiter," he said. "Well, it's no use thinking about it. You say that you will be leaving about seven. I'll be hanging about outside from half-past six—there's sure to be the usual staring crowds outside. If you've nothing better to do, look out for me and follow me. When we are well out of view, we can go into some place and you can tell me anything that you think may be useful to us."

On the day appointed, Leonard went to Curzon Street. His afternoon had been a pretty busy one, and he did not arrive there till close upon six. The rooms were quite full and it was a little time before he met his hostess, who had abandoned her position at the door some time ago. She greeted him cordially, and after a few words with her he passed on.

Presently he found the Stormont party. The portly Howard was looking very happy and radiant. "A thorough success," he whispered to the young man. "Zillah's a born hostess and seems immensely admired. Most of the people here are the husband's friends; she has been so seldom in London that she doesn't know many people yet. But it won't be long before she does. I'm delighted it is going off so well. I'm very fond of Zillah; she's such a sweet girl."

Lydon thought grimly that the unfortunate Calliard had said the same thing. He inquired if Mr. Whitehouse was there.

"No," was the answer. "He was awfully disappointed he could not be here to witness her triumph. But he was prevented by important business. I

111

believe he is dining with them after the show."

The mother was not there. Well, her parents were supposed to be dead and the uncle was absent. No doubt, Mrs. Edwards had her own good reasons for not having her own family round her. Casually he said to Stormont: "I've just caught a glimpse of Edwards; he hasn't seen me yet. Do you know he's a member of my club, the Excelsior?"

Was it fancy, or did he detect a rather shifty look in Stormont's eyes as he replied to him? "Yes, he told me when I first mentioned your name. What a small place the world is, eh?"

"It came as a surprise to you all, Gloria told me. Did you or her uncle know anything of Edwards before she married him?"

"Never set eyes on him," came the prompt answer. "Zillah has been a very sly little puss over it; they seem to have met abroad first. But he's a delightful fellow with lots of money. There's no doubt she has done wonderfully well for herself. And he knows heaps of good people. As you know, I don't go about in London, but this seems to me decidedly a smart party."

Lydon was intensely disgusted with the hypocrisy of the man, his effrontery in denying any previous knowledge of the man whom he had sent to Paris with his instructions to his "clever Zillah." But he quite agreed with his last remarks, it certainly was a smart gathering, with so many beautifully gowned women and immaculately dressed men. The Excelsior Club, he noticed, had sent up its contingent to a man. Mr. Joyce was ubiquitous, and seemed to know a great many of the guests. Leonard was sure that the host had a footing in one world. He seemed to have an equally sure position in a more reputable one.

"He knows people in every walk of life—artists, authors, fashionables," went on the garrulous Stormont, who seemed in the very highest of spirits. "He belongs to half a dozen clubs, from the quite exclusive to the frankly Bohemian."

Gloria had been annexed by a very dandified young man. Mrs. Barnard was engaged with an elderly person of the well-preserved type. There came a sudden hush, a well-known professional was going to sing. Lydon left his companion and made a tour of the rooms.

When he stopped, he found himself standing next to Edwards, who gave him a cordial nod and a whispered: "Will speak to you presently."

The song was finished and his host turned to Lydon. "Very pleased to see you here. I little thought when we used to meet occasionally at the club that we should become so closely connected, as it were. Stormont has known Zillah from a child; he is a sort of adopted uncle. Delightful fellow, Stormont, so genial, so unaffected."

112

"Quite," said Lydon, in a tone the reverse of enthusiastic. Not greatly relishing the prospect of a prolonged conversation with Edwards, he was about to move when his host stopped him.

"Do you see that young man talking to my wife, over there by the door? You know who he is, don't you?"

Lydon looked in the direction indicated. Zillah Edwards was conversing with a handsome, elegant young fellow of about twenty-five. There was something distinguished and aristocratic about his appearance, and Leonard fancied that the face was familiar to him, but he could not recall where or under what circumstances he had seen it.

"That is Lord Wraysbury, the eldest son of the Earl of Feltham, one of the oldest families in England," whispered Edwards in an impressive voice; and guided by this information, the young man knew why the face was familiar to him. He had seen the portrait of the young fellow in some of the society papers.

"He often comes here," went on the host. "You know all about his history, I suppose?"

"Very little," was the cold answer. "My acquaintance with the great world is negligible, I am sorry to say."

"It is quite a romance," continued the other, who did not seem to have noticed the coldness of his companion's manner. "His father, as I said, can boast of representing one of the oldest families in England, but he is not rich. The estates are in Suffolk, and I am told don't produce much more than twenty thousand a year; that is not much for a nobleman in his position, you know, and he has a large family."

"I suppose not," assented Lydon, who was not particularly interested in this good-looking young aristocrat.

"Well, thanks to an extraordinary bit of luck, Wraysbury is very rich, one of the richest young men in London. He owes it to his aunt, a very beautiful woman. She married twice. The first match was a fairly good one, but nothing out of the common. She was left a widow when she was just nearing thirty. Her second husband was an enormously rich American who had settled in England, a multi-millionaire. He died soon too, five years after their marriage. The bulk of his fortune was left to his children by a first wife; but his widow, Wraysbury's aunt, got a comfortable two million left to her to dispose of as she liked.

"She was devoted to Wraysbury. Never having had a child by either of her husbands, she looked upon him as a son. She died two years ago and left him every penny, with the exception of a few insignificant legacies."

"A very fortunate young man," commented Lydon, interested in spite of himself by the romantic story. "And what sort of a chap is he? Is he taking care of his money, or making ducks and drakes of it?"

"He is a most delightful fellow in himself. With regard to your question, he spends a lot, of course. He has the handling of a very big income, but I should say he has a fairly good head upon his shoulders and knows how to manage his affairs."

"Is he your friend, or your wife's?" asked Lydon bluntly, hastening to add, "I mean of course in the first instance."

"Oh, Zillah's," was the answer. "They knew each other abroad before he came into his aunt's money. The acquaintance dropped till quite lately. We were dining one night at the *Ritz* and met him in the lounge as we were going in. She introduced me and of course gave him an invitation to Curzon Street. He has dined with us twice and called several times. I like him immensely; he is a dear chap."

Lydon stayed for another half-hour and noticed that Lord Wraysbury was never for long away from the side of his hostess. He did not appear to know more than a couple of people in the room and Leonard had a suspicion that they had been introduced by Zillah. It was a smart party certainly; but although he knew little of fashionable or semi-fashionable society, he did not think it was quite up to the standard of a young man of such aristocratic lineage.

He managed to obtain a few words with Gloria. "Are you enjoying yourself, my sweetheart?" he whispered.

"Oh, in a way, it is rather novel," she replied. "But I don't think I should care for too much of this sort of thing. Zillah has been quite kind, introduced me and aunt to a lot of people. Uncle Howard is enjoying himself immensely. I have not seen him look more beaming at one of his own dinner-parties. But I'm afraid I haven't his temperament. I'm not fond of strange crowds."

Soon the party began to break up; only a few determined stayers were left behind. Stormont collected his women-folk and they bade adieu to their host and hostess. Lydon took his departure with them. As he shook hands with Zillah, he observed that the good-looking Wraysbury was still in close attendance.

Stormont's car was waiting. As they went out, Lydon saw Grewgus standing amidst the small crowd that had gathered to watch the departing guests, and made a hasty signal to which the detective answered with a slight movement of his head.

What was the young man's astonishment to see amongst the waiting crowd the weather-beaten face of Tom Newcombe, and a hasty glance at him revealed the fact that, if not actually drunk, he was certainly not strictly sober. As soon as he caught sight of his "old pal" he rushed forward and shouted out what he intended to be a welcome, in a husky voice.

Howard Stormont's face went white when he saw him. "Get out of the way, you drunken dog," he said in a low voice, full of fury. "Never dare to accost me again when you are in this state."

The Colonial, no longer shabby-looking, but dressed in very loud attire which he doubtless considered to be the height of fashion, slunk away, his face working, and muttering, "Drunken dog! Drunken dog!"

Stormont pushed the women into the car and it drove off, the occupants waving a farewell to Leonard as he stood on the kerb.

When he turned round to look for Grewgus, that gentleman had gone. He saw him a few yards off, stealthily tracking the Colonial.

He knew by this action that the ever-vigilant man had overheard what had passed and was on a fresh scent. It was no use waiting for him.

CHAPTER SIXTEEN

It was not long before the quarry came to a halt at a public-house in a side street off Piccadilly. When he reached this hostelry, his intense indignation had exercised a remarkably sobering effect upon him, his gait was quite steady, and when he asked the barmaid for refreshment his voice had recovered its normal tones.

Grewgus had followed him in. After a little while, Newcombe went and sat down in front of one of the tables. After a decent interval the detective followed him and opened up conversation by some remark about the weather. Mr. Newcombe made a somewhat gloomy response; it was evident his mind was still full of the epithet which Stormont had hurled at him as he hurried into the car.

As Grewgus saw that he was not disposed for general conversation, he thought he would try him on something that would interest him. He judged him not to be too well blessed with the world's goods, in spite of his loud but evidently cheap apparel; he thought, therefore, he would start on a democratic note.

"Awful lot of money these nobs do waste on themselves. When you walk down these parts, the luxury that meets you on every hand makes you fairly sick, it does. Many a poor bloke has got to keep his wife and family for a week on what they spend on one meal."

He was a very good actor, and he put on a ripe Cockney accent for the benefit of his companion. He did not want to be taken for a man of too superior class, or else he might easily excite suspicion.

Mr. Newcombe grunted assent to these propositions, and drained his tumbler. Grewgus put on a genial smile and did the same.

"They give you precious little stuff for the money in these days," he remarked in the same dissatisfied tone. "I feel a bit fed up to-day with thinking of all these things; I always feel that way when I see much of this quarter of the town. I'm going to have another; I should be rather glad if you'd have one with me."

Mr. Newcombe hesitated for a second, then accepted. Grewgus had judged his condition pretty accurately. He had had too much when he stood outside the house in Curzon Street; the abuse hurled at him by Stormont, and the indignation it created, had momentarily sobered him. But another glass or two would stir up the old drink and reduce him to his previous condition. When he got back to that he would be disposed to talk. The second tumbler accomplished the desired result. The detective saw he could now get to work.

"I've just strolled down from Curzon Street, and it was the sight of a big party going on at one of the houses that set me thinking. Motor-cars galore waiting for the beautiful ladies with frocks that cost a small fortune, men coming out with their expensive suits. It gave me the hump, it did, so I cut it and dropped into the first public I could come across."

Newcombe looked at him with a perfectly unsuspicious eye. "Was you there too? So was I. Did you happen to see me?"

"No," answered the detective unblushingly, feeling that he was lying in a good cause. "Rather rum that when you come to think of it, isn't it? That we should be looking at the same thing, and then meeting a few minutes after in this place, I suppose for the same reason, that we both felt a trifle dry. I say, we'd better have another. I always feel reckless when I'm a bit fed up."

The Colonial accepted the hospitality for the second time. Grewgus went to the counter to get the drinks; he did not wish the Colonial to entertain any doubts of his own sobriety, which was fast tottering under the last glass.

When he returned, Mr. Newcombe began to give vent to some of the thoughts that were harrowing his indignant soul.

"It isn't often I come in these parts—I live King's Cross way. But it being a fine day, I thought I'd just take a stroll up here, and have a look at the nobs. Well, I wandered about a lot, then I sat down in the Park, and afterwards I got into that street where you were. I forget what you said the name of it was."

Grewgus supplied the necessary information, and the Colonial rambled on, in a voice that grew thicker as he proceeded.

"Well, presently I come to that house where the show was. I stood looking at the motor-cars and the dainty ladies stepping into them. Suddenly I see come out a man I have known for years, with his sister and niece. He was a pal of mine in Australia when we were both young men. Many a good turn I done him, once I nursed him back to life through a bad fever. Well, remembering the good old days, I go up to him in a cheery sort of way. And what do you think I get in return?"

"Haven't the slightest idea," replied the mendacious Grewgus.

"He called me a drunken dog, a drunken dog, and dared me to speak to him in the street or anywhere else. What do you say to that?"

Grewgus shrugged his shoulders and spoke in a withering voice: "A rich man, of course, got on in the world. Well, I should say it was just what he

117

would do, like the snob he is. I suppose he wouldn't chuck you a shilling if you were starving."

It was evident, in spite of his resentment, that Newcombe could not tell an absolute lie. "I won't say he hasn't given me a bit, but there's a reason for it, a reason for it."

"A reason for it," repeated the detective. "I expect a pretty good one too?" Was he going to get something out of this sot?

Mr. Newcombe went on muttering to himself: "I could make him smart, if I chose to, the ungrateful dog. He to lord it with his flunkeys and his fine motor-car while I live on a pittance."

"You know something about this fine gentleman who calls you a drunken dog?" insinuated the detective, repeating the offensive epithet with the view of keeping the man's resentment at white heat.

Perhaps Grewgus had overdone it. Something seemed to stir in the drink-soddened brain, and told him he had gone too far. The Colonial seemed to pull himself together.

"That's neither here nor there," he said in a surly tone. Then he harked back in his maudlin state to his original grievance. "A drunken dog indeed, from him who for years never drew a sober breath! Tell me, mister, did I look drunk? But I forget, you said you didn't see me. Am I drunk now?"

Grewgus knew that the moment had gone. He would get nothing out of this creature now. There was no need for him to dissemble any longer. "If you ask my candid opinion, I think you have had too much. The last glass has knocked you over. I am not sure you can stand properly. Have a try."

Mr. Newcombe did as he was told, but the effort was not successful. He got up for an instant, but relapsed promptly into his seat. Grewgus found himself confronted with an awkward situation. He did not for a moment regret his hastily conceived pursuit of Newcombe; he had come within an ace of accomplishing his object. It was by the merest bad luck, at the last moment, some sudden flickering of intelligence had caused the inebriated man to exercise discretion.

All the same, he found himself saddled with a companion, drunk to the point of incapacity, and unable to look after himself.

Grewgus made up his mind at once; it was necessary to do so, since Newcombe showed signs of sinking into slumber.

"Look here," he whispered into the man's ear as loud as he dared. "If you don't want to be locked up for the night, I shall have to get you home. Tell me quickly where you live."

In a thick voice, the incapacitated Colonial muttered the name of a mean street in the King's Cross district. Grewgus knew the place well, and, as was his custom, drew a rapid inference. Either Stormont was allowing him a very small pittance, or else Newcombe was averse to heavy standing charges as they would curtail his opportunities of purchasing his beloved alcohol.

A very decent young man had come into the bar, whom the detective judged, by his appearance, to be of the Good Samaritan sort, disposed to help in a case of trouble. Propping the almost comatose man well against the table, he went up to this individual and besought his assistance.

"My friend has been overcome, been taking too much before I met him, I expect," was his explanation. "I want to get him away without fuss, if I can. If you would kindly call a taxi, and come back here and lend a helping hand, I am sure I can manage it. I doubt if he can walk very well, but between us we can manage to shove him along and get him in the taxi."

The decent-looking young man responded nobly to the appeal. In a very short time, Mr. Newcombe, still half asleep and almost deprived of the powers of motion, was being borne in the direction of King's Cross.

About half-way on the journey, he made one of those remarkable recoveries which are frequently to be observed in the devotees of alcohol. He was still far from sober, but his partial slumber, and the rather keen fresh air blowing through the open taxi-windows on his inflamed face, had cleared his faculties to a certain extent. He was able to appreciate and thank the detective for what he had done.

"The act of a pal, that's what it is," he hiccoughed. "If ever your turn comes and I'm there, I'll do the same with you. If you had sneaked out and left me, I should have been run in as safe as eggs." His mind suddenly reverted to the events of a short time ago. "By gosh, if it had been that fellow with the flunkeys and the fine car, he'd have left me in the lurch. I say, mister, I don't know your name, perhaps I was a bit gone; he bawled at me that I was a drunken dog."

There was something very comical in his almost abject aspect as he put this question. Grewgus could hardly keep from laughing.

"I should say more than likely, my friend. You strike me as one of those chaps who can get drunk and sober again three or four times in a day. We shall be there in a very few minutes. I expect you will find yourself able to walk without assistance when we get out."

And so it proved. When the taxi drew up before the shabby-looking house in one of the meanest streets in the locality, Mr. Newcombe was able to comport himself with a certain amount of steadiness. He apologized for not being able to ask his companion up, as he occupied one apartment at the top of the house, and there was, alas! no refreshment to offer a guest when he got there.

"I've sense enough not to keep it in the house," he said with a cunning smile. "Having to go out for it does put a bit of a stopper on me. You see, I know my weakness. But I tell you what—I want to prove to you that I look upon you as a pal, one of the right sort. If you'll make an appointment to meet me to-morrow, not perhaps at the same place, we'll have a return match."

Grewgus thanked him and hastily explained that he would not be in London on the morrow, nor for some little time after. Then, having seen his companion put his key in the door, and enter the unprepossessing premises, he went on his way. With his usual methodical habit, he posted in his note-book Mr. Newcombe's address, in case he should require it in the future.

Early the next morning he rang up Lydon while the young man was at breakfast.

"A thousand apologies for running away from you yesterday. But after that little scene with Stormont, I thought I ought not to let the chance slip. Got nothing out of it though, will tell you all when I see you. I want very much to know what you have to report to me. Shall I come to you, or vice versa?"

"I'd rather come to you," was Lydon's answer. "We shall be less liable to interruption in your place."

The young man went round to him after lunch. Grewgus related how he had nearly brought the Colonial to the blabbing point, and how the man had suddenly shrunk back into his shell. On his side Lydon gave a full account of the reception in Curzon Street, omitting no detail.

"There is no doubt what the game is," said the detective when his companion had finished. "They have evidently got this young chap into their clutches, and they mean to bleed him to the utmost."

"Do you think these elaborate preparations, the taking of the house in Curzon Street, this purchase of expensive furniture, etcetera, are a part of the plot?"

"Undoubtedly. I have heard a good deal of this young Wraysbury from one source and another. I should say he's rather a silly sort of chap, intoxicated with his good fortune, and an easy pigeon to be plucked. I am told he has a lot of hangers-on who are thriving on his bounty, regular parasites and leeches. On the quiet, he goes in for the theatrical business, has put money in one or two shows, and I need hardly say lost what he put in."

"Edwards, who seems immensely proud of the acquaintance, spoke in very warm terms of him, says he is a delightful fellow in himself, very generous, but by no means a fool."

Grewgus laughed derisively. "Of course, that is just what a man of that stamp would say of somebody he had designs on, make him out cleverer than himself. No, I think my version is the true one. I don't say that the young man is vicious or anything of that sort, but he is pleasure-loving, gambles pretty heavily, and of course goes racing."

"He is evidently very thick with the woman. He was sitting in her pocket all the afternoon."

"Ah! I understand he has a great *penchant* for female society, and that he is far from discriminating in his choice of fair companions. I believe his parents live in terror that he will one fine day make some actress or dancer Lady Wraysbury. Probably you don't know anything about the Felthams; in my line I get a lot of information about people. They are a very pious, straight-living couple. The old man is a pillar of the Established Church, his wife is equally devout. At their London house in Eaton Place she is surrounded with parsons. His youthful lordship has certainly not taken after his parents."

"And I suppose they would be shocked beyond expression if they knew he was hanging about a married woman?"

"Go off their heads, I should think," was the detective's reply. "But they are not likely to hear of it. They live in a very narrow set, to whom such doings don't penetrate. They won't know unless some scandal arises suddenly out of it."

Presently Lydon suggested that, in view of what they knew about Mrs. Edwards, otherwise Elise Makris, Wraysbury ought to be warned. How could it be done?

Grewgus looked doubtful. "You see, the difficulty is that we have no evidence of her having previously blackmailed anybody. Your friend, Mr. Craig, was very vague on the point, you say. Of course, I don't suppose they would dare to take any action if we did such a thing, wouldn't court having their past ripped up. But if this young ass is infatuated—and it looks very like it—he wouldn't believe much stronger evidence than it is in our power to produce."

"But you have no doubt of the character of all these people yourself?" asked Lydon, who did not perhaps quite realize the habitual caution of a man who followed Grewgus' profession.

"In my own mind, certainly not. But what we do know is of such a purely circumstantial kind that we should have great difficulty in getting the average person to agree with us. One can feel a thing without being able to prove it."

"It seems to me that we have come to a deadlock," said Lydon in a tone of disappointment.

Grewgus reluctantly admitted that it looked like it. He added more cheerfully that something might turn up at any moment. The French police were still pursuing their inquiries into the mystery of Calliard's death, and they might still be able to connect Edwards, if not Zillah Mayhew, with that tragedy. Then there would be something to go on of a tangible nature.

It was some few days after that Grewgus sought another meeting with his client. Perhaps in their last interview he had sensed a certain dissatisfaction on Lydon's part at the slow progress of affairs.

"I have been thinking a good deal over that fellow Newcombe," he said. "I have not the slightest doubt he could tell us something about Stormont that would make a certainty of what now is not more than a very strong conjecture. I wonder whether you would care to bribe him. There is no doubt that at the moment he is very incensed with Stormont; those bitter words, although he has half a notion they were deserved, will rankle for a long time. Also I doubt if Stormont pays him much to hold his tongue. Now would be the time to strike while the iron is hot, so to speak. Of course, the drawback is that you will have to put down more money, in addition to the expenses you have already incurred, as it were, for no practical result."

Lydon thought a little. "I would give a great deal to have the thing settled," he said presently. "To find out something which would definitely justify our suspicions, our almost positive suspicions, of Stormont. As you have pointed out, we cannot prove that Calliard was done to death at his instigation, but we have little doubt of it in our own minds. We cannot actually prove that this Curzon Street couple are out to fleece this simple young Wraysbury, but we are sure of it; and Stormont, perhaps also Whitehouse, is at the bottom of that. What sort of a sum do you think would be required?"

"I should say five hundred at once would be a big temptation to a fellow of that sort."

Lydon rose. "Then set about it at once. I will go to that. If necessary, a bit more. Anything to get rid of this state of suspense."

It was five days since Grewgus had escorted Newcombe home to his mean little lodging. He had received Lydon's permission to embark on his new scheme shortly after the luncheon hour, their usual time for meeting. Directly after his client had left, he went up to King's Cross.

The door was opened by a slatternly woman of middle age, whose appearance was in keeping with the house. She was the landlady.

To his inquiry as to whether Mr. Newcombe was in, she replied in the voluble and indirect manner of her class.

"You're the gent as brought him home in a taxi a few days ago, ain't you, when he'd had a drop too much? I saw you through the door when he let himself in, and I never forgets a face. Yes, he's in right enough, but nobody can see him. He's that bad, we don't know whether he'll pull through yet. The doctor ain't sure."

"What's the matter with him?"

"The doctor says the symptoms are those of a man who has been poisoned, whether by bad food he can't say."

"When did the attack commence?"

122

"Two days after you brought him home. On the next day somebody called for him, dressed like a toff, a very genial, red-faced man. Said he was an old friend and he went upstairs. They were in Newcombe's room for over an hour, and then they went out together."

"Do you know where they went to?"

"I'm coming to that in a minute, mister. I didn't see him again that day; he came back about ten o'clock and went up to his room. The next morning he had his breakfast in my kitchen as usual; he always told me he was poor now, but had seen better days. Said he had been to dine last evening with an old friend of his who had known him in his prosperous times, and had been given the best dinner he had ever had in his life. He didn't come to tea, and I went upstairs to tell him it was ready; he was a nice, pleasant feller, very free with his money, when he had it, and always grateful for any little kindness or attention. He was sitting huddled up in his chair, and couldn't speak. I sent for the doctor at once, for I was sure he had some money. We put him to bed, and there he's been ever since. He's still unconscious. I and my daughter look after him."

Grewgus pulled out his ever-ready note book. "I should like the address of that doctor, please, in case I want to see him. Your lodger was once a friend of mine, and I've only lately learned he is down on his luck. I called to-day to propose something for his benefit; I will come again to-morrow or next day. Many thanks, sorry to have taken up your time; you must be a busy woman."

He slipped a pound note into her hand, and went straight to Lydon's office in Victoria Street. But he just missed him; Leonard had left to catch an early train to Brighton.

He called on him early the next morning, and told him what had happened. The two men looked at each other. There was an inquiry in Leonard's glance which Grewgus answered at once.

"Yes, I surmise what you surmise. The genial, red-faced man was Stormont, and there is no doubt he is at times an active member of his organization. You may depend upon it, he is devilish clever, and this last thing may still remain a matter of conjecture incapable of actual proof."

He paused a moment, then added: "But if this poor devil lives, he is clever enough for the same idea to occur to him. And if it does he will speak out what he knows about Stormont."

CHAPTER SEVENTEEN

IT was a long time before Newcombe struggled back to convalescence; during that period Grewgus had several interviews with the doctor who was attending him, a young, harassed-looking man who had a large but not particularly remunerative practice in a poor neighbourhood. The detective came to the conclusion at their first meeting that he was not a very brilliant member of his profession. He said there were symptoms of poisoning, certainly, probably ptomaine poisoning. The landlady had said the patient told her he was dining at some restaurant the previous evening. Possibly some cheap one where there was little care exercised in the selection or cooking of food. Undoubtedly he had partaken of some dish which had produced this disastrous result.

Then came the day when Grewgus was permitted to go up to the ill-furnished room where the Colonial lay, a shadow of his former robust self. He stretched out a wasted hand. "Very good of you to come and see me, mate. My landlady told me a gent had been inquiring after me. For the life of me I couldn't guess who it was. I've no friends in this infernal country. And what made you look me up?"

Grewgus played a waiting game, till he could see his way more clearly. "Well, just blind chance, as it were. I was in this district, on a bit of business one day, and remembering where you lived, I thought I'd look you up, to see if you had recovered from the effects of that rather warm evening we spent together. I was shocked to hear you were so bad."

"I've had a close shave, mister; the doctor told me he thought my number was up. But he says now, if I keep quiet for a few days, I shall pull through."

He paused and added grimly, "If I do, I guess it will be a disappointment to somebody."

So the same suspicion had crept into his mind. Grewgus proceeded in the same quiet way: "You dined out with a friend, your landlady told me. No doubt you partook of some food that poisoned you?"

The man's calm manner left him. His eyes blazed out in sudden fury. "And a dog-goned idiot I was, knowing the character of the man I went with. At my time of life I ought to have had more sense."

For a little time he kept silence, but his eyes were blazing, his face was working all the time. When he spoke again, it seemed as if he had, for the moment, forgotten the other man's presence, as if he were muttering his thoughts aloud.

"The dirty dog, the dirty dog to try and do me in for the sake of saving a few paltry quid! Me that stood by him when he hadn't got a pal in the world, me that nursed him when he was sick to death as well as his own mother would have done. The treacherous swine."

Suddenly he seemed to realize the presence of Grewgus, and his mood underwent a sudden change. The fury in his glance died down, the voice lost its tone of hatred.

"Don't take any notice of me, mate. I'm weak after this infernal bout and perhaps a little bit light-headed. I was just rambling, that was all."

Grewgus leaned forward and looked the Colonial straight in the face. "You are not light-headed, and you are not rambling," he said in a firm voice. "You did not partake of any bad food. You have in your mind the same suspicion which I have, and that is that you were deliberately poisoned, by some subtle means, by the man, your pretended friend, who took you out to dinner."

The man's jaw dropped. He looked at the detective in a dazed kind of way. "How did you guess that?" he cried.

It was evident to the keen-witted Grewgus that Newcombe's feelings were making deadly war on each other. On the one hand he wanted to speak, to give full vent to the terrible ideas that were surging in his mind. On the other hand, he feared the consequence of a too frank revelation.

He resolved to put his cards on the table. "Now, look here, my friend, you don't know me from Adam. I will tell you frankly I am here for a purpose. I'm not a detective in the usual meaning of the term, although I was for some years at Scotland Yard. I am no longer a recognized officer of the law, I am on my own, as a private inquiry agent. Here is my card. My office is in Craven Street, and my name is Grewgus."

The man's mind took in the situation swiftly. "Ah, I see it now. You followed me that night from the street where the party was—I forget the name of it now—you followed me into the pub. You took me home, not because you were a particularly good sort of a chap as I thought, but because you wanted to find out where I lived."

"You're a smart fellow, Newcombe, I can see that quite plainly," said the detective, thinking a little flattery might be judicious. "I think you and I shall get on quite well together presently, when we know each other better. Now, first of all, I want you to get this thoroughly into your head, that I am not acting on behalf of the law. Unless you recognize that, it is not likely we shall go very far. Do you believe me?"

Mr. Newcombe hesitated a little before he replied to this straight question. "Suppose I say I do, just to make things more comfortable between us," he said presently. "You are here on behalf of somebody."

"Quite true," answered Grewgus promptly. "On behalf of private parties."

A cunning smile overspread the Colonial's features. "What is it you want to find out?" he asked bluntly.

"I want to find out as much as I can about that man you had the altercation with the other day, Mr. Howard Stormont, the owner of Effington Hall, and apparently well off. At any rate, he seems to spend a pretty good amount of money."

Mr. Newcombe thought things well over before he spoke again, in a disjointed sort of way as if he were giving utterance to his own thoughts. "Private parties you said. Well, I'd wager a bit I can guess who the private party is—that nice-looking young fellow I met down at Effington who's going to marry the pretty niece. He thinks there's a bit of mystery about, and he wants to get to the bottom of it."

It was evidently not much use fencing with this shrewd, hard-headed Colonial. "I won't say you're right, and I won't say you're wrong, Newcombe. Think what you like. Of course, you'll understand that in my delicate position I can't afford to be too frank."

"Neither can I, in my position," said the Colonial with a grin.

"Granted. Well, now let me put things as they appear to me. You can tell me presently whether I am right or wrong. It is evident you know something about this fellow who appears prosperous enough now. You had fallen upon bad times, that we know from his own admission."

"Oh, he has told that, has he?" cried Newcombe, with something of a snarl in his voice. "He didn't mind giving me away, did he?"

"In a sense he was forced to; he had to explain your sudden arrival at Effington. Well, to continue, you had fallen upon bad times. You went to see your old friend, and no doubt represented to him that it would be highly inconvenient for him in his present position if you made certain disclosures about his past. Not being a fool, he saw that."

Mr. Newcombe listened to this reconstruction of what had taken place between himself and the owner of Effington Hall without interruption. Not wishing his countenance to betray him, he kept his gaze steadily averted.

Grewgus looked round the ill-furnished room in a disparaging fashion. "He recognized the fact that he could not allow you to talk, and he agreed to make you some sort of allowance. Judging by the condition of this apartment, not a very handsome one."

The Colonial indulged in a derisive grunt at this allusion to his surroundings, but he did not break his obstinate silence.

"Small as that allowance is, he begrudges it. Or perhaps it is not the money he minds so much; what weighs upon his mind is that you are a standing menace to his safety, the fear that one day, when you've had a drop or two too much, you'll blurt out the very thing he wants to hide. He feels he'll have no real security till you are safely out of the way. Hence that apparently hospitable action the other day."

Grewgus had the satisfaction of seeing a vindictive scowl steal over the man's face at this reference. He hoped to appeal not only to the Colonial's cupidity but in an equal degree to his thirst for revenge.

"If you ask me, I don't think your position is a very safe one, my friend. From what I do know of Stormont, I have reason to believe him to be possessed of diabolical cunning, and unscrupulous to a degree. If he has made up his mind to get you out of the way, it is long odds that, in the end, he will accomplish his designs, either on his own initiative or with the help of his numerous friends."

And then Mr. Newcombe spoke: "He's a cunning devil enough, you're right about that. Well, mister private inquiry agent, let's come to the point. What is it you want to propose to me? You've been a long time leading up to it. Let's have it without any more beating about the bush."

"If you'll tell me the secret of Stormont's past which he is paying you some paltry pittance to hush up, I'll pay you down in hard cash the sum of five hundred pounds."

"And supposing you got that information—mind you, I haven't said that I can give it you—what use are you going to make of it?"

Grewgus was a bit puzzled what to answer to this plain and very natural question. Would Lydon take any steps against Stormont if he found himself in a position to do so? The young man had carefully kept Gloria's name out of the matter, but the shrewd detective had originally guessed there was a woman in the case. Newcombe's statement that Lydon was engaged to Stormont's niece confirmed that suspicion absolutely.

No, he felt sure that his client would never lift his hand against the uncle of the girl he loved, however great his guilt might be. He was quite safe in making the Colonial's mind easy on that score. Strange perversity of human nature that this man, presumably a crook himself, shrank from giving another crook away, even although he had been treated so vilely. Or was Newcombe's hesitation due to a sense of self-preservation? In giving his old pal away, would he be forced to implicate himself?

"I understand what is in your mind, but I think you may be quite sure nothing of the kind will happen. Certain suspicions having arisen, it is necessary to confirm or remove them."

The Colonial was evidently thinking very deeply, looking at the matter from every point of view. "And supposing, mind you, I only say supposing, that the suspicions were confirmed, I presume the young fellow would chuck this pretty girl."

"I am sure of the contrary," answered the detective, speaking quite warmly; he had taken a great fancy to Lydon and was convinced he would never act shabbily to a woman. "It is not pleasant to have a criminal for an uncle, of course, but I understand her father is a man of the highest probity."

Again the Colonial put on his thinking cap. "That settles that, then." And now he began to relinquish, to some extent, his rather futile attempts at caution. "And now let's consider the position as it affects me. If I give Stormont away, I shall have to make a clean bolt of it; there'll be no further help from that quarter. Besides, I shouldn't be safe, if he happened to find it out, and it's a chance one must reckon with. He wants to get me out of the way as it is."

"You're quite right, Newcombe. If he ever got a hint, he would be doubly, trebly anxious to remove you. If we do come to an arrangement, you'll have to quit in double-quick time. Now, let us discuss terms. If you can tell me something definite about this man, as I have said, there is five hundred pounds waiting for you. You are a man of brains and resource; with that sum you can start life again. And, in my candid opinion, the sooner you get out of Stormont's reach, the better for your own peace of mind."

"Not enough," cried the Colonial promptly. "One can't do much in making a fresh start with five hundred. Besides, it's worth a thousand."

But if Newcombe was hard at a bargain, Grewgus was by no means a bad man of business. He joined issue at once, and for a long time they fought each other strenuously. A compromise was finally reached at seven hundred. Grewgus was sure his client would go to this extent, from what he had said.

But the victory was not quite won yet. Newcombe wanted further time for reflection. "It's a very serious step you are asking me to take. I've got to look at it all round. Don't think I have any consideration for that dirty dog, Stormont; you wouldn't expect it, would you? If we were out in some parts I could name, I'd plug him without the slightest compunction; he'd deserve it. But I've got to think of myself, to be sure I'm not making a false step."

From that position he would not budge. He must have a clear day to think it over. If Grewgus would call at the same time to-morrow, he would give him his decision.

Grewgus saw his client later in the day, and got an open cheque from him for the seven hundred pounds which he would cash on the following morning. It was no use going to the Colonial without the money in his pocket. His knowledge of human nature told him that Mr. Newcombe, if he had made up his mind to betray his old pal, would stipulate that the money should be handed over before he opened his mouth.

"My own impression is that he will bite," remarked the detective. "It is perfectly obvious that he knows something damaging, or he would not have gone so far in the preliminary negotiations. We are buying a pig in a poke, and what he has to tell may not be worth so much money. Still, if Stormont suffers himself to be blackmailed to the extent of three or four pounds a week, it must be something rather bad, if not so bad as we think."

Lydon agreed. Anyway, if Newcombe took the seven hundred pounds, the suspense would be ended, they would know something definite.

"The thing I want to assure him positively of is that nothing he tells me will be used against himself or Stormont. I gave him this assurance off my own bat, as it were," said the detective as he took his leave. "I take it that, whatever we find out, you personally have no intention of setting the police upon Stormont. In other words, this is strictly a private inquiry, with which the official police will have nothing to do?"

Lydon assured him that this was so. He could not yet quite bring himself to disclose his relations to Gloria. He simply said that the man belonged to a highly-respectable family which he was determined to spare so far as it lay in his power.

The French police were still probing the mystery of the death of Calliard, the jeweller. If they were successful, it was more than probable that Stormont might be implicated. That contingency could not be averted.

"Of course, I shall mention nothing of that affair to Newcombe," was the detective's reply.

CHAPTER EIGHTEEN

GREWGUS did not pay his visit the next day as arranged. In the morning he received a wire from Newcombe, asking him for a respite of another twenty-four hours. It was evident the Colonial wanted to think the matter well over, in other words to consider which course would be the most beneficial to his own interests.

On the second day the detective presented himself with the seven hundred pounds in his pocket, the money which he devoutly hoped would soon pass from his keeping.

Newcombe was much better, had recovered marvellously in that couple of days. His lean face had filled out; there were no longer about him the signs of a deadly and wasting illness. He greeted his visitor with a rough good-humour. Grewgus, a shrewd judge of men, put him down as a good-tempered fellow in the main, inclined to be quarrelsome and vindictive when the drink overtook him, rather a man of moods and apt to act on impulse.

"Come along, mister, glad to see you. The doctor says I have made a marvellous rally. I'm a different man from what I was when you last saw me. A lot of fight yet left in old Tom Newcombe."

Grewgus paid him handsome compliments on his changed appearance and laid on a little flattery. "Even now you look as if you could knock spots off some of the young ones. I should say you would be as fit as a fiddle in another week or ten days."

The Colonial laughed his loud, hoarse laugh. "I guess a certain person will be bitterly disappointed to find his old pal is so tough. Ha ha! he's wondering what has become of me. His money has come right enough, but I haven't acknowledged it yet. I don't quite know what I'm going to do about that. It depends."

Grewgus did not answer. He was fairly confident he had won the day, but he did not wish to spoil matters by hurrying them unduly. He smiled agreeably and waited for Newcombe to speak again. "Well, mister, I've decided to accept your offer. Have you brought the 'boodle'? If you haven't we can adjourn this meeting till to-morrow. Another day will make no difference to me."

Grewgus drew out a bulky pocket-book and flourished it invitingly in front of his companion. "I'm a man of my word, Newcombe. I wasn't, of course, absolutely sure of what your decision might be, but I brought the money on the off-chance. You would like me to hand it over to you at once, eh?"

The man's eyes had an avaricious gleam at this invitation. The detective thought it was a long time since he had handled such a sum. "What do *you* think?" he said with a chuckle. "The money first, the information after. You would do the same in my place now, wouldn't you, if you had the brains of a mouse?"

Grewgus could be as frank as anybody, when there was no necessity to beat about the bush. "I trust you more than you trust me, Newcombe. Here is the money. Count it over before you start."

Newcombe began to count over the money. Suddenly he looked up at his companion with a rather aggrieved air. "I say, you didn't answer that question. Wouldn't you do the same in my place? It's a matter of business, ain't it, pure and simple?"

"Of course, my good fellow, I am not complaining. If I were you I would certainly have the money before I opened my mouth."

Mollified by this rejoinder, the Colonial stuffed the notes in his pocket, and again burst into his loud laugh.

"Now, you're a clever man, mister—a darned sight cleverer than I am, I expect—and I suppose you haven't overlooked the fact that I might take the money and give you practically nothing for it."

Grewgus intimated in his suavest manner that such a contingency had not escaped his intelligence. In some cases he would have taken greater precautions. He ended with a handsome compliment. "I don't know much of you, Newcombe, but I'm pretty sure you're not one of that sort."

The Colonial looked pleased. "You're right, Mr. Grewgus, I don't pretend to be much, but if people play fair and square with me, I play fair and square with them. I've never rounded on a pal yet; I shouldn't round on this swine if he hadn't played the dirty on me. Why, a week or two ago I would have been cut into little bits before I would have given Howard Stormont away. That was when I believed him to be a pal, not a too generous one perhaps, but still a pal. Have you got me?"

"Perfectly," answered Grewgus smoothly. "You would be a bit of a soft, I think, if you showed Stormont any quarter."

The man's eyes flashed with sudden fury, it was evident his hatred of his old friend was very intense, and that once having made up his mind, he rejoiced in getting even with him.

"Yes, that was a bad evening's work for him, cleverly as he thought he had managed it. He was always very keen on the poisoning business, although mind you, I can't honestly say that I ever knew of any case in which he had given it. But he was always fond of reading books on the subject. He used to laugh when he told me how people in the old days used to polish off their enemies with a poisoned glove or flower. He dropped a little drop of something into my drink that night, you bet—something that this fool of a doctor could not detect anyway."

"And if you don't get yourself out of this neighbourhood he'll try it again. I shouldn't say he is the sort of man to be baffled by a first failure," commented Grewgus, whose object it was to keep the Colonial's indignation at white heat. "And now, Newcombe, let's get to business. You've counted the money and found it right. It's for you to carry out your part of the bargain."

There was just a touch of shamefacedness in the man's expression, hardened character as he was, as he began his story.

"I'm not going to say more about myself than I can help, Mr. Grewgus. You won't blame me for that, I'm sure."

"Not in the least. To be quite frank, I'm not interested in your career, Newcombe. Stormont's is the only one that concerns me."

"Right-o! And if anything comes of it, you're not going to drag me in. You promised that at the beginning, didn't you?"

"Practically I did, and I repeat that promise now," confirmed Grewgus.

"Well, mister, I'll start with the days when I first came across Howard Stormont, when we both were young men. No need to tell you I wasn't a model youth. If I had been, I shouldn't have picked up with him, or rather he with me. Upon my word of honour, Mr. Grewgus, I never had much of a chance. My mother, I know, was a good woman, she died when I was a kid, I should say of a broken heart. My father was a ne'er-do-well, drunken, callous, dishonest. Unfortunately I took after him, but never in my life have I had decent luck. If I went straight for a bit, misfortune dogged me, and on the crook I didn't fare much better."

Proceeding with his narrative, the Colonial explained that at this period he was associated with a set of men who were not particular as to how they got their living, although they could not boast of being scientific or high-class criminals. The one thing to which they had definitely made up their minds was that they would not work, except under the direst compulsion. They preferred to beg, borrow, or, when necessary, cheat and steal.

Stormont, then quite a young man, a little while before was introduced to this promising association, and in spite of his youth soon evinced qualities that marked him out for leadership. It was whispered about presently that he had got into some trouble at home and that his relatives had insisted on his going abroad.

"I never knew precisely what the trouble was," Newcombe explained, "but from all I could gather from a few things dropped by him when he had a little—for he was a heavy drinker in those days—it was about money. His

132

people—he always used to boast that he came of a highly respectable family—paid his passage out and gave him a few pounds over. I understood he was not to go back to England till he could return with a clean bill of health.

"Him and me took a great fancy to each other. I don't quite know what he saw in me, for I was rather a dull, plodding sort of chap compared with most of the men I associated with, who told me I wasn't quite clever enough for the game. What I admired in him was his high spirits, and first and foremost his wonderful cunning and cleverness: he was always alert and up to every move on the board. He was also very generous, spent money like water when he had it, and most popular with his mates. They thought a wonderful lot of his abilities and prophesied that he would one day become a crook of the first water."

"I take it, these associates of yours were not in the front rank of their profession?" interjected Grewgus.

The Colonial shook his head. "Certainly not; with the exception of Stormont they had neither the nerves nor the brains. A great deal of card-sharping, plucking raw young pigeons who had just come out, a little bit of easy swindling here and there, that was as far as they could go. Stormont was altogether on a higher plane. He had the brain to invent and elaborate big things."

"And of course, he joined you in these agreeable pursuits, the card-sharping, the plucking of young pigeons, even although they did not give full scope for the exercise of his superior talents."

"That is so, mister, and in a minute I'm coming to what you want to know. I take it, you've been making a lot of inquiries, but up to the present you haven't been able to prove definitely he is the criminal you believe him to be. That goes without saying. If you could have got that information yourself, you wouldn't chuck away seven hundred pounds on me."

The Colonial, when he could keep off the drink, was evidently a clear thinker. With great modesty he had spoken of himself as a dull and plodding fellow, but Grewgus did not consider him as dull as he pretended to be. Probably intemperance had stood in his way: prevented him from being a successful crook and reduced him to his present position of subsisting on Stormont's bounty.

"Well, the game wasn't fast enough for him; the profits out of this petty kind of roguery were too small for a man of his ambitious nature and expensive tastes. Three or four times he launched out on things of his own—things that the others were too timid or too slow-witted to join in. And the last one brought him to grief."

Grewgus leaned forward in an attitude of expectation. At last he was going to get something definite about the apparently prosperous owner of Effington Hall.

"It was rather a neat little bit of forgery. He had laid his plans well too, thought it all out very carefully, almost succeeded in fixing the guilt upon another chap, a perfectly honest man."

"As big a scandal as that, eh?" was the detective's surprised comment.

Newcombe indulged in a sardonic laugh. "Stormont wasn't the sort of man to think of anybody but himself. As long as he could swim he didn't care who sank. An innocent man sacrificed didn't weigh heavily on his conscience. But clever as he was, the police just went one better. The other fellow's innocence was proved and the guilt clearly fastened on the right person. I forgot to tell you that when he began to launch out on these dangerous *coups* he changed his name from Stormont to Manvers. Under the name of Manvers he was convicted and sentenced to a pretty tidy term of imprisonment. Now, I've kept all the papers describing the trial and evidence. I shan't give them up, of course; but if you give me your solemn word of honour to return them to me, I'll lend them to you to make copies of."

"Thanks very much; I'll take them away with me when I leave. Does the name of Stormont occur in them?"

"Yes, they discovered he had been passing under the two, but they inclined to the belief that Manvers was the real one, and as Manvers he was convicted. Of course his old pals knew better."

"And what became of him after he came out of prison?"

"He went back to England; I expect that sharp dose of imprisonment sickened him of Australia. He had been clever enough to put away the swag somewhere; it was quite a nice little sum. I've a notion he had a confederate, although I'm sure it was not one of the old lot, somebody much cleverer than we could turn out. He came to say good-bye to me and one or two others who had been his particular pals. He bluffed us that when he got back to his own country he was going to lead an honest life. For my part, I never believed it. Howard Stormont was a crook by instinct and he'd never do a bit of honest work if he could get money by any other means."

"What do you know of his career between the time he left England and when you paid him that surprise visit at Effington Hall?"

"Practically nothing," was the answer. "In the rough and ready life out there, one soon forgets things, anyway you don't think continually of them. I had a lot of bad luck and after many years I worked my way back to the old country. As I was looking about for any kind of job that would keep my head above water, I began to think a good deal about him and wondered what he was doing, if he had struck oil or not.

"By the merest accident I got on his track, saw him coming out of some city offices unseen by him. A telegraph boy was passing at the time, and I asked him if he knew anything of the gentleman, slipping into his hand a shilling which I could ill afford. He seemed to know a good deal about him. He was a Mr. Howard Stormont—that of course I was sure of as, with the exception of growing stouter, he had not altered since the Australian days— that he was engaged in business, and lived in a fine house in Surrey at a place called Effington. I smartened myself up as well as I could, for I had very nearly come to the end of my tether, and went down there. Lord, he was struck all of a heap when he saw me, so was the flunkey who opened the door.

"He was always a quick-witted fellow, so as soon as he had recovered from the shock, he made the best of it, and took me into his study, where we had a long jaw. He told me he had gone in for finance—perfectly straight business, he swore—but it was terribly hazardous, and he owned he was living up to the hilt. Knowing his extravagance of old, I thought it very likely, but he might be pretending this in order to choke me off, as he could be pretty certain I hadn't called upon him merely to inquire after the state of his health. He was devilish civil all through, of course; he knew I was acquainted with that nasty little episode, and he didn't dare to ride the high horse."

"And in the end you came to some little financial arrangement?"

"Why, naturally. But he made a hard bargain. When he had money, he was generous in a spasmodic sort of way; he would stand you any amount of food and drink, but he was never fond of parting with actual cash. The sort of man that would give you a dinner costing five pounds, and button up his pockets when you asked him for the loan of a quid. He said he'd try and find me a good job, and in the meantime he would allow me four pounds a week."

"I should say you found it a tight fit," remarked Grewgus, thinking of his companion's fondness for liquid refreshment.

"You never spoke a truer word. But I couldn't get him higher. He pretended that he was frightfully hard up, and that any moment he might have to give up his fine house. Of course, he knew I wasn't in a position to bargain."

A smile of reminiscence stole over the Colonial's face as he continued: "I'm afraid I didn't behave very well on that visit. He had on a swell dinner-party that night, which of course I didn't expect to be present at, I wasn't dressed for the part. I had a fine dinner by myself, and after his guests had gone, he came in and chatted with me for a few minutes, and set a bottle of whisky in front of me before he left.

"I'd been going very much on the teetotal lately, through lack of the ready, and when I saw that tempting bottle before me, I went at it with a vengeance. When I take a drop too much, I get quarrelsome, the stuff brings the worst of me to the surface. I began to think he wasn't treating me too courteously, and I followed him into the billiard-room to have it out with him.

"He smoothed me down after a bit, and I had some more drink—there was plenty of it about—and I got from the quarrelsome into the stupid stage. I made a silly reference to a little prank of ours when we followed up a young greenhorn with a view to relieving him of some of his money. Luckily, he stopped me in time; his niece and her young man were there, but of course it was a silly thing to do. I think he was afraid of me from that moment, was never sure of what I might let out when I was in the same condition."

Grewgus interrupted the flow of reminiscences relating to that embarrassing visit to Effington Hall. "Now tell me, please, all that took place on that day when Stormont took you to the restaurant."

The Colonial's face darkened at the allusion. "The scoundrel showed his usual cunning. You know of that little scene that occurred outside the house in that street, the name of which I never can remember. Ah, yes, Curzon Street. You remember how upset I was about it, how very near I was to giving him away on the evening you came across me. Well, I suppose Stormont had been thinking it over too, and came to the conclusion he had gone too far, offended me beyond forgiveness. Well, the next day, while I was brooding over it, he walks into my room, with his hand outstretched, and smiling all over his red face.

"'Tom, old man, we've been too good friends in the past to quarrel now,' he says. 'Let us forget and forgive, and shake hands on it. I was so riled when you came up to me in that state, before all the crowd too, that I lost my head. I'm sorry if I spoke too harshly, but you must allow it was a bit rough on me. Let us both bury the hatchet.'

"I don't think I'm a very vindictive man, except when somebody plays the real dirty on me," urged Newcombe in his own defence. "And I was forced to admit to myself it was a trifle rough on him, as he said. Well, after a bit, we made it up and agreed to be friends again. He seemed awfully relieved, and proposed I should go out to dinner with him, not to one of the swagger places, which he knew I shouldn't care for, but to a quiet little restaurant in Soho.

"We went there, and I had a splendid dinner, and as much drink as I cared to take. He drank plenty too, but his head was always harder than mine, and he would be sitting up in his chair when I was under the table. When I got home, I felt a bit muddled, and when I woke in the morning I knew I had had a warm night. But it wasn't till the middle of the day that I began to feel really queer. I heard the doctor whispering to the landlady, and I caught the word 'poisoned.' When I was able to think things over, I began to tumble to what had happened. I understood why he had been so devilish civil. I had given him away in a sense twice. He was afraid of me, and thought there would be no peace for him till I was out of the way. The dirty dog! The dirty dog! I must try and not think of it more than I can help. It makes me see red when I do."

There was a long silence after this rather furious outburst. Grewgus broke it with the question: "And have you any ideas as to what he has been doing all these years in England?"

Newcombe indulged in a rather cunning smile. "That's not quite in the contract, is it, mister? I ought to ask a bit more for that, but still you have played fair and square with me, I don't mind answering you. Mark you, I have never been able to get a word out of Stormont; he swears through thick and thin he's on the square. But I've done a little spying on my own account, and I've come to the conclusion he's after the same old game, but much bigger game. There's no legitimate business done in that tinpot office in the city. There's nobody there but himself and a man named Whitehouse, a solemn-looking sort of cove who puts in an appearance about three or four times a week. Have you come across Whitehouse?"

The detective nodded. "Yes, I know a little about him, not very much. A very old friend of Stormont's, according to Stormont's account."

He did not tell him that the man carried on a solicitor's business also, under the name of Glenthorne. It was a fixed policy with him to obtain confidences, not to make them.

"And I am pretty sure he *is* a very old friend," observed the Colonial. "The first time I spotted him coming out of that office in the City—I had placed myself where he wasn't likely to see me—his face seemed familiar. There was a young chap, not one of ours, whom I've seen several times with Stormont in the old Australian days. He wasn't known to any of our lot, and Stormont never said much about him, never mentioned his name, but I always had a notion they were in some jobs together. When Stormont went to quod under the name of Manvers, this chap disappeared altogether. Now, I'm not prepared to swear to it, but I've got more than a notion that this fellow—he was a young man then—and Whitehouse are one and the same person."

Grewgus left presently, very satisfied with his day's work, taking with him the papers which contained a full account of the trial and conviction of Manvers, otherwise Stormont. The next day he had a long interview with Lydon.

"Well, I don't begrudge the money," said the young man, after listening to what had passed between the two men. "We have now proved absolutely that the man is a criminal, and a pretty desperate one at that."

The thing that was worrying him was this—had things now come to such a pass that he ought to pass on the information he had acquired to Jasper

Stormont? Was it right that Gloria should ever return to her uncle's custody?

Without mentioning his exact relations with the girl, relations which Grewgus already knew of from Newcombe, he put this question.

"Let's wait a bit, something else of a confirmatory nature may turn up," answered the detective. "You still want me to watch the little game going on at Curzon Street. Something may come to light there."

And so it was left. Lydon would not approach Jasper Stormont just yet. There was still some time before he would return to China, and until then Gloria was safe from further association with her criminal uncle.

A week later there came to Grewgus a telephone call from the offices of Messrs. Shelford and Taylor, the solicitors.

"Is that you, Grewgus? Good morning." It was Mr. Shelford speaking. "I am sending a client of mine, Lord Wraysbury, round to confer with you. A very serious business, I fear. He will explain it all to you. Divorce proceedings are threatened, but I think blackmail is the real object. You might know something or find out something about the people. Will twelve o'clock suit you?"

At the mention of Wraysbury's name, Grewgus had a premonition of what was in the air.

"Perfectly, Mr. Shelford, I will be in," he said. "What are the names of the parties?"

The reply was what he expected. "A young married couple of the name of Edwards. They live in Curzon Street."

CHAPTER NINETEEN

THERE was a decided feeling of elation in Grewgus as he waited the advent of Lord Wraysbury. The loose strands were being gathered together by this unexpected visit.

He formed a rapid impression of the handsome young man as they exchanged a few conventional words of greeting. Rather impulsive, generous, easy-going, not burdened with any great excess of mentality, likely to be easily exploited by designing persons, trusting and unsuspicious.

The young nobleman was perfectly straightforward as to the object of his visit, and made no attempt to beat about the bush.

"The plain truth, Mr. Grewgus, is that I have made a fool of myself," he told him. "Shelford, whose firm has acted for us for years, since my grandfather's time, says there is no doubt it is a blackmailing case, and advised me to come here and tell you the whole story from the beginning to the very unpleasant end."

"That will certainly be the best plan, Lord Wraysbury; Mr. Shelford told me as much over the 'phone. When I have learned all the details, it will be possible for me to tell you if I can help you."

The young nobleman, in his pleasant, well-bred voice, proceeded to unfold the history of the relations with Mrs. Edwards—perfectly innocent relations he urged with a warmth that was undoubtedly genuine, which had led to the present trouble.

A couple of years ago he had met at Monte Carlo a Mrs. and Miss Glenthorne, mother and daughter. Miss Glenthorne was a very charming and attractive girl; the mother seemed somewhat of a nonentity and kept herself in the background, giving pride of place to her clever and particularly fascinating offspring.

At this point Grewgus interrupted his client.

"One moment, please. Is this Mrs. Glenthorne a stoutish woman, with a Jewish type of countenance?"

"Yes, I should certainly say there was more than a touch of the chosen race about her," was the reply. "You know her, then?"

"I can hardly say as much as that, Lord Wraysbury. I have seen her once or twice, but I have never spoken to her. The point of importance so far as you are concerned is that I know something of her, also something of the daughter. Tell me, does not the young lady wear on every possible occasion

139

a pendant of a very peculiar design, a big sapphire set in an unusual manner?"

Again the answer was in the affirmative. The young man was naturally greatly surprised at the detective's display of knowledge.

"It seems I've come to the right place," he remarked with an almost boyish glee. "I infer from your manner that what you know about them is not anything to their credit."

Grewgus smiled with his somewhat enigmatic smile. "I think I would rather wait till the end of your story before I say anything, if you don't mind. I shall interrupt you as little as possible, and when I do it will only be for the purpose of clearing up some point that suddenly suggests itself."

The young nobleman proceeded with his story. The two women were staying at one of the less expensive hotels in the place; he gathered that the mother was a widow, and had been left an income that was comfortable, but not large, that enabled her and her daughter to enjoy life in a moderate and modest way. He first made their acquaintance at the tables, where the young woman occasionally risked a few francs. The mother never played.

Wraysbury made no secret of the fact that the girl interested him very considerably; she was clever, bright, amusing, and also beautiful. He was never at any moment seriously in love with her. The fact that she was a mere casual acquaintance, of whose antecedents he knew nothing, forbade any such happening. But in the free and easy atmosphere of Monte Carlo the acquaintance ripened considerably. Possibly onlookers might have considered it an obvious flirtation on both sides. All the time he was perfectly heart-whole, and he felt pretty certain that the young woman was in the same condition.

He took her to dinner on a few occasions, and every time the mother was present. He bought Miss Glenthorne flowers and chocolates, nothing of a more expensive nature, and no letters, not even the briefest note, had ever passed between them. There had never been the slightest attempt on his part at love-making.

His reasons for this attitude were perfectly honourable ones, as he explained to the detective. Everybody knew that he had come into possession of a considerable fortune, and that he was a more than usually eligible person from a matrimonial point of view. He was too modest to flatter himself that he had any special attractions for women, but his money was bound to have. Miss Glenthorne appeared to him then to be a well-conducted, modest girl, but no doubt, like the majority of women, she was anxious to settle herself well in life. Under such circumstances, it would have been conduct little short of dastardly if he had led her to entertain false hopes of becoming Lady Wraysbury.

"It was just a most agreeable acquaintance, nothing more," concluded the young man as he finished this portion of his story.

In due course Wraysbury left Monte Carlo, and said good-bye to the two women. There was nothing of a sentimental nature in their parting, no reference to further meetings in the future. He learned that they did not visit Monte Carlo frequently, and they very seldom came to England. He thought it extremely improbable that he would ever come across the couple again. In due course the memory of the dark, handsome girl faded away from his active recollections.

Then one day, as Grewgus already had learned from Lydon, he met the young woman at the *Ritz*, after this considerable period. She was accompanied by a smart-looking man, whom she introduced as her husband by the fairly common name of Edwards. She pressed him warmly to call at their house in Curzon Street, an invitation which was heartily seconded by the husband.

"You knew nothing, of course, of this man Edwards?" queried Grewgus.

"Nothing at all. We had a rather long chat, in which he did a good deal of the talking, and he seemed to know his way about. He spoke of attending Ascot and Goodwood and Henley; said he had seen me at all these places. I had certainly not seen him, should not have known him if I had," was Wraysbury's answer.

"I take it, he was not at all in your world?"

"Most certainly not, but my impression of him was that he was a very pleasant and gentlemanly fellow. Well, when we parted, I certainly said that I would call; I could not very well hurt their feelings by a positive refusal. But really I had no intention of going. As a single girl, Miss Glenthorne was a most pleasant casual acquaintance, but I did not particularly wish to mix myself up with the Curzon Street ménage."

"And, later on, I suppose you changed your mind?"

A slight wave of colour swept over the young man's face at the question. "Unfortunately, as it turned out, I did. I'm afraid I'm rather a vacillating sort of chap, making good resolutions one minute and breaking them the next. I don't quite know what led me to break them in this case. I think principally a silly sort of curiosity to know how she would comport herself in her new rôle of married woman. I was, to a certain extent, interested in her, but by no means unduly fascinated. And perhaps, Mr. Grewgus, you may not believe me when I say it, but I am not a libertine, and have no desire to run after other men's wives."

Certainly, Lord Wraysbury gave the detective the impression of being a quite honourable and clean-living young fellow. But possibly the seductive Zillah had exercised over him a fascination which he would not admit to himself.

So he made his first call in Curzon Street. Edwards happened to be at home, and laid himself out to be especially agreeable to the visitor. The wife was charming, too, but she seemed a little pensive and *distraite*, as if she had something on her mind. Lord Wraysbury noted that the married couple did not seem to address much of the conversation to each other. He left the house with a distinct impression that the pair had had a recent quarrel, or that there was just a little rift within the lute in their married life.

He left in due course, but not before he had accepted an invitation to dine informally with them a couple of days later. He had done his best to get out of it, but Edwards, to whom he had rather taken a fancy, had been so insistent that his resistance was overborne. And here again curiosity played a large part in his decision. He could easily have thrown them over, but he wanted to test his suspicions, to see if all was right between this very charming woman and her equally charming husband.

But he had not so far the least idea of the game that was being played. Everything seemed square and above-board. There was evidently plenty of money about; the house was run on a liberal scale. Edwards himself was a most companionable and gentlemanly fellow. He was not quite sure there might not be some ulterior motive in this extreme friendliness, this insistent hospitality. But he fancied it might be a social one. Probably they were ambitious, and wanted to climb in the world. If they made a friend of him he might be disposed to help them in their designs.

He went to dinner. "Quite an informal affair," he explained to Grewgus. "There was only one other guest, a very breezy, red-faced man, just a trifle vulgar. His name was Stormont, and Mrs. Edwards addressed him as uncle. I gathered he had known her from a child and was excessively fond of her, but he was no actual relation. My original suspicions were rather confirmed; there seemed a certain coldness between husband and wife, veiled under the appearance of great politeness. I couldn't understand it. Mrs. Edwards' conduct as a young wife seemed to me to be quite perfect. I could not help thinking it must be his fault."

He went again very shortly to a second dinner. As on the previous occasion, there was only one other guest. This time it was her real uncle, a man named Glenthorne, a rather gloomy, taciturn fellow, whom he judged to be altogether of a superior class to Stormont. But of the two he preferred the adopted uncle.

He went to Curzon Street three or four times after that, once to the big party which the pair had given as a sort of house-warming. All the time, from various signs and symptoms, his conviction grew that Mrs. Edwards' life was not a happy one, in spite of her efforts to mask the fact under an assumption of cheerfulness and high spirits.

The climax was quickly reached. On a certain day Wraysbury received a note from her, asking if he would call that evening after eight o'clock. She could not ask him to dinner for reasons she would explain when she saw him. She was about to take a very important step, and, presuming on their old acquaintance, she would like to consult him as to the prudence of it. If he were engaged that evening, would he make it the next, or the next after that?

"Of course, now I come to think of it, there was something suspicious in that note," said the young nobleman. "I ought to have told her to write to me what she wanted to consult me about, and I would preserve absolute silence and destroy the letter; but I'm foolishly unsuspicious, and I went, being disengaged that night.

"To my great surprise, the door was opened by Mrs. Edwards herself. She appeared in a state of great agitation; I thought at the time she had been crying.

"'Oh, Lord Wraysbury, I am in the greatest trouble,' she said in a distressed voice. 'Come up to the drawing-room for just a few minutes, so that I can tell you about it. There is no danger. My husband is in the country and won't be back for a week. I have sent the servants out to the theatre, so that we might be alone. That is why I couldn't ask you to dinner.'"

Wraysbury did not quite like the look of things, the absence of both husband and servants, but he was still unsuspicious. The woman played her part so well that he attributed her rather foolish act to her acute distress of mind. He was quite sure it was connected with her husband, and that his suspicions of the unhappiness of their married life were going to be confirmed by her revelations.

He went up to the drawing-room with her, resolving to get out of the embarrassing situation as soon as he could, and she at once burst forth into an impassioned account of her wrongs and sufferings.

According to her account, Edwards, so genial and gentlemanly in public life, was a bully and a brute. On many occasions she had suffered personal violence at his hands. She rolled up her sleeve and showed a shapely arm on which appeared a big bruise which had been inflicted a couple of days ago. She had no positive evidence of infidelity, but she had grave suspicions of his relations with other women. On Wraysbury remarking that it was very early in their married life for such a thing to occur, she made a confession.

"I must tell you a little secret. We have been married for some time; it was kept quiet for certain reasons of his own. The truth is, Lord Wraysbury, he is tired of me. I feel I can stand it no longer. I have made up my mind to leave him. I'm sure you can't blame me."

143

This was evidently the subject on which she had wanted his advice, and still unsuspicious, the young man answered her question.

"But after all, Mrs. Edwards, I am not the person to whom you should come for advice," he had told her. "You are not without friends, who would not feel the responsibility as I should. There is your mother, your uncle, this man Stormont, who has the same regard for you that he would have for his own niece. Have you spoken to them, or if you have not, would it not be wise to do so, before taking such a serious step?"

She had answered him with a profusion of tears that her mother was a woman of weak character, who would make any sacrifice for the sake of peace. She would advise her to bear her burden with as much fortitude as she could. Both Glenthorne and Stormont would oppose her. They were very worldly men; they would point out to her the folly of forfeiting the advantages which her position as the wife of a rich man gave her; they would remind her of the equivocal status of an unattached woman who was neither maid, wife nor widow.

Suddenly she burst into a fit of passionate weeping, drew her chair close to his and laid her hand upon his arm. "Oh, please befriend me," she wailed. "The others will give me advice that will suit themselves. Be my friend. Tell me what to do."

And at this moment, the most compromising one in their interview, the door opened, and Edwards walked into the room. Not the smiling, genial man he had known up to the present, but another person altogether, his eyes glaring, his face contorted with fury. He thundered at the weeping woman to go to her room and leave him alone to deal with her lover.

He turned to the discomfited young nobleman and spoke with an angry snarl in his voice when she had obeyed his order.

"And what have you to say, my lord, in explanation of this vile outrage upon an unsuspecting man?"

Wraysbury made the best defence he could, a perfectly truthful one. He had come there in answer to a note from his wife, asking him to call upon her in reference to a subject on which she wanted advice.

Edwards listened in stony silence. His fury had died down, but his voice had an inflection of cutting sarcasm when he replied:

"Do you believe such a story would take in a child? You must think me a simpleton to credit it. I had not intended to return for another week, but the sudden illness of a friend caused me to change my plans," he said. "I came home, as I imagined, to the society of a faithful wife. After I had put my key into the door, I noticed an unnatural stillness in the house. I go down into the lower regions; there is not a servant left in the place—they have been got out of the way by some cunning means. I go up the stairs to the drawing-room. As I ascend I hear the sound of voices—presently that of a woman sobbing. I open the door and see her with her hand upon your arm. What conclusion am I to draw from that? You have stolen her in my absence, and the servants have been got out of the way. You can show me twenty letters; they are a part of the game to try and avert suspicion in the remote event of discovery."

Wraysbury was nonplussed. To any husband the situation might have borne the interpretation he put upon it.

Edwards spoke again in a peremptory voice. "Leave this house, Lord Wraysbury, at once; your presence has polluted it too long. But don't think for a moment that, because you occupy a high position in the world, and I am in your eyes a mere nobody, that you are going to go scot-free. Neither shall this worthless woman whom you have dazzled with your fine manners and your great fortune. Before long you will hear from my solicitors."

Wraysbury knew that argument was useless. He left Curzon Street feeling bitterly humiliated.

And as he walked along there dawned upon him the conviction that this was no unrehearsed scene to which he had been subjected, that there had been a cunning plot between husband and wife to entrap him. The woman's tears were simulated; her story of ill-treatment was a myth. That bruise she showed him had been purposely made to lend colour to her story.

Two days later a letter arrived from a firm of solicitors, stating that they were instructed by their client Mr. Edwards to bring an action for divorce, and requesting the name of a firm who would act for him in the matter.

He made an appointment with Mr. Shelford, but before the time arrived for him to keep it, he had a visit from Glenthorne, whose usually grave face looked graver than ever when he met Wraysbury.

CHAPTER TWENTY

"A VERY terrible affair, Lord Wraysbury," were his first remarks. "Very terrible for all parties concerned. Zillah has been to me; she is distracted. They had an awful scene after you went, and the same evening Edwards left the house. He raved that he would not spend another night under the same roof with her. Much as I deplore her conduct, I could not help pitying her."

Mr. Glenthorne seemed to make no secret of his belief in the guilt of the parties. "Of course, she swore to me that her husband had no ground for his suspicions, that unfortunately appearances were against her, that she was perfectly innocent. Well, any woman in her position would naturally say the same thing."

"Mrs. Edwards has simply told the truth," answered Wraysbury, speaking with the warmth he felt. "She is innocent, and so am I."

"Lord Wraysbury, you will understand that I should espouse my niece's cause if I felt I had a leg to stand upon," said the usually taciturn man. "In that case, I would go to her husband and force him to hear reason. But how can I, in the face of such strong circumstantial evidence? How would it appear to you, if I told you the same story of somebody else? Her husband away, as she was quite sure, the servants packed off to the theatre, she alone in the house! What would a jury say?"

It was on the tip of the young man's tongue to answer that he was convinced that it was an elaborate plot, engineered by one or both and carried out with scrupulous regard to detail. But he could not say this very well to the woman's uncle, at any rate till he had received capable advice. He took refuge in silence, till suddenly what he considered a bright idea struck him. It was his general rule to destroy all correspondence that he considered of little importance, and at the time he had certainly classed Mrs. Edwards' letter under that category. But by the merest accident he had preserved it, and he showed it to his visitor with the observation, "If that doesn't prove to you my visit was an innocent one, nothing will."

The grave-faced man read it with the closest attention, and in due course handed it back. "This cuts both ways, my lord. You probably are not possessed of what we call the legal mind. I am, being in the profession of the law myself, I am a solicitor. If I were acting as your counsel, I should urge this as an almost convincing proof of your innocence. But how would the counsel on the other side argue? He would say that letter was written with a purpose, as the result of an agreement between both parties, the purpose being to avert suspicion if, by an unforeseen accident, you were discovered together. He would also say that if the visit were a perfectly innocent one, there would be no necessity to get the servants out of the way. Mind you, I am endeavouring to show you what would present itself to the legal mind. It would give me the greatest pleasure to prove Edwards in the wrong, but I fear that letter won't help me."

It might be a mere coincidence, but he was using just the same argument that the husband had employed. Having once allowed the suspicious side of his nature to develop itself, Wraysbury suspected this grave-faced man.

"What is the object of this visit, Mr. Glenthorne?" he asked sharply.

"My deep concern for my niece's welfare," was the reply. "It is an awful thing to contemplate a beautiful young woman's career being blasted almost before it has begun, as it must be if this affair comes into court."

"Had you not better show that letter to Edwards, and point out to him the consequences of the step he is taking?"

Mr. Glenthorne spoke, Wraysbury thought, in a less assured tone.

"Unfortunately Edwards is a very obstinate man, a very vindictive one. The only thing one could appeal to, perhaps, would be his cupidity. He is very fond of money for its own sake, not because he hasn't plenty of his own."

Wraysbury repressed a smile. Sharpened by his experience of recent events, he divined that this solemn-faced, not very prepossessing person had come as an emissary. Realizing the delicacy of his mission, he experienced some embarrassment in coming to the point. He was now evidently on the road to it.

"Will you speak a little more plainly, sir? I am not a very subtle person myself. Will you tell me what is in your mind?"

And Glenthorne told him. "If this matter comes into court, Lord Wraysbury, it will not only ruin my niece for life, it will be a very serious thing for you, it will damage you greatly, and cause terrible grief to your most worthy parents. I think it is worth a considerable sacrifice, even from your own point of view, to prevent it reaching that stage."

The man was showing his hand very plainly now. Wraysbury, with a face as grave as his own, led him on. "In plain English, you suggest this injured husband, as he pretends to be, can be bought off?"

Glenthorne lowered his voice. "Between ourselves, my lord, I believe it might be possible. As I have told you, he is a very greedy man; I believe greed to be the predominant feature in his character. He will, of course, go for heavy damages, and, with your well-known wealth, he is likely to obtain them. I think it possible that, if you anticipated those damages, as it were, made him a firm offer, he might withdraw from the action. Of course, I cannot speak positively, but I think it would be worth trying."

"I could say nothing on that point until I had consulted with my own solicitors, Shelford & Taylor. You will understand that."

"Quite," agreed Glenthorne. "Shelford & Taylor, a most respectable firm, their reputation is second to none. But, although I have the highest respect for my profession, may I suggest that, in certain cases, lawyers are not always the best judges? I think in the present instance the advice of a man of the world would be more helpful to you. Of course, for all I know to the contrary, this firm may be men of the world as well as solicitors. In that case I have very little doubt as to how they would advise you."

"You think they would advise me to pay hush-money to this person. And do you happen to know at what price he values his fancied wrongs?" asked Wraysbury in a sarcastic tone. The reply confirmed his conviction that Glenthorne was in the plot as well, and had come for the purpose of sounding him.

"I can give you some indication, I think. When my niece told me the painful story, I felt it incumbent on me to do something, to use my best endeavours to avert the impending catastrophe. Edwards is staying at the *Cecil*, that was the address he sent to me the day after he had left Curzon Street. I did not call upon him at once; I thought it wiser to give him time for his anger to cool down. I used all the arguments I could think of to dissuade him from the drastic course he had resolved upon. I met with a very stubborn resistance, as I expected. But my impression when I left was that he would abandon the idea of a divorce, if a sufficient sum were offered him. In that case he would never live with his wife again, but settle upon her a quite decent income."

"And what is his idea of a sufficient sum?" queried Wraysbury.

"I am sorry to say a very high one. For my own part, I thought an amount round about fifty thousand would meet the case. He laughed at me, and said he wouldn't move for twice that. If two hundred thousand were offered, he would probably consider it, nothing less."

At this point in the interview, Wraysbury rose, controlling his indignation with a great effort. "In an hour I am going to see Shelford, and shall tell him what has passed between us."

Mr. Glenthorne took the hint and prepared to depart. "If the suit goes on, I shall act for my niece, and all communications as regards Edwards and yourself will be conducted by your own firms. But if you entertain the idea of the course I have suggested, it might be as well to deal through me. Edwards is a touchy fellow, and requires a good deal of handling. Here is my card."

Wraysbury afterwards saw Shelford. When the whole details were explained to him, including the tentative suggestion of Glenthorne, whose name as a practising solicitor was unknown to him, he at once agreed that it was a put-up job, out of which this shady practitioner was to have his bit. They talked for a long time, and then the idea of Grewgus occurred to Shelford. These people most probably belonged to the underworld of which the detective had a considerable knowledge. He advised him to see Grewgus at once, and fixed up the appointment.

"So now you have the whole story," said the unfortunate young nobleman when he came to the end of it. "Two alternatives face me, and only two; either I must pay this big sum to this infamous set of swindlers, or suffer my name to be dragged through the mire."

"Which course does Shelford advise?" asked the detective.

"He is almost as undecided as myself. I don't pretend that the two hundred thousand would break me; they know that as well as I do. But it is unspeakably humiliating to pay such a big sum for what was not even an act of folly, rather an absence of discretion. On the other hand, if the action goes on——"

The young man paused a moment to conquer his emotion. "You see, Mr. Grewgus, I have a very vulnerable place and these thieves know it. I am the only child of my parents, God-fearing, devout souls who have lived lives unspotted from the world. If I alone were concerned, conscious of my innocence, I would brave the shame and scandal of it. But it would break their hearts. They would believe me, because they know my good points as well as my bad ones, but they would know half our world wouldn't share their belief, and they would never hold up their heads again."

And then Grewgus spoke. He had great sympathy with this manly young fellow; he had heard his voice tremble when he spoke of his mother and father. Thoughtless and careless perhaps, like many young men of his age, but a loyal and affectionate son.

"I don't want to send you away from this office in a too optimistic frame of mind; I cannot absolutely promise to get you out of the clutch of these cunning blackmailers, but I'm going to have a devilish good try. It is a most fortunate thing that Shelford has sent you to me, instead of to one of my confrères, for it happens that through my investigations on behalf of another client I know a great deal about all these people which they would be very sorry to have come to light. I think—mind you, I cannot be sure—that what I know will be sufficient to deter them from going any further. Leave it to me. I will arrange with Shelford to allow me to act upon your behalf. When I have got that formal permission, I will see this man Edwards, and throw my bombshell into his camp."

Lord Wraysbury was delighted with the turn of events. "But this is simply wonderful," he cried. "Do you know something of every one of them?"

Grewgus was delighted too, to such an extent that he relaxed his habitual reticence. "Not so much about Edwards, except one very damaging thing, but a good deal about Stormont, Mrs. Edwards, even the smooth-tongued Glenthorne, who, of course, paid you that visit in the interests of his pals. Well, good day, Lord Wraysbury. I shall lose no time, I assure you. I expect to fire my bombshell to-morrow, and after the interview I shall at once let you know what I expect the result will be."

The young nobleman departed in much better spirits than he had entered. Being a very generous fellow, he resolved that if Grewgus did extricate him from his unpleasant position, he should receive a fee that would astonish him.

Having conferred with Mr. Shelford over the 'phone, the detective sent a note to the *Hotel Cecil* addressed to Edwards, in which he told that person he was acting on behalf of Lord Wraysbury in a certain matter and begged the favour of an appointment.

The boy who took the letter was to wait for an answer, if Edwards was in. He returned with it.

> "Dear Sir," wrote the *débonnaire* person who belonged to so many respectable clubs,—"In reply to yours, I beg to say that I shall be at your disposal any time between eleven and twelve to-morrow. Yours faithfully, BERTRAM EDWARDS."

The detective smiled grimly as he wondered if this elegant crook had any idea of what was in store for him. Hardly. He probably conjectured that the detective was paying him a visit for the purpose of beating him down.

Before he went to the *Cecil*, he paid a flying visit to Lydon at his office and told him what had passed between himself and Wraysbury on the previous day. He had no hesitation in doing this, as it had been agreed that he should watch what was going on at Curzon Street on Lydon's behalf.

It was, of course, what they had expected from the day when the young nobleman had attended Mrs. Edwards' reception.

"I'm glad we have got confirmation," remarked the detective. "But I do wish we could have directly implicated Stormont in it, that he had, for instance, taken the rôle in it played by Glenthorne, alias Whitehouse."

"We can guess he was at the back of it anyhow," continued Grewgus. "Rather amusing his being at that first dinner. I expect he couldn't resist the pleasure of hobnobbing with such a distinguished person as Wraysbury. But I think we have got enough against Stormont now, with the help of our venal friend Newcombe. He has kept himself pretty well in the background in this affair, but we have sufficient proof that he is the friend of blackmailers. And a man is known by the company he keeps."

"Quite true. Well, now that I know this, I shall tell Jasper Stormont at the earliest opportunity. I am staying with him at Brighton. I haven't told you before, but I may as well tell you now, I am engaged to Jasper's daughter. He is a bank official in China and she has been living with her uncle since she was a child. She is now with her parents at Brighton, and she must never return to the criminal atmosphere of Effington."

Grewgus had learned the fact of the engagement from Newcombe, but he affected to hear it for the first time. He fully concurred in the young man's determination that she should not return to Effington.

Later on, he was shown into a private sitting-room where he found Mr. Bertram Edwards, looking as smart and gentlemanly as ever. He could not help thinking that this elegant young crook, with his charming manners, must be a great asset to the gang. If he did not move in the most select circles like Wraysbury, it was evident, from what Lydon had told him of the Curzon Street party, that he had a foothold in quite respectable society.

"You have come about this wretched Wraysbury matter, I understand?" he said in his pleasant, urbane tones.

The detective intimated that this was the object of his visit.

"And have you anything to propose, Mr. Grewgus?"

"My client, Lord Wraysbury, has received a sort of unofficial intimation from a man named Glenthorne, who claims to be the lady's uncle, that if the sum of two hundred thousand pounds is paid to you, you will abandon proceedings. I beg to tell you, Mr. Edwards, I shall advise his lordship not to pay you a single farthing."

Edwards tried to assume an expression of indifference, but it was easy to see he was taken aback by this blunt declaration.

"In that case, sir, the action will proceed, and I shall go for heavy damages. I am not going to permit a young sprig of the nobility to violate the sanctity of my home, without making him smart for it in the only place where he can feel it—in his pocket."

Grewgus bent upon the dandified man his very penetrating and expressive glance. "This is a business interview, Mr. Edwards, and there is no necessity for heroics. You know as well as I do that Lord Wraysbury is quite innocent of any desire to violate the sanctity of your home, or, for the matter of that, the home of anybody. He's not that sort of man. Let me warn you that if you do proceed with this action, it is at your own peril and that of the lady who bears your name."

"My own peril! What the devil do you mean?" blustered Edwards. But, in spite of his assumed bravado, Grewgus saw an unhealthy pallor creeping over his usually high-coloured cheek.

Again that penetrating gaze, that distinct and deliberate utterance: "I don't know very much about you at present, Mr. Edwards; I have no doubt I shall add something more to my knowledge shortly. One little thing I do know, that you were in Paris a short time before the discovery of the dead body of Léon Calliard in the river Meuse. And that every day you were meeting the woman who is now Mrs. Edwards in the outskirts of the city."

He paused, expecting a bold-faced disclaimer. But it did not come. For the moment, the man was stricken dumb.

"Of the woman now calling herself your wife, I know a great deal more, under her different names of Elise Makris, Zillah Mayhew, Miss Glenthorne. I also know a fair amount about your friend Stormont. And the same applies to another friend of yours, Glenthorne, otherwise John Whitehouse. Have I said enough?"

Still there was no reply; the man could not find speech, and he had aged in those few seconds.

"Please understand me once and for all. If, in a reckless moment, you persist in this baseless charge against my client and your wife, who is your accomplice in the matter, I go to Scotland Yard and give my information, which, as I have told you, is rather extensive."

Edwards rose to his feet and pointed with a shaking hand to the door.

"Leave the room, you wretched spy. Tell your client the action will proceed," he shouted with a last attempt at bravado.

Grewgus laughed derisively, and flung at him a Parthian shot as he left.

"Don't forget when you reckon up the pros and cons that the Paris police are still investigating the case of Léon Calliard, the murdered jeweller."

As he walked along the Strand, Grewgus felt very satisfied with himself. In spite of Edwards' bluff, he felt sure that he had won the day.

And presently a man brushed past him as he was within a few yards of Charing Cross Station, walking at a rapid pace; it was the man he had just left.

As he hastily crossed the road at Villiers Street, Grewgus had a sudden idea that he was going to the telegraph office to dispatch a wire. He could have sent it from the *Cecil*, of course, but no doubt he had good reasons for not doing so.

Grewgus was a past-master in the art of shadowing. Behind the hurrying man came the tall, thin form of the detective. And over his shoulder, as he wrote the message, Grewgus read the words: "Stormont, Effington, Surrey. It must be dropped. See me to-morrow without fail—EDWARDS."

After reading it, Grewgus crept stealthily away, and was in the street again, while Edwards, unconscious that he had been watched, was presenting the telegram at the counter.

Circumstantial evidence, it is true, but of the very strongest character. What did that wire mean? One thing, and one thing only. Edwards had been so thoroughly frightened that he was afraid to go on with the Wraysbury affair, had advised his friend Stormont of the necessity of dropping it, and urged him to see him to-morrow to tell him what had happened. It was convincing proof that Stormont was in the plot.

CHAPTER TWENTY-ONE

It was a couple of days before Lydon found an opportunity of breaking to Jasper Stormont the painful news about his brother. In the meantime he had received from Grewgus an account of the interview at the *Cecil*, and the dispatch of the telegram to Effington.

On his return to Brighton in the late afternoon, he was fortunate enough to find his future father-in-law sitting alone in the lounge; Gloria and her mother were out shopping.

There was a somewhat worried expression on the banker's face. "Had a letter from Howard by the last post in," he explained. "It looks to me as if he were within measurable distance of the end we have foreseen and predicted. He writes that the big *coup* on which he was engaged has unexpectedly fallen through, and this places him in a most awkward predicament for the immediate future. He has made up his mind that he must give up Effington, reluctant as he is to part from a place to which he has become so attached. He adds, what I suppose we both suspected, that it is heavily mortgaged, and that when a sale is effected, there will be very little left for him. He has already apprised my sister of the alteration in his fortunes, and begs me to break it gently to Gloria. Somewhat to my surprise, he has made no request for money. I suppose he finds the future so dark, that any little help I could give him would be useless, and that he must make a drastic change in his mode of life. I must own candidly, my sympathy would be keener if his own insensate folly were not the cause of the disaster."

Here was a splendid opportunity, thought Lydon. The big *coup* on which Stormont was engaged, which was to repair his tottering fortunes, had failed to come off. It was easy to guess what the *coup* was—the extraction of that immense sum of money from young Wraysbury. The abandonment of the prospect which had been nipped in the bud by the visit of Grewgus to the *Hotel Cecil* had brought him to the ground.

"There is something I have to say to you about your brother, Mr. Stormont, something which I am sure will give you the greatest pain, but which it is right you should hear. But this is too public a place, and the ladies may return at any minute. Do you mind coming up to my room?"

Wondering and uneasy, the banker went with him upstairs. When they were seated, the young man told him all the details with which the reader is acquainted. Jasper Stormont listened with a set and rigid face, as Lydon explained to him how his suspicions had first taken definite shape on the arrival on the scene of Zillah Mayhew, whom he had at once associated, from the two facts of the scar and the sapphire pendant, with Elise Makris; of his engagement of Grewgus to follow up the clues and the various discoveries of that zealous detective, down to the latest episode in connection with Wraysbury, and the despatch of the wire from Edwards to Howard Stormont, which clearly involved the owner of Effington Hall in the dastardly plot.

"If I have not explained it as lucidly as I might have done," were the concluding words of the long recital, "I can take you to Grewgus, if you wish it, and he will, I am sure, give you a much more coherent account than I have been able to do."

Jasper Stormont lifted his haggard face: "There is no necessity, Leonard. You would not say these things if they were not true, and I can quite understand how, even before the advent of this woman, Howard's unnatural reticence about his business affairs had created in you a feeling of uneasiness. I had that same feeling myself."

Lydon drew a deep breath: "Ah, the same thing struck you, then?"

"Yes, I was suspicious, but very far from guessing the ghastly truth. I came to the conclusion that my brother had spoken truly when he said he was a financier, but he was not engaged in the highest walks of his profession. I guessed he was concerned with enterprises which men of strict integrity would describe as shady, but that in pursuing them he kept well within the compass of the law. That he bore to a financier of high repute much the same sort of relation that a blood-sucking moneylender bears to a reputable banker."

There was a long pause before Jasper Stormont spoke again. "And now I must tell you something that would never have passed my lips but for what you have told me, and which proves that moral turpitude was engrained in the man from his early years. You know that he went to Australia? Do you know why he went?"

Yes, Lydon did. He had refrained from telling Jasper a certain portion of the revelations made by the Colonial, Tom Newcombe, from a feeling of delicacy. His reply was that he knew he had got into some trouble about money, but was not aware of the precise nature of it.

"Well, I will tell you. My father, who, although poorly blessed with the world's goods, was a man of the strictest rectitude, and highly respected by all who knew him, procured him a post in a most respectable firm where, unfortunately, he had the handling of money. You can guess the sequel. To gratify his always extravagant tastes, of which Effington Hall is an illustration, he diverted several sums to his own use, displaying in their appropriation a remarkable ingenuity and cunning. When his defalcations came to light, the firm sent for my father. But for the respect in which they held him they would have prosecuted his son. My father and I between us—I had not very much money then—paid back the sum abstracted. We saved him from prosecution, on the condition that he should go out to Australia."

"Did Mrs. Barnard know of this?" asked Lydon. He had never yet been able to make up his mind whether this self-contained, rather silent woman knew anything of her brother's actual pursuits. Jasper Stormont's next words solved the problem.

"Not a word. She had been recently married, and lived with her husband at a considerable distance. It was easy to keep the affair from her. I may say, in passing, that she is as honest as Howard is the reverse.

"He went to Australia, keeping up a fairly regular correspondence with his father, in which he made out that he had seen the wickedness of his ways, and was in honest employment. Of course, at that distance, we had no means of testing his assertions. He and I had never been particularly good friends, and his proved dishonesty had snapped the frail bond between us. We never wrote to each other for years.

"And then one day the long silence was broken. I married and went out to China, where I had secured a good post. Our parents had died before he returned to England. The little money my father had accumulated out of a continuous struggle with fortune was left to my sister, as being most in need of it. One day I received a long letter from Howard in which he told me that, having made a little money in Australia, he had determined to come back to the old country, and see what he could do with the small capital he had saved. He had gone in for finance, of course in a very modest way, and he had no reason to complain of his success.

"It is perhaps not greatly to my credit when I tell you that I am very hard against evil-doers, offenders against the moral law. I had not forgiven that early transgression, and I would have preferred not to renew relations with my brother. But I reflected that such sentiments were unchristian, and if the man was now walking in the straight path, it was not for me to withhold the hand of fellowship. I answered the letter, and from that day we corresponded more or less regularly.

"As that correspondence proceeded, it was apparent that he was prospering greatly. I was not surprised at that, for he had plenty of brains, and if he chose to employ them in a right direction, I saw no reason why he should not succeed. Mrs. Barnard's husband had died, leaving her a small annuity which, joined to what my father had bequeathed her, formed a modest competence. Howard had pressed her to make her home with him, as he was a bachelor. He would not accept a penny from her towards the housekeeping; her own small income she was to look upon as pin-money."

At this point in the history of his renewed relations with his brother, Jasper Stormont confessed that Howard's generous treatment of his sister had strongly impressed him in his favour. It was more than probable that that early lesson had sunk into his soul, and he had really undergone a process of complete moral regeneration.

And then had come the request to adopt Gloria, and make her welfare one of the principal objects of his life. That further established him in the good graces of a brother who was disposed to be critical. Criminal as he had been, there were some good instincts in him, and these he had displayed to the full in the case of these two members of his family.

"It will be a terrible shock to Gloria when she is told, as told she must be," said the banker. "She is a shrewd girl and you can see she has a sort of pitying contempt for some of his weaknesses, his extravagance, his vulgar love of ostentation. But she realizes he has shown unexampled kindness to her; if she could be spoiled, he has done his best to spoil her. I wish I could spare her sensitive nature the shock, but that cannot be. She must never go back to that man's roof. So far as my influence goes, she must hold no further communication with him. The money he has spent on her during these several years I shall refund to him. As I doubt if he will be in a position to dictate terms, I may make it a condition that he shall cut away from his evil associates. Heaven knows if he would keep such a promise. I fear the spirit of evil is too strong in his crooked nature."

For some little time the banker sat in agitated meditation. Then he suddenly roused himself from his painful thoughts and spoke again. "I feel as if my own small world had tumbled about my ears, Leonard; you will understand that. There is one thing we have got to face first and foremost as a consequence of this hideous discovery. Gloria cannot become your wife."

The young man looked at him in astonishment. "But, my dear Mr. Stormont, in the name of justice, why? Do you think me such a cur as to visit the crimes of her relative upon a pure and innocent girl? Gloria has promised herself to me. Depend upon it I shall exact that promise."

But Jasper Stormont could be a very obstinate man when he chose, and he held very rigid views of what was right and what was wrong. "No child of mine shall carry her tainted name into an honourable family," he said firmly. "And you cannot get away from it that he has communicated a taint to the whole of his kindred. Besides, how do we know what is going to be the end of it? How can we be sure that, long as he has succeeded in evading justice, it will not overtake him one of these fine days. Even if I could succeed in persuading him to lead an honest life for the future, how can we guarantee the past? You say the Paris police have not yet given up their researches into the mystery of the jeweller's death. At any moment something may come to light in that direction. No, my dear boy, I appreciate your no-

bility of choice, but Gloria must give you your freedom. If she is her father's daughter, I think she will take the same view as I do."

Lydon was not so sure. In his own mind, he thought that love would pre-
vail. For a long time they wrangled over the point, the decision being finally reached that Gloria should act exactly as her feelings prompted her.
Her father would state his views, but he would not use his influence over
her to adopt them.

It was natural they should still talk further over the subject, painful as the
discussion was to both.

"That *coup* he pretended to be the outcome of some financial speculation
was clearly the mulcting of this young simpleton of that tremendous sum,"
remarked the banker presently. "The fact that it had fallen through as soon
as he received that telegram from his accomplice proves that. And yet I do
not see, if it had come off, that it would have made his position as sure as
he told me. I do not know in what proportion these miscreants divide their
villainous gains. There were certainly four of them in it, Howard, his friend
Whitehouse, and the husband and wife, to say nothing of the gang who I
suppose have an over-riding percentage on everything. Even if Howard got
a quarter of the amount, the interest on that would not keep a place like Effington Hall going."

Lydon smiled ironically. "Would a man of your brother's temperament
bother about such things as investments and interest? If he received that
sum, he would simply draw on it as long as it lasted, trusting to further luck
to replenish his waning store."

"Horrible idea," said the banker with a shudder. "But I think you have
seen more clearly than I did, Leonard. To me, the idea of a man living on
his capital is unthinkable. Well, I shall make these awful disclosures to Gloria after dinner; she shall have a little more peace, poor child. And, later on,
you and she shall have a heart-to-heart talk."

That talk took place later on in the evening, when the young couple went
for a stroll. At first Gloria, tearful and agitated, took her father's view. It
was impossible she could intrude herself into his life, with such a ghastly
secret in the background, a secret that in all probability could not be kept
indefinitely in the background. It would break her heart to part with him,
but, for his own sake, she must insist upon giving him back his freedom. If
he was angry with her now, he would be grateful in the future. So she
pleaded amidst her plentiful tears.

But by degrees he wore down her resolution, dictated by the judgment,
not the heart. If Howard Stormont's past should ever be revealed to an astonished world, he would help her with all his might to live the hateful
thing down. When they returned to the hotel, he had proved the victor, and

announced the result to Jasper, who, loyal to his promise, acquiesced, if he found it impossible to approve.

"I shall come up to London in the morning with you," he said to the young man, "and ascertain on the 'phone what are Howard's movements. I should say that, as his *coup* has failed, he will be bewailing his ill-fortune at Effington. He will hardly have the heart to resume his usual habits for a few days."

And so it proved. Mrs. Barnard, who answered the 'phone call, explained that her brother was rather out of sorts, and Jasper would find him at Effington at almost any hour of the day. If he went out, it would only be for a stroll in the grounds or to the village.

Jasper Stormont went down after luncheon; he had not committed himself to any particular time. To one thing he had firmly made up his mind; he would not take another meal at Effington Hall, in the society of the man he had the misfortune to call brother. He took a taxi at the station and drove in due course through the big gates of the stately mansion, which he devoutly hoped he was entering for the last time.

The owner was out, the new butler informed him, but was expected back shortly. Mrs. Barnard was in.

She was pleased to see her brother. "But why couldn't you come to luncheon?" she asked him. "Surely you are going to dine and stop the night?"

She had received him in her own little boudoir, in which she wrote so many letters. "This may be the last time I shall see you here," she remarked, not without symptoms of emotion. "Howard told me he had written to you about his misfortunes. For a long time I have feared this would be the end of his reckless extravagance. Well, it has come, and the only thing to do is to face it as well as one can. Thank Heaven, it won't affect dear Gloria very much personally, but I am sure she is terribly grieved for us."

Jasper Stormont was a lovable enough man in many ways, but the sight of Effington, with its pretence of wealth, had made him feel very hard. Still, he could not show hardness to this poor woman who had lived for so long in a fool's paradise.

"She feels intense pity for *you*," he said, laying a strong emphasis on the pronoun.

Mrs. Barnard looked wonderingly at him, and a flush dyed her face. "What does that mean? Has she no pity for poor Howard, who gratified her every whim, and spoiled her from the day she entered the house? I will not believe it of her. He has been weak, but not criminal, Jasper."

And then Jasper raised his voice in righteous wrath. "My poor sister, you little knew, I have only known for the last few hours, that this brother of

159

ours has been leading a double life. He is one of the biggest criminals that ever walked the face of the earth."

Mrs. Barnard's face froze into a look of horror. If any other man had spoken those awful words, she would have told him he lied. But she knew Jasper's character too well. He would not have made such a charge if it were not true.

As briefly as possible he told her what he knew, through that chance opening of the letter to Zillah Mayhew by Lydon. The unhappy woman burst into a passionate fit of weeping.

"Jasper, you must take me away with you when you leave," she said when she had recovered herself a little. "I could not stay another night under the roof after what you have told me. The associate of thieves, blackmailers, a potential murderer himself. It is like some hideous nightmare."

And at that moment Howard Stormont walked into the room, with a smile of welcome on his harassed countenance. Perhaps he thought his brother had come to help him in his financial difficulties.

But as he took in the scene, the still weeping woman, Jasper standing beside her with a hard and inflexible look upon his face, he knew that the visit portended nothing of the kind.

He looked from one to the other and his own face grew paler as he noted his sister's averted countenance.

"What the devil does all this mean? And you, Jasper, why do you refuse to take my hand?" he cried in a harsh voice that showed traces of fear.

At a sign from her brother, Mrs. Barnard withdrew, and the two men were left alone—Jasper stern, rigid; Howard with terrible forebodings in his guilty soul.

CHAPTER TWENTY-TWO

HOWARD was the first to break the strained silence; he spoke in a toneless voice. "I Suppose you will presently tell me what all this means, the reason of this extraordinary attitude. I suppose you have been talking over the state of affairs with Maud, and are angry with me for having made such a muddle of things. You will stay to dinner, of course?"

Swiftly came the reply: "If I would not take your hand, is it likely I would accept your hospitality? I hope never to see you, nor set foot in this house of evil, again. Howard Stormont, I know you for what you are; I know the double life you have been leading since you left England and since you returned to it. I know you to be the associate of criminals, yourself not the least criminal amongst them."

The face of the detected crook went livid: "We can't talk here," he said hoarsely. "Come down to my room and let us have it out."

They went into the handsomely furnished study. As soon as they got there, he opened the door of a small sideboard, from which he extracted a bottle of uncorked brandy. He filled a tumbler half full of the raw spirit and gulped it down. For the moment, the potent draught steadied his nerves, and he sank into a chair, and looked with a certain amount of hardihood at his brother.

"Now let me hear what you do know, or think you know." He had made no attempt to repel Jasper's charge. He knew the man's cautious character too well to think he would speak as he had done, except on evidence that was satisfactory and convincing.

"I know of your association with the woman known at present as Mrs. Edwards, who has gone under the different names of Elise Makris, Zillah Mayhew, Zillah Glenthorne, the woman who was connected with the tragedy at Nice in which poor Hugh Craig figured, the woman you dispatched to Paris along with the man Edwards to carry out your designs against the rich jeweller Calliard, who was robbed and murdered."

Howard Stormont interrupted in a choking voice. He knew it was useless to protest innocence. "Murder was never intended. The fool who carried out the job exceeded his instructions."

"Do you think I should believe a word you said?" was Jasper's scornful comment. "Lying, even perjury, would be a venial offence in the eyes of one so steeped in crime. But even if the murder of Calliard cannot be laid directly at your door, what have you to say to your own attempt on the life of your old Australian associate, Newcombe, the man whom you feared for his knowledge of your past?"

"I made no attempt upon his life," was the dogged reply. "I only wanted to give the drunken fool a fright."

"A miserable lie," said Jasper sternly. "You miscalculated the dose of your devilish poison, or the man would be dead now. For some days he hung between life and death. And I also know that you were concerned in this last dastardly attempt to extort money from young Wraysbury, with the help of the two confederates who had carried out your schemes in Paris."

Stormont rose and helped himself to another dose of brandy. "And how did you find all this out?" he asked presently.

"That is my business," was the curt answer.

It was some time before the wretched man spoke again. "I think I can guess how the information came. That young Lydon had his suspicions from the day he met Zillah here, and put a detective on our track. My sister told me she had given him some letters to post which I had forgotten to take with me; one of them was to her. He opened it and what he read gave him the clue, and he set this fellow Grewgus to work. But what beats me is how he suspected Zillah; he had never seen her. When he and Craig were at Nice, she took good care to keep out of his way."

Jasper did not enlighten his brother on this point, and presently Howard put to him, point-blank, the question: "And now that you know all this, what are you and this precious young Lydon going to do? Do you intend to play the part of virtuous citizens and denounce me to the police?"

"We ought to do it, if we performed our duty," said Jasper coldly. "But I have a proposition to make to you. Your letter shows me that you are broke to the world. Your interview with your confederate Edwards, after Grewgus had foiled his plot against Wraysbury, must have convinced you that a continuance of this criminal life is fraught with peril; that at any moment Nemesis may overtake you."

Stormont looked up sharply, "How did you know that I had an interview with Edwards?" he asked, in evident surprise.

But Jasper declined to enlighten him. "Again I repeat, that is my business. This precious young Lydon, as you call him, has behaved like the honourable Englishman he is. I told him emphatically that he must give up Gloria, that he must not connect himself with a family that had this black stain upon its records. Gloria took the same view, and insisted upon releasing him, although she told me that to do so would break her heart."

For the first time in their interview, the hardened criminal showed an overwhelming sense of shame. "Poor Gloria!" he muttered in a broken voice. "Poor Gloria! It is indeed hard upon her. And Lydon would not accept his dismissal. Well, I will admit he is a noble fellow."

"I am glad you do him that justice. Well, my proposition is this. It is horrible to me to think that my innocent and unsuspecting child has lived all these years upon the proceeds of infamy. The money you have expended upon her for something like fourteen years I will restore to you on the condition that you abandon this life, and break away for ever from your criminal associates. Even then, there is not absolute safety. At any moment the past may yield up its secrets, and all the world may know you for what you are."

Howard Stormont kept silence. His active brain was no doubt weighing the advantages and disadvantages of his brother's suggestion.

"As I shall be very liberal in my estimate of what she cost you," continued Jasper; "you could exist upon the interest of the capital sum I should hand over to you. But you are not without brains, and you might use that money to embark in some honest business."

"It is a very generous offer," Howard said at length. "And I am very disposed to accept It without further reflection. Still, I would like to go into matters a little closer first. I admit your visit here to-day has taken the courage out of me. You will laugh at me, I suppose, and consider it a further proof of my hypocrisy when I say that I would prefer not to live upon your bounty. But I should like to reckon up what I am likely to get out of the sale of Effington, when the mortgages have been paid off."

"It is not a question of bounty; it is an act of reparation to my own conscience," said Jasper hastily. "I would prefer to return the money to its rightful owners, if I could find them. But that is impossible. If you refuse to accept this sum, I shall devote it to charity, so as to make some sort of amends."

"Give me till to-morrow, and I will let you know definitely. I presume you have told Maud?"

"Certainly," answered Jasper. "She is as much horrified as I was when I learned the horrible truth. She is coming back with me."

A ghastly smile spread over Stormont's white face. "It is what one might expect. Rats always leave the sinking ship, don't they?"

Jasper made no reply to this cynical remark, which showed the naturally hard and callous nature of the man. He moved towards the door with a few last words. "I must have your decision not later than the time you have stated."

He went out into the hall and summoned a servant to find Mrs. Barnard and ask her to come to him in her boudoir. He had kept the taxi waiting. As soon as she was ready, they could quit this house of evil where the owner of it had plotted and thought out his criminal schemes.

163

She came to him ready dressed for her journey. She was taking with her a couple of small trunks; the rest of her belongings, which had all been bought with her own money, could be sent after her. Jasper explained that he was taking her down to Brighton, where she could make a long stay till she had made her plans for the future. Together they went down into the hall.

And suddenly, in a burst of womanly feeling, she whispered to her brother, "Vile as he is, I cannot leave him without a word."

She turned, and walking swiftly to the study, opened the door and entered. Howard was sitting huddled up in his chair, looking a ghastly object of misery and despair. She laid her hand lightly on his arm for an instant. "God forgive you, Howard, and turn your heart before it is too late."

His dry lips muttered a faint "Good-bye," and she turned from him and rejoined Jasper.

They got back to Brighton in the evening, and in the private sitting-room the banker explained to Lydon and his family what had passed between the two men in that final visit to Effington. Leonard was rejoiced that Mrs. Barnard had come back with her brother. He had never quite been able to make up his mind about her, whether or not she was in Howard's confidence; but her action showed that, like her niece, she had never guessed his guilty secret.

The next morning, Jasper Stormont, according to his usual custom, went for a stroll before breakfast, and on his return to the hotel found a telegram awaiting him. It was from the butler at Effington Hall and informed him that his brother had committed suicide early that morning. He had thought he would never set foot in Effington again, but in the face of such news he must go there at once.

When he reached the house, the butler gave him the details. On entering the study, one of the housemaids discovered her master lying dead in his easy-chair, a bottle of brandy standing beside his elbow, an empty pistol lying on the floor to which it had dropped after he had shot himself. He had been dead some few hours, the doctor said, when she had found him. At the time of his suicide, for the perpetration of which he had fortified himself with large doses of alcohol, the household was fast asleep, and nobody had heard the shot. Jasper could only conclude that the wretched man had come to the conclusion life was played out for him, and had nerved himself to make his exit from the world on which he had preyed for so long.

He had been careful to preserve appearances. He had written an open letter lying on the table in which he stated that utter financial ruin had come upon him, and that at his age he lacked the courage to begin the battle of life over again. He gave the address of his brother at Brighton, and requested that he should be communicated with at once.

There was a good deal of sympathy in the neighbourhood, where his benefactions and lavish hospitality had made him popular. The inquest was held in due course, and the usual compassionate verdict recorded. When Howard Stormont was laid to rest nobody guessed that the body of an arch-criminal was being committed to the earth. Jasper Stormont's visit was explained on the grounds that he had come to take his sister for a long stay at Brighton.

So the future was secure. A sum was offered for Effington Hall which, after payment of the various charges and debts, left over a balance of about a couple of thousand pounds. Stormont had left no will, and his property therefore devolved upon his next of kin. But as none of them would touch a farthing, Jasper made a donation of the money to a necessitous hospital.

It was a great relief to Jasper and his sister that he had solved the problem of the future in the way he had, before the old instincts came to life again and led him to the commission of further crime. But tender-hearted Gloria sometimes shed tears when she remembered the numerous acts of kindness to her, proving that even the basest of men can possess some good qualities.

Lord Wraysbury heard nothing further from Edwards' solicitors. Grewgus had settled that little matter, and for doing so he received a very handsome cheque from the grateful young nobleman. The house and furniture in Curzon Street were up for sale. Neither Edwards nor his wife was any longer in residence there. Grewgus chuckled as he thought this frustrated scheme must have cost the gang a pretty sum.

Glenthorne had also suddenly left Ashstead Mansions, and abandoned his solicitor's practice. That interview of Grewgus with Edwards and the suicide of Stormont seemed to have produced far-reaching consequences. Edwards had disappeared and was not heard of at any of his usual haunts, and the dark, handsome Zillah had vanished as suddenly as her uncle. It looked like a wholesale dispersal of that portion of the gang.

Lydon and Grewgus settled up accounts. The detective informed his client that the Paris police had given up the case of Léon Calliard, after following several delusive clues. There was now practically no chance that the details of the unfortunate man's murder would ever be known, unless he communicated the information he had acquired about Edwards and Zillah. Even then, it would be almost impossible to connect them with the affair.

But of course Lydon strongly discountenanced such a step. One could not take it without bringing Howard Stormont into the matter; it would also involve Jasper, who would have to testify that his brother had practically admitted his participation in it.

"Best to let sleeping dogs lie, for the sake of the family," said the young man. "If one did discover the actual murderer, it would not bring the unfortunate Calliard to life, and it would inflict the greatest pain upon innocent people."

Grewgus agreed, rather reluctantly. He had the true instincts of the sleuth-hound; he loved to hunt his quarry down. He would dearly have liked to go to Scotland Yard, but he was bound to respect his client's wishes on the subject. All the same, he felt it was a tame sort of inquiry which had not resulted in a triumphant finish. As a consequence of it, Stormont had been driven to suicide, and the other persons concerned had found it expedient to lie low for a while. But for him, there was no public kudos in it.

On the same day on which he squared up accounts with Lydon he came face to face in the Strand with his old friend Tom Newcombe. The gentleman's appearance had altered very much. He had discarded his beard and moustache, and a less keen eye than the detective's might have failed to recognize him. But Grewgus had a wonderful memory for faces, and it required a very clever disguise to baffle him. They exchanged greetings.

"Hardly knew me, did you?" inquired the Colonial. "You see, I clean-shaved myself directly after we had settled matters. I got out of that house as soon as I could, but I was mortally afraid I might run across Stormont, and he might get me into his clutches again. Well, it's all right now, he has passed in his checks. I can tell you it was a relief when I saw it in the papers. I thought, as I read it, that you might have had something to do with it."

"Perhaps I had, in a very indirect fashion," was the cautious answer.

"Well, he's gone to where he wanted to send me. Gad, that man did make me see red when I thought of his attempt to put me out of the way. Many a time I've half made up my mind to sneak down to Effington and plug him if I got the chance. But a bit of prudence stepped in, fortunately. It wasn't worth swinging for a fellow like that. And so he came to a bad end, after all. It makes one think a bit, mister, it does."

"It makes you think a bit, eh?" repeated the detective. "And what turn do your thoughts take? The wages of sin is death, or something of that sort?"

"You've hit it," said the Colonial, speaking with great seriousness. "I told you my mother was a good woman; she did her best to bring me up religious, but my father always scoffed at her for her pains. How many times have I heard her use that very phrase; it has always stuck in my memory. I thought of her a goodish bit when I was struggling back to life. I began to feel quite sick of the past, and all the evil I had done. But you know, mister, when you've once got into the crooked life, it's precious hard to get out of it. But now I've got that bit of money, I've made up my mind to go straight."

"I'm exceedingly glad to hear it," said Grewgus heartily.

"Most crooks come to a bad end. Stormont, who was clever and cunning as the devil, took his life at the finish, and most of 'em overreach themselves and get into quod. So I'm making a fresh start. Till I read that in the papers, I was going out to Canada, for fear of Stormont. But now he's out of the way, I shall stick in the old country. I shall buy a snug little business, a tobacconist's by preference. Gosh, it will be pleasant to pass a policeman without fearing he's going to lay his hand on you."

They chatted for a little time longer, and at parting Grewgus offered Newcombe his hand, which the Colonial shook heartily. Since he had now resolved to lead an honest life, the detective felt he was justified in showing him this mark of esteem.

He got back to his office about four o'clock and busied himself with his correspondence. In the midst of it, a clerk entered and said that a lady wished to speak with him for a few minutes, but would not give her name.

Rather impatiently, for he was very occupied with his letters, he ordered the visitor to be shown in.

What was his astonishment when the mysterious lady entered, and he recognized in the dark, handsome young woman who had refused to give her name, Elise Makris, otherwise Mrs. Edwards.

CHAPTER TWENTY-THREE

THE handsome young woman addressed the detective with the charm of manner that had no doubt beguiled so many men, notably Hugh Craig and the susceptible Léon Calliard.

"I take it from what you told my husband, Bertram Edwards, that you are acquainted with me—at any rate, my appearance. I suppose, Mr. Grewgus, you must have been in Paris at the same time I was there."

"That is quite true," was the answer. Grewgus had certainly formed the opinion at one time that the young woman's sudden departure had been occasioned by her discovery of the fact that she was being watched. But her next words settled this point once and for all.

"And I suppose you followed me about from place to place. It is rather strange that I did not spot you; as I flatter myself that I am rather a keen observer. From what you know of my career, you may be sure I have had to cultivate the quality of alertness. You must be very clever at your business. I should have said it would be impossible for anybody to shadow me continuously for even a day without my being aware of it."

Grewgus smiled. "I think I may say, without undue vanity, I am rather clever at it. In your case, I took somewhat elaborate precautions, as I felt I was dealing with a very resourceful woman. I shadowed you under perhaps a dozen different disguises. Well, Mrs. Edwards, I need hardly say I am very astonished to see you in my office. I suppose you will tell me in good time the object of your visit."

A very hard look came over the handsome face. "I need not keep you waiting a moment longer. My object is revenge."

"Against your former associates in general, or some particular person?" suggested the detective quietly.

"Against my former associates, with one exception, I have no rancour. They did their best to make my life pleasant, so far as such a life can be made pleasant. I was one of those unfortunate creatures whose mode of existence is determined for them at a very early age by others, from whose domination it is impossible to escape. My father was a crook; my mother, so long as she retained her good looks, followed the same calling. And I was trained to follow in her footsteps. You can say it was easy to break away, to separate from these evil counsellors, and earn my living in some honest way. Mr. Grewgus, it was not easy. More than once I have tried and I had to go back."

Grewgus looked at her curiously. She had spoken very calmly up to the last few sentences, and then her manner had suddenly changed. Her voice had in it a vibrating ring; her attempt to break away, and the futility of it, had aroused in her very bitter memories.

"They would not allow me to sever my bonds," she continued, speaking in the same intense tones. "Once I thought I had succeeded, and hidden myself away from them, I had taken a situation as a shop assistant. Somehow, they tracked me down. One of the gang went to the proprietor, and representing himself as a police official, warned him that he had a thief in his service, a girl who had lately come out of gaol. It was a lie. I have deserved prison many times, but luck has kept me out of it; but it was a lie that served its purpose. I was dismissed there and then, turned out into the street with the few miserable francs I had saved out of my poor wages. My mother was waiting near by to take me back. I think in a way she pitied me, but she told me it was useless struggling against them; they would never let me go. I was too useful to them."

"Your natural advantages proved, no doubt, a great asset to them," remarked the detective. "Your appearance made you an ideal decoy."

"Yes, good looks are not invariably a blessing," said the beautiful young woman with a melancholy smile. "Had I been an ordinary-looking girl, they would have allowed me to remain in that humble shop, and troubled their heads no further about me. They were the cause of my being devoted to a life of evil by which I enriched others more than myself. But the greatest curse of all which they brought upon me was my association with the man you lately called upon, my husband, Bertram Edwards."

Her voice, as she spoke the name, was full of passion and hatred. Grewgus guessed now why she had called upon him.

"You know something about him, a great deal too much for his comfort, but you cannot know the utter callousness of his brutal nature. Stormont was hard and ruthless in a way, where he encountered opposition, but he had his good points, he was genial, he was generous. If you knew how to handle him, you could get on well with him. The same might be said of John Whitehouse, who for a long time has passed as my uncle, although there is not the most remote relationship between us. But after the first few months of glamour were over, I could never find a single redeeming quality in Edwards. I think the man had all the vices it was possible to amalgamate in a single temperament."

"You were in love with this man, then, when you married him?"

"Passionately," was the reply. "Nobody could have been more successful than he in masking a vile nature under a prepossessing exterior. But even in the early days of our honeymoon he showed the cloven hoof. During the whole of our married existence my life has been one long experience of infamy, insult, brutality and outrage. And the love I bore him has turned to a hatred so intense that I would risk anything to procure him the punishment he deserves."

So, when she had shown Wraysbury the bruise on her arm, and told him her husband was a brute and a bully, she had been speaking the truth, thought Grewgus.

"Have you come to me with the idea of getting him punished?" asked the detective. He would have dearly loved to aid her in such a laudable object but for the express wishes of Lydon to let sleeping dogs lie.

"That is my sole reason. I can give you so much evidence about him and put you in the way of corroborating it without having to appear myself. But, of course, a wife is not allowed to give evidence against her husband in a criminal charge."

"That is the worst of it," said the artful detective, who wanted to get all he could out of her, to turn her hatred to his own advantage. "But let me know some of the details, and I will see if anything can be done. Let us start with the murder of Calliard. Was Edwards the murderer?"

Reluctantly, as it seemed, she had to admit he was not. In the course of her confessions on the subject, she confirmed what Stormont had insisted on to his brother, that murder had never been intended. Edwards had not been on in the final act of the tragedy. As at first resolved upon, it had been a case of simple robbery. She had not even sought the jeweller's society with the object of blackmailing him, but solely to ascertain his movements.

After she had left Paris, two members of the gang had been dispatched to Brussels to wait for the unfortunate man and entrap him. In rendering him senseless, one of the miscreants had given him too strong a dose of chloroform, and it proved fatal. To cover up their crime, they had thrown his body in the river. She had learned these details afterwards from Whitehouse, but she did not know the names of either of the men. Stormont, who was the leading spirit of the gang, and had originally marked down Calliard for a victim, was alone acquainted with their identity. It was always his policy to keep the subordinate members of the association as far apart as possible. They worked in little coteries, and, in the majority of cases, one coterie knew nothing of the other.

But dearly as she would have loved to implicate Edwards in the tragedy, she had to confess she could not do so. As a matter of fact he was in Spain on other business when it happened.

"Our married life would have been intolerable, but for the fact that we did not spend a great deal of it together; when we did, I suffered physically and mentally," she explained at this point. "His vile temper vented itself upon me on the slightest provocation, in spite of the fact that both Stormont and Whitehouse frequently intervened on my behalf, and remonstrated with him. When the plot against Wraysbury was hatched, it was a necessary part of it that we should live together. That was a time of terrible torture to me. When it failed, thanks to your intervention, he wreaked his disappointment on me. On the day he left England, frightened by your knowledge, he beat me almost into a state of insensibility."

Was she exaggerating, or was Edwards such a monster as she made out? But Grewgus, a shrewd judge of demeanour, guessed by her emotion, her fervent accents, that she was telling the truth, that this man had terrorized and ill-treated her, that but for his devilish power over her she would have broken away. She remarked incidentally that she and her mother had a fair amount of money put by, their share of the proceeds from the various schemes in which they had taken part under the leadership of Stormont and Whitehouse.

She gave him a great deal of information about Edwards. This rascal had specialized chiefly in blackmail, using her in most cases as a decoy, and his activities in this direction had almost exclusively been practised abroad. The affair with Lord Wraysbury was the only serious *coup* he had attempted in his own country. This unscrupulous scoundrel was intensely proud of his birth and social connections, and that perhaps was the reason he did so little in England.

"But, from what he said to Whitehouse, on the day after you had so thoroughly frightened him, I don't think he will ever return. You see, he is not sure how much you know. He guesses your inquiries were made on behalf of a private person, but he also remembers you threatened him with Scotland Yard," said the young woman when she had concluded this portion of her story.

Grewgus explained to her that he could not very clearly see his way to assist her in her schemes of vengeance on her brutal husband, as he had appeared to confine himself almost exclusively to acts of blackmail abroad. "In all these cases," he told her, "there is no chance of securing the co-operation of the victims. If we could have connected him with the kidnapping of Calliard, which resulted in unintentional murder, you yourself could assist the Belgian police, who have abandoned the case. But you emphatically say he was somewhere else at the time. All he did, I suppose, when in Paris was to convey the instructions set out by Stormont, and meet you from day to day to learn what progress you were making. When you both left that city, I presume others were engaged in the affair."

Mrs. Edwards admitted that this was so. In spite of the prejudice engendered against her by his knowledge of her evil past, Grewgus had to admit that the woman had extraordinary powers of fascination. They influenced him so far that he found himself pitying her profoundly for being tied to such a brutal husband, so much so that he voluntarily offered his services to her if Edwards should again seek to intrude himself into her life.

She thanked him very sweetly. "I have a notion I shall never see him again," she said. "But one never knows. He has made a good deal of money, but he is a very greedy man. He is very frightened just now, but his fear may pass away, and he will want to further enrich himself by the same old means. In that case, he would seek me out with the object of compelling me to help him. In that case, I should be glad to come to you in the hope that you could terrify him again."

"What are your intentions as regards the future?" asked the detective presently. "It would hardly be safe for you to go abroad, would it? You would be pretty certain to run across him some day."

"Yes, I would prefer living on the Continent, but I dare not run the risk of falling in with him again. After the design upon Lord Wraysbury miscarried, thanks to your intervention, and both Whitehouse and Edwards judged it prudent to clear out, I telegraphed to my mother to come over from Rouen, where she was living quietly. We talked over matters very thoroughly, and we made up our minds that we would hide ourselves in some corner of England under an assumed name."

Grewgus could not help smiling at this last remark. This fascinating young woman had gone under so many different names, that the adoption of another alias would come very naturally to her.

"I understand, then, that you propose for the future to go straight."

"Most certainly," was the reply given in a tone that showed absolute sincerity. "Through you, the particular coterie to which I belonged has been practically dispersed. Howard Stormont, for whom I had something like a feeling of affection for his kindness to me, took his own way out of it; he was a thriftless, improvident man and he saw ruin staring him in the face. Whitehouse was altogether different. He was careful, not to say parsimonious. By now he must have saved a great deal of money, and I know it was his intention to give up the life as soon as he had amassed enough to live on. I think he was only waiting for the Wraysbury *coup* to come off to execute that intention. Its failure has made him forestall it."

"You know where he is at the present moment, of course?" asked Grewgus.

"No, I do not," was the emphatic answer, and the detective believed that it was a truthful one. "When we talked the matter over, we both agreed that it was best we should know nothing of each other's movements. I suppose we had both lived in such an atmosphere of suspicion and secrecy, that he did not care to trust me; I was equally disinclined to trust him."

"Why did he carry on that solicitor's business? He had no genuine business, had he?"

Mrs. Edwards smiled. "Although I did not particularly like the man, I had no grudge against him, and we always got on comfortably together, and I should not care to do him a bad turn. But I think now I can answer that question without doing him any harm. He had practically no legal business, but he acted for the organization in cases where they wanted advice. He was actually a money-lender, and having got his articles when a young man, before he took to a life of crime, set up as a solicitor in order to present a more respectable appearance. I believe he made a great deal of money that way."

"And I suppose you know how he and Stormont became first acquainted?"

Mrs. Edwards was perfectly frank about the matter. "Whitehouse and he met originally in Australia. Whitehouse had been affiliated to a rather high-class gang for some time, and I suppose he recognized in Stormont a very promising recruit. They engaged in some enterprises there, and Stormont got into trouble. When he came out of prison he returned to England and hunted up his old friend. In due course, Stormont became a leading member of the organization. I was one of his assistants, and I am sure he had several others. But he was a very cautious man, in spite of his bluff and genial manners, and he never allowed us to know much of each other. He and Whitehouse directed affairs in their own particular branch."

Grewgus was feeling very well satisfied with the result of the interview. The candour of the fascinating young woman had led her actually to confirm his different discoveries and suspicions. There was one other matter, however, on which he wished to obtain further enlightenment.

"The affair with Hugh Craig at Nice, was Stormont at the back of that?"

Mrs. Edwards did not appear to answer quite as readily as before.

"Yes, it was he who first set me upon it. He knew that Craig, although not a wealthy man, had some money."

"And you were married to Edwards at the time, of course?" was the detective's next question.

"Not at the time I first met Craig. Our marriage came later. But, as I told you, we lived only occasionally together. The exigencies of our calling rendered it necessary for us to be apart the best part of our married life."

"And I know that you relieved poor Craig of a good deal of his money."

"I had to obey orders in this case as in the others," was the young woman's answer; and Grewgus could perceive that she was speaking with considerable emotion. "It was the most painful episode in my career, for the poor young fellow was desperately in love with me. When a foolish blunder on my part roused his suspicions, I think his mind became unhinged. He

173

would never have tried to kill me if he had been in full possession of his senses. I can guess you know all the details of the ghastly story from his great friend, Lydon."

Grewgus nodded, and Mrs. Edwards, conquering her emotion, went on in a calmer voice:

"I always felt a premonition that Stormont made the greatest mistake of his life when he cultivated Lydon's acquaintance with the view of providing a good match for his niece. He should have steered clear of anybody who had a knowledge at first hand of that tragedy. I told him so when I first heard of it. I told him again when I met Lydon that day at Effington. He laughed at my fears, said that we had never met, and that if I kept my mother out of the way, all would be well. Dozens of girls had a similar blemish. How was he likely to connect me with Elise Makris? Lydon, I must say, acted very well. I did not suspect for a moment that he recognized me. I cannot guess to this day how he did."

"I think I can enlighten you on that point," said Grewgus, who felt, after her attitude to him, that he could afford to show a little candour. He touched the sapphire pendant which she was wearing, and told her what Lydon had learned about it on the day he saw it lying on the table in a room of the Villa des Cyclamens.

"If it had been the blemish only, Mrs. Edwards, he might not have identified you," Grewgus concluded. "But it was *that* which gave him the clue— your mascot which your mother said you always wore, and which she had taken from you that day in the hospital."

"Ah, now I understand. The incident must have passed completely from my mother's mind, for although we have often talked together of young Lydon, and the necessity of keeping her out of his way, she never spoke of it. Strange, very strange," she added in a musing voice, "that this little mascot in which I so firmly believed should be the cause of all that has happened, should have set you, through Lydon, on the track of myself, Stormont and the others."

Grewgus presently brought the conversation round again to Hugh Craig directly, and artfully cross-examined her as to the manner in which she had blackmailed him. But to his questions he did not get very distinct replies. He gathered that, in his infatuation for the beautiful girl, the young man had parted with large sums, ostensibly to defray debts incurred by herself and her mother, sums which were divided in certain proportions between the confederates in the schemes. But he failed to get any precise details. She sheltered her reticence under the plea that it gave her inexpressible pain to dwell upon those miserable days.

She left him shortly, with renewed thanks for his promise to help her in case Edwards should return and endeavour to force his society upon her.

And after she had left, he sat for a long time meditating on herself, her strange charm, and all she had told him.

Had she been only playing a part in order to excite his sympathy, or had she always hated the life which had been thrust upon her by her environment, and was only too thankful to embrace this opportunity of quitting it?

CHAPTER TWENTY-FOUR

LEONARD and Gloria were married a month before Jasper Stormont and his wife left England for China. That last month they spent in London. It was a very quiet wedding; a cousin of the bridegroom officiated as one of the bridesmaids, the two others were girl friends of the bride, and had been her bosom friends at Effington, where the memory of Howard Stormont was still held in kindly remembrance by those who would have been horrified if they had known the truth about him. Mr. Grewgus was present at the ceremony, and presented dainty gifts to both bride and bridegroom.

Leonard had bought a charming house in the neighbourhood of Godalming with some four acres of pretty grounds. It could not compare with the magnificence of Effington Hall, where Howard Stormont had played the rôle of country gentleman what time he was hatching his evil schemes in conjunction with his taciturn fellow-criminal, John Whitehouse. But to Gloria it was a haven of peace and delight, with her flowers and dogs and the sweet sounds and scents of country life. She and her young husband are devoted to each other, and although they have the most friendly relations with their neighbours, are full of happiness when they are alone.

Twelve months had passed, and the villainy of Stormont and his associates had become almost a faint memory to the young wedded couple. Grewgus was always engaged in fresh investigations, and the case to which he had given so much time and attention had almost been jostled out of his mind by fresh problems.

Then one morning in the newspaper he read something that greatly startled him and sent his thoughts travelling back to the strenuous time when he had made that journey to Paris in pursuit of the woman suspected to be Elise Makris.

His eye caught sight of the headline. "Murder and suicide in a small Devonshire village." Two very clear portraits of the victim, a woman, and the murderer who had shot himself after killing her, stared at him from the pages of the newspapers. The woman was Elise Makris, to call her by the first name under which he had known of her in these pages; the man was Bertram Edwards.

The report stated that a Mrs. Mayhew and her daughter Mrs. Baradine had come to this village about a year ago, where they had purchased a house of moderate size. They led a quiet and secluded life, only mixing infrequently with the few neighbours of a respectable class around them. Both women gave themselves out as widows. They attended church regularly and visited at the Vicar's house. Although little was known about them, they had made a very favourable impression on everybody with whom they had come in contact. The daughter was quite a young woman and of remarkable beauty.

No visitors except those in the immediate neighbourhood had ever been known to enter their doors. But one day their comparative isolation had been disturbed. According to the account of one of the two maids, a handsome man about thirty with very urbane and courteous manners had called and requested that his name should be taken in to the ladies. The name he gave was Edwards.

The mention of this name, when the maid took it in to the drawing-room where the two women were seated, seemed to arouse consternation in both mother and daughter. After a whispered conversation between the two, Mrs. Baradine went into the hall and took the strange visitor to her mother. The door of the room was closed, and the three sat together for over an hour. At the end of that time, Mrs. Baradine went out with the man Edwards and they did not return till it wanted a few minutes to dinner.

The visitor stayed the night, sleeping in one of the spare bedrooms at the back of the house. He stopped on the next day. From a remark dropped by Mrs. Mayhew to the maid after breakfast, she gathered that Edwards was taking his departure on the following morning. During the whole of his visit, the demeanour of both mother and daughter exhibited symptoms of great depression and anxiety.

They all dined together on the evening of the second day. After dinner Mrs. Mayhew went out for a stroll, leaving Edwards and Mrs. Baradine in the dining-room by themselves. The housemaid also went out, and the rest of the story was finished by the other servant, the cook.

This woman, very curious as to this strange visitor, admitted that twice she went into the hall and listened at the dining-room door. The second time she heard voices high in altercation, but could not gather what was being said. Suddenly, as she sat in the kitchen, speculating on what was taking place between her young mistress and the man Edwards, a shot rang out, followed in a fraction of time by a second one. Sensing that a tragedy had happened, she rushed into the room and was confronted with a ghastly spectacle. Mrs. Baradine was lying on the floor dead, and beside her Edwards with a bullet through his brain. Screaming, she fled into the village in search of the local constable, whom she brought back to the house. Five minutes after they came back, Mrs. Mayhew returned from her walk and fainted at the awful sight.

Later on, the mother told her story. Mrs. Baradine was not a widow; her real name was Edwards and she was the wife of the man who had killed her, and who, realizing the impossibility of escape, destroyed himself. Hers had been a most unhappy marriage, and, to escape from her husband's brutality, she had left him and hid herself, as she fondly hoped, in this quiet Devonshire village under an assumed name.

By some means he had tracked her down, and had visited her with the view of obtaining her forgiveness of the past, and inducing her to resume their married life. To his request she had returned an obstinate refusal, in which he seemed to have acquiesced, as he announced his intention of returning to London on the following day. On the evening of the fatal day, Mrs. Mayhew had left them alone after dinner, apparently on fairly amicable terms. She could only conjecture that, during her absence, he had sought to alter her daughter's resolution, that high words had ensued, and that in the violence of his passion he had first taken her life and then his own.

Mrs. Mayhew, otherwise Madame Makris, was a clever woman and had told her story well; she had kept out of it anything that would arouse suspicions of the past. But Grewgus, with his knowledge, was able to read between the lines.

Edwards had felt his old criminal instincts rising within him. So long a time had elapsed without any action being taken that he had concluded the past was done with. To the successful accomplishment of any future schemes, his wife was necessary. He had tracked her down to this lonely Devonshire village, and used all his arts of persuasion to induce her to return to him. A man of brutal and violent passions, he had been maddened by her refusal, and in a fit of frenzy bordering on delirium had killed her.

After he had mastered the facts, Grewgus went round to Lydon's office. The young man knew what he had come for. He and Gloria had read the same news at breakfast.

"I wonder if she was wearing her mascot when he killed her?" said Lydon in a musing tone. "It saved her from the consequences of her lover's bullet, but not from her husband's."

"And so that is the end of three out of the four," observed Grewgus in the same thoughtful voice. "I wonder if Nemesis has yet overtaken that gloomy miscreant, John Whitehouse, or if he is living somewhere a life of smug respectability on his ill-gotten gains?"

But that question has not been answered yet. For all that is known to the contrary, John Whitehouse, as great a criminal as the others, may be leading the life suggested by the detective.

THE END.

www.ingramcontent.com/pod-product-compliance
Lightning Source LLC
Chambersburg PA
CBHW011445170626
46816CB00008B/2530